OLD ENOUGH

THE AGE BETWEEN US (BOOK 1)

CHARMAINE PAULS

Published by Charmaine Pauls

Montpellier, 34090, France

www.charmainepauls.com

Published in France

Cover design by Angela Haddon (www.angelahaddon.com)

Photography by Wander Aguiar Photography LLC

ISBN: 978-2-9561031-4-1 (eBook)

ISBN: 978-1-7208111-5-2 (Print)

❁ Created with Vellum

PROLOGUE

One month earlier, lunch hour

Jane

Damn this Pretoria Brooklyn traffic. I should've made a reservation in Menlyn, but no other restaurant comes close to Kream in terms of cuisine. The maître d'hôtel knows me thanks to the three-digit sums Orion Advertising spends on company lunches. He'll hold our table, but punctuality is Francois' pet peeve.

It's only spring, but a freak heatwave makes the car's interior stifling hot. The full effect of the air-con hasn't kicked in. A trickle of sweat runs from my armpit down my side under my dress. I tap my fingers on the steering wheel, counting the traffic lights as I pass the stately embassy residencies. Six left to go. Francois will let ten minutes slide, but not fifteen. I hoped I wouldn't have to call, because he's going to sound irritated, which makes me nervous, and our date will be tense even before it starts. Filling my lungs with positive vibes, I dial Francois on voice commands, but his phone goes straight to voicemail. I leave a quick message,

1

apologizing about the traffic. For the next ten minutes my stomach is in a knot, until I pull into the parking, right next to his Porsche. I don't relax until I'm inside and spot him in the booth at the back.

When my husband looks up, my heart sinks. His face is perfectly expressionless, which is worse than irritated. He's angry. As the waiter pulls out my seat, Francois flicks back his sleeve and checks his watch.

"Sorry." I sit down and offer the waiter a smile before he leaves. "The traffic was terrible. I left a message." I reach over the table to take his hand. "Did you get it?"

He doesn't pull away, but he doesn't close his fingers around mine like he usually does.

"I have to be back in the office at two," he says.

"I know." He's in the middle of a big architectural project. "We'll eat quickly." Letting go of his hand, I take the gift box from my bag and put it on his plate. "Happy anniversary."

He stares at it, eyes cast down, and frames his head between his hands while running circles over his temples with his thumbs. Several seconds pass. Disappointment dampens my mood. I've put a lot of thought and effort into the gift. Giving a man who has everything something meaningful isn't easy. We may not be the most passionate couple, but we have a solid, good relationship based on genuine friendship. Twelve years say something. It says we're making this marriage work and it deserves to be celebrated. Francois can be awkward and unresponsive when he's annoyed, but the way he leans back, opens his jacket, and wiggles loose his tie, confuses me. It's as if it's too hot in here when the air-conditioner gives me goosebumps on my arms.

I motion at the gift and say with renewed enthusiasm, "Open it."

With a firm motion, he puts the box aside and leans his elbows on the table, looking at me intently, but still he doesn't speak.

"Are we playing a silent game," I touch my shoe to his under the table, "or are you going to say something?"

Tapping his fingers together, he doesn't break our stare. He continues to delve deep into my eyes for four more heartbeats, and then he says, "I'm leaving you."

The words come out of nowhere and everywhere. They're wrong, because he'd never do that to me. He promised. Our start wasn't easy, but I've tried my damnedest to be the good wife for him, the wife he wanted. We have Abby. He won't do this to his daughter.

"I wanted to tell you before," he says, "but the right opportunity was never there."

Lowering my voice, I motion at the full restaurant. "This is?"

A shutter drops in his regard, and his demeanor turns distant, inaccessible. "I thought it best to move as soon as possible. I don't want a drawn-out drama."

I can't process what's happening. There were no warning signs, except for his recent withdrawal, but he always pulls into himself when work gets stressful.

"I'll be out by tomorrow," he continues.

"Why?" My question has nothing to do with him moving out tomorrow.

He doesn't hesitate in his answer. "Debbie."

I only know one Debbie. "From your office?"

"She resigned." He adds, "Obviously."

As if that's a consolation. "How did this happen?"

"We fell in love."

Tears prick at the back of my eyes, but I blink them away, not wanting witnesses for my pain and humiliation. "How long?"

He gets that closed-off look again. "It's not important."

"The hell it is."

"Jane." His tone is chastising. "Your language, please."

"Can we talk about this at home?"

"There's no point. My mind's made up."

"Yes, there is a point. There are things to be said, explained. If you're so certain of your decision as you say you are–"

"Jane, stop. It's hard enough as it is. There's nothing else to say."

My heart feels as if it's going through a blender. Rejection and betrayal are the rotating blades in my chest. A masochistic part of me argues I deserve this for not loving Francois like he loved me when we started out, but our beginning was anything but normal. No one, least of all Francois, can judge me.

It's hard to keep my voice even and not give in to the hysterics that hover beyond the threadbare limit of my self-control. "You owe me this at least."

His answer is not to answer.

"You'll walk out on me, *and* deny me closure?"

Still no answer. Suddenly, I know why he chose the restaurant over the privacy of our home. In public, he doesn't have to deal with the breakdown I feel coming.

Pushing back my chair, I get to my feet. "Excuse me, but I don't have an appetite."

Relief washes over his features. "I understand. Maybe you should take the rest of the day off, and we'll discuss the logistics tonight when Abby's in bed."

No. I fought for this career, which happened late in my life. I'm not calling in with a family emergency to hide at home with red-rimmed eyes and a hole in my ribcage. If I ever needed to throw myself into work, it's now.

"You take the rest of the day off." I push the gift back to him. "It's a fruitcake with marzipan." It took hours to make the tiny Rubik's Cube–Francois' only weakness–that decorates the miniature cake. The Rubik's Cube is how we met. It's a perfect replica of our wedding cake. "Give it to one of the beggars outside."

With as much pride as a rejected woman can possess, I turn my back on the man who's given up on us. Every step I trace back to my car cracks and breaks under my feet, my world falling away.

How did this happen?

I don't know, and I do. It happened twelve years ago, with the tragedy that set the course of my life.

I just can't face it, yet.

Couldn't then. Can't now.

Brian

IT'S LUNCH HOUR. The restaurant is full. Golden globes serve as lampshades. The white tablecloths look heavy and rigid, like they've been starched to the tables in forty-five degree angles. A pianist plays an unrecognizable tune on a grand piano, the notes subtle enough to provide background music without hampering conversation. The dining room is surprisingly quiet. The hushed conversations are as inhibited as the soft clink of the silver cutlery.

Depressing.

Men in fancy suits and women wearing expensive dresses sip mineral water or wine, their gazes stealing over me as my work boots thud on the shiny floor. The room and everyone in it feel fake. I should leave. I don't have time to piss, never mind to waste in a place I already know I'm going to hate. Instead of swinging back for the door, I press forward. This is the least I owe Mike for securing the job for me. I'm not going to kick him in the teeth after he'd put his ass on the line to hire me. The headwaiter's eyebrows pull together at the trail of caked mud I leave behind. They seem a lot like crumbs, in case I have to find my way back to who I am, which is not what's inside here.

I take a seat at the bar from where I have a view of the room so I can spot Mike when he arrives. A couple of blondes are staring openly. They're either twins or not far apart in age. When I boldly return the stare, both turn red and giggle. I'm not interested, but I'm not a circus attraction or fuck-toy to be gawked at. The woman across the table from them with the same wheat-colored hair, who I assume to be their mother, turns slightly in her seat, her eyes measuring me with cool hostility as she takes in my attire. Her gaze lingers on my hands, and then she looks away, leaning over the table and whispering to the girls. They lower their heads, but the giggling continues. I stare at my fingernails, black from grime that no scrubbing can erase, and shrug inwardly. Screw her.

The barman places a coaster in front of me. "What will it be, sir?"

He's dressed in a stiff white shirt and black waistcoat. Poor fellow must be feeling like he's in a straitjacket.

"Coke, please."

From my vantage point, I observe the floor. What's it like to be one of them, to order a meal without looking at the price? What's it like to say, "Hey, let's have lunch at Oscars on Friday," like it's grabbing a quarter pounder at McDo? Rubbing a hand over the stubble on my chin, I feel my troubles bone-deep. Fifteen grand deep, to be exact. Fifteen grand or Sam doesn't go to a decent school. She's my kid sister, and I'm all she's got, which is why I'm busting my balls slapping bricks at the building site instead of taking notes in my Consumer Behavior class.

I check my watch. Mike's late. Staring out the window, I look beyond the sculpture of the applauding hands to the State Theater doors. I'll give it another ten minutes before I pay the outrageous price for the Coke and be gone.

A suave male voice speaks up on my right. "I bet you're the kind of guy who makes panties drop with the flick of your fingers."

I turn toward my neighbor. He's lean, regal, and tall. He wears a dark suit and white shirt with a silk scarf. His black hair is combed back, not a strand out of place. On his left hand, he sports a golden ring with a square onyx stone. If it weren't oversized, it would've seemed old-fashioned, like my grandfather's wedding ring. His nails are trimmed and clean, his hands soft and white.

He plays with the stem of his wineglass as he studies me. "That one over there, for instance." He motions at a brunette who I judge to be in her thirties. "I bet you can have her bent over the vanity in the toilet and fucked in less than ten minutes."

The bartender puts my drink down in front of me. I mumble a thank-you and take a sip.

"That one," the guy points a finger not so discreetly at a woman in the corner who meets my eyes squarely and gives me a broad smile, "will be on her knees under the table in under ten seconds."

I scoff at that. "I think you underestimate women."

"I know a sex magnet when I see one."

"Thanks, but I'm straight."

He chuckles. "I'm not hitting on you."

"Then what are you doing?"

"*Sussing* you out."

"For what?"

"A job."

I always need a job, but something about this guy makes my sixth sense stand on end. "I'm not looking."

"No?" He runs a gaze over my faded cotton shirt, torn jeans, and have-seen-better-days boots. "Are you sure?"

The asshole has me. Half of the time, I feel as if I have *poor* carved on my forehead, and the other half I feel like I'm naked, like everyone can see into my soul.

He faces forward and brings his glass to his lips. "Ten grand," he says over the rim.

"Excuse me?"

"Ten easy grand to seduce a woman."

He looks back at me without as much as a blink. The guy's serious.

"You're offering me money to seduce a woman?"

"That's what I said. I'll need proof. A photo."

"Whoa."

I push back my barstool, but his hand on my arm stops me with a surprisingly strong grip.

"Hear me out," he says.

"No thanks."

"Ask me why."

I shake off his touch and fish for a bill in my pocket.

"Drinks are on me." He flicks his fingers at the barman. "Put it on my tab." Then he turns back to me. "Go on. Ask me why."

Fine. I'll play his game. I've got time to kill, anyway. "Why?"

"She was engaged to my friend. Had an affair not even a week before the wedding."

Classic case of cold feet. Nothing I haven't heard before. "Your friend caught them red-handed, and it broke his gentle heart."

He chucks back the rest of his wine. "Then he killed himself."

Fuck. That's heavy. Feeling like a jerk about my mocking remark, I utter a sorry-assed apology.

"It's not like he put a gun to his head," the guy says, giving a soft laugh. "He took off on his bike and crashed it on the highway."

There's nothing I can say to that, so I sip my soda, letting the guy get his friend and the cheating fiancée off his chest.

"Now you know," he continues, "why I want revenge."

"What are you going to do with the photo?"

"Nothing. I just need proof."

"This will make you feel better?"

He looks at me again. "A whole lot."

"I don't get it."

"I want her to fall off the high and mighty throne she managed to mount through the years. I want her to remember who she truly is and that the fake life she created for herself is nothing but a fairy tale. I want her to remember she's a whore."

"You want me to make a woman feel like a whore," I say with disbelief.

"As long as you fuck her, I don't care *what* you make her feel."

"I don't want to preach, but–"

"So don't." He takes a photo from his pocket and pushes it toward me.

Despite my intention not to get further involved in whatever crazy fuck this dandy has going on, my gaze is drawn down to the piece of paper lying on the counter between us. The woman in the picture is looking away from the camera, like she's not aware of the photo being taken. Her gaze is proud. It's fixed on the horizon, and I have an overwhelming urge to know what she's staring at so intently. Her short, blonde hair is the color of moonlight. It's styled in waves around her face, accenting her good bone structure. Pale, glossy lipstick makes her full lips look lush. Between those lips and gray-blue eyes, I can't decide which her best feature is. Whatever the case, she's a looker. She's also a lady. I can tell from the fancy dress with the matching jacket and shoes, but most of all from the way she carries herself. She seems self-assured, wealthy, and cultured. Way out of my league.

"She's pretty. I'm sure you won't battle finding a gigolo to take up your offer." My stomach churns. The thought doesn't sit right with me.

He pockets the photo. "Ten grand."

Fuck. Ten grand is half of my problems gone, and two thirds of a private school year covered. Still… "Nah."

"A little bird told me she'll soon be single, so it's not like you're risking breaking up a marriage."

I want to remain indifferent, but that changed the minute I laid eyes on her. I'm curious with an interest that goes deeper than what it should. I won't admit it, but I'll be damned if I don't feel it in my gut.

"How long ago?"

"That my friend died?" He blotches his brow with the paper napkin. "Twelve years."

"Why now?"

"She's getting divorced."

I want to ask if it's because of his consideration for her marriage that he didn't act on his plan before, but he speaks before I can utter the question.

"Go check her out before you make up your mind."

The idea of stalking a woman–*this* woman–makes my insides crawl, but this guy won't give up. This isn't a plan he concocted today. It's obvious he's been walking around with the fantasy in his head for years. It's taken root and grown in his soul. That's what revenge does. A man can't unearth it like a weed. It seeps into your heart until your blood is as black as your intentions. I want no part of his revenge.

As I open my mouth to tell him so, he says, "Name your price."

I laugh. How easy everything seems for people with money. "Fifty."

I throw the word at him, meaning to end this game with the ridiculous sum, but he regards me with the same, unblinking stare from earlier.

"Done." Reaching inside his pocket, he takes out a business card, flips it over, and slides it my way. "Write down your name and email."

This time, my laugh is forced. "I agreed to nothing."

"Understood."

His easy admittance catches me off guard.

He takes back the card, produces a pen from his inside jacket pocket, and scribbles something on the back before slipping it into my shirt pocket. "Her name and address. Go check her out and decide if she's worth a fuck for fifty grand. When you send me a photo of the two of you naked doing the deed–and I want a clear shot of her face *and* the action–I'll transfer the money. Don't even bother with Photoshop. I'll know." He puts the pen on my napkin. "Name and email address. That's all I need."

It's not a deal, not until I've decided, or so I tell myself as I pick up the pen and start writing.

"Good," he says when I'm done, pocketing the napkin with my details. He holds out his hand.

After a second's hesitation, I accept, returning his firm shake. "It's a deal."

His smile is polished and toothy, reminding me of a crocodile, but there's something melancholic about him, a presence of sadness. I'm still gripping his hand when he gets to his feet.

He studies my face. "How old are you?"

"Twenty."

His smile is knowing. "How many months before you turn twenty?"

The man is no fool. "Eight."

"Perfect. I'm looking forward to hearing from you."

He lets go first, leaving me sitting there with an outstretched hand and a business card burning in my pocket. My gaze follows him out of the restaurant to the street where a car waits. The chauffeur gets out and opens the door. A few pedestrians pass, obscuring my view, and then the car takes off, and he's gone.

Did this just happen? Did a man in a black suit just offer me fifty grand to seduce his dead friend's cheating fiancée? Taking the card from my pocket, I stare at the embossed print on the white paper. It's an email address. Nothing more.

I don't have to do it. Just because I said I'd check it out and shook hands on the deal doesn't mean I'm committed. Then again, I've done worse. I'm not going to pretend to be a good man.

Mike walks up to me, his smile easy. "Hey, mate." He slaps me on the back and takes a seat. "Sorry I'm late. Got held up by one of the ever-complaining contractors. How's things?"

"It's a strange world."

"You're in a philosophical mood."

"Just saying that everything happens for a reason."

I do believe in karma. I believe what you think is what you get. Haven't I been thinking fifteen grand when I walked in here?

He motions at the card in my hands. "A girl gave you her number? Already?" He gives me a mixed look of admiration and envy. "I can't leave you alone for ten minutes, and this is what happens."

"It's nothing."

I don't sound convincing, least of all to myself.

1

Jane

Splash.
"Fuuuck!"
Splash. Splash.

Turning my head on the pillow, I dig my face deeper into the linen, drowning out the sounds. My body and brain are finally in a deep state of relaxation after having tossed for a couple of hours. I'm not ready for another day. Specifically, not for *this* day.

"It's freezing."

"Pussy. It's great."

Male voices. An internal alarm jerks me fully awake. The noise didn't come from my dream. It's coming from my backyard. A blaze of shock heats my skin. I glance at the clock on the nightstand. It's two in the morning.

"I've wasted good money on working up a buzz, 'cause now I'm sober."

"You're the one who wanted to cool down."

Reflexively, I reach out to the space next to me, remembering too late it would be empty.

"Not in ice water. My dick's the size of a cocktail sausage. Look at this."

"Jesus, Clive. Keep it in your pants."

Are they breaking into my house? What kind of thieves take a dip in the pool before they rob you? My fingers tremble as they fumble for the lamp. Wait. If I switch on the light, I'll not only alert them to my location in the house, but also to the fact that I'm awake, not that anyone can sleep with the racket they're making.

Slipping from the bed, I yank on the leggings and T-shirt I'd put out for morning. By fluke or God-sent mercy, Abby is sleeping over at Francois' place after a parent evening at school. My heart drums an uneven rhythm as I pad to the window and pull the curtains open on a crack.

What the hell?

Three guys are bouncing around in my pool, a flash of red passing between them. Abby's ball.

Sons of bitches. Indignation replaces the shock. The gate is locked. They either climbed over or jumped the wall. Fists balled and heart still pounding, I tiptoe to the nightstand and grab my phone. A push of a button and a ringtone sounds in my ear. My call is promptly answered.

"Groenkloof Police Station. How may I help you?"

"Three men broke into my pool." I keep my tone hushed and ramble down my address.

The female voice on the other end is authoritative. "Ma'am, what's your name?"

"Jane Logan."

"Ms. Logan, are you inside the house?"

"Yes."

"Alone?"

"Yes."

"Are your doors locked?"

"Of course."

"Do you have a visual on the men?"

"Yes."

"Are they forcing entry into your home?"

"They're in my pool. They broke into my garden."

"I heard you the first time. Are they displaying signs of violence?"

"Isn't forced entry into someone's property a form of violence?"

"Ma'am, please answer the question so that I can help you."

Gritting my teeth, I say, "The fact that they're in my pool would mean they're swimming, so no, for the moment, they're not displaying *signs of violence*."

I move back to the window and peer outside. One is knocking the ball around while a second is pushing the third's head under the water.

"Right." The clacking of a keyboard sounds over the line. "I'll dispatch a vehicle as soon as one becomes available."

"How long will it take?"

"All our officers are currently on call-out. Can an officer reach you on this number to let you know when they're on their way?"

"This number's fine. An hour? Two?" I crumple the T-shirt in my fist against my chest.

"As I said, all our officers–"

"Give me a rough idea."

She sighs. "A few hours. It's hard to say. It depends on how quickly the call-outs are dealt with."

"Thank you."

She mumbles, "You're welcome," and cuts the line.

Unless I'm being murdered, the police won't come. Even then, it'll be too late. Stuff that. If the guys having a party in my pool meant me harm they would've already tried to break into the house. They're up to no good, but they're not here to steal anything or kill someone. I iron out my T-shirt with a palm and make my way down the hallway. In front of the patio doors in the lounge, I pause. For an embarrassing moment, I consider calling Francois. No. I can only imagine him explaining to Debbie he's going to rescue his ex-wife from pranksters. Besides, Francois is a realist. He'd never take on three men bigger and stronger than himself. He'd do the same as what I did–call the police.

Another bout of hurling laughter seals the deal. My hand is already reaching for the key before I've taken the conscious decision. Unlocking and yanking the sliding door open, I step out onto the deck. The spot comes on, announcing my exit, and for a moment I'm filled with trepidation again, but I straighten my back and make my voice hard.

"What are you doing in my pool?"

The males turn to me in unison. They're younger than I'd thought, maybe closer to boys than men. The chubby one gapes. The redhead squeezes the ball between his palms. The blond flicks his hair back, scrutinizing me with a fearless gaze. His stare is intense, as if he's not just seeing, but really looking at me, and the light in his eyes is mocking. His regard angers me more than them swimming in my pool at two o'clock in the morning.

"I asked what you're doing in my pool," I say as silence prevails.

Chubby lifts his shoulders up to his ears. "We're swimming."

"I called the cops. You better leave before they get here."

The redhead snort-laughs. "Yeah, right. Like they'll come."

It was a foolish threat. I should've said I phoned my ex-military neighbor or something. "If you're not out in five seconds, I'm letting the dogs out." More bluffing. I don't have dogs.

Red waddles toward the shallow end. "Oh, come on. It's thirty degrees. Give us a break."

"You can have your break in the dam or river where it's a free for all. This is private property."

"You look like you can do with a dip yourself," Red says. "You're all flushed, like you're overheating."

"Is that advice you'll give your mother or girlfriend, wisecrack? Go swim with three criminals you don't know from Adam?"

At least he has the decency to look somewhat ashamed.

"Come on," Chubby says, slapping the water next to him. "We won't bite."

The blond speaks up for the first time. "Shut up, Clive."

When he swims to the shallow end and pushes himself out onto the side, I suppress the urge to flee back into the house. I need to show these bullies I don't scare that easily, or they'll have the upper hand.

Straightening, the blond turns to face me. Our eyes clash over the distance. I make quick work of taking in everything about him. I may need a description for the police. He's a giant, taller than Abby's basketball net on the wall. Maybe not as young as I'd judged him, but not a day older than twenty. His body is defined in a way I've never seen in real life, not even in the gym. Mind you, it's mostly retired people who frequent our gym. His arms and legs are powerful, almost too well cut. His shoulders are broad and his abs a slab of solid muscle. Drops roll down his chest, a small rivulet running into and down his navel. Green swimming trunks mold around his hips, leaving no guesswork as to how well-endowed he is. It's embarrassing that I'm staring, but his body demands to be heeded. I don't mean it in any sexual way. It's just impossible not to notice all that perfection and beauty.

When I meet his eyes again, there's amusement in his. He knows he's pretty, and he's used to being looked at. He flashes me a smile, exposing a dimple in his left cheek.

"Get out," I say, for some reason even angrier than earlier.

He raises his palms. "Easy now."

How dare he address me like a dog? "The party is over. I said get out."

He takes a step forward. Instinctively, I take one back.

"We don't mean any harm," he says. "We're just cooling down."

"I want you to leave."

He advances a few more paces. The intensity of his eyes cut

through me. It's as if he's calling my bluff, knowing I'm not nearly as collected or brave as I'm trying to appear.

"What are you going to do?" Clive chirps from behind. "Throw us out?"

As the blond closes more distance between us, I hold up a finger in warning. "Stop right there."

To my surprise, he obeys.

"We're not going to hurt you."

"I don't know you, and I don't trust people I don't know."

"Wise." He nods his approval.

"You have ten seconds." Shit, I sound like when I scolded Abby in her toddler years.

He grins. All teeth. "What happens after ten seconds?"

"You'll be forcefully removed."

"I don't think so," Red calls from the pool. To demonstrate his point, he hops out and stretches out in a deckchair.

The invasion of my privacy is infuriating, but my helplessness even more so. "If you don't leave right now…"

I'm starting to lose my composure. I can feel it in the shaking of my hands and the way my heart hammers with something heavier than fear. Injustice and powerlessness.

"I'm not afraid of you." Lie. "Don't make me drag you out by your ears." No idle threat.

I walk to the deckchair with brisk strides, but the blond cuts me off, putting himself between his friend and me.

"Go back inside," he says. "We're leaving."

"Like fuck we are," Clive says.

The blond turns on him with an expression hidden from me, but one that makes Clive shut up and get out of the water.

Red huffs a grunt, but lifts his butt from my chair to follow his buddies to the garden table where they'd left their T-shirts. Crossing my arms, I watch as they dress, determined to see them off my property. It's the blond who turns back to me. The fabric clings to his wet chest, somehow making his body seem even more impressive than when it was naked. He flicks a brow, letting me know he's caught me staring.

"Ready?" I ask sarcastically.

He wipes back his wet hair. "Just about."

"What are you waiting for? A written invitation to leave?"

"We'll leave as soon as you've gone inside and locked the door."

"This is my property. I don't take orders from you."

"No?" Another cocky lift of his brow. "Do you really want to fight me on this?"

"What I want–"

He gives a step in my direction. "We can always hang out here until we're dry. I'm not keen on soiling my truck."

There's steel in his eyes. Now that he's standing closer, I can see their color. They're fudge-brown with specs of melted caramel. For another couple of seconds, we're locked in a stare-down. Shit. I'm not going to have an argument I won't win. I turn on my heel and walk back to the house. His voice stops me on the doorstep.

"Sweet dreams, princess."

The urge to flick him a middle finger is overwhelming, but I'm not going to lower myself to that level. Not for him.

Inside with the door locked, I watch through the window as they make their noisy exit down the driveway and jump over the gate with a lot of hooting. I don't move until I hear a vehicle start up and drive away. Only then do I allow myself to blow out the breath trapped in my chest.

Damn, I'm wide awake now. There's no way I'm going back to sleep with the adrenalin coursing through my body. With a tremulous sigh, I go return to the bedroom and call the police station to cancel the call-out before settling in bed with my laptop. I may as well work on the Monroe account. One of the advantages of sleeping alone is that no one complains about your screen light.

Brian

NOTHING HAPPENS WITHOUT A REASON. There's no such thing as coincidence. Being in Jane Logan's pool after midnight certainly wasn't. Neither was the event that took me there. I was meant to be at a time and place that set me in Ms. Logan's path, and now that I've seen her in real life, I'm glad it's me and not someone else.

I'm quiet in the truck, playing our first meeting over in my mind. She's a woman, not a girl. Too much woman, maybe. For me, I mean. But Jane's also a lady. She's in a class that exists on the other side of the tracks, the kind who is well-bred and polite. They don't raise their voices or lose their cool, not even when a no-good asshole like me invades their privacy. They don't have to ask the waiter what hors d'oeuvre is, because they were brought up to know shit like that. They look like they've just stepped out of Young Designers Emporium, even at two in the morning dressed in a clingy T-shirt with no bra and leggings that hug the sweet swell of their hipbones. Seducing her won't be a chore, but she's a princess. It'll take more than giving her ten minutes of my attention or buying her a drink.

"What's up with you?" Clive shoulders me none too softly. "Why so broody?"

I grip the wheel harder not to steer us into the ditch and silently curse him for interrupting the image in my mind.

"The cops weren't coming," he continues. "Why did you make us leave?"

"She lives alone," I grit out.

"So?"

"Imagine how she must've felt waking up to three assholes in her pool."

"What's with the gentlemanly behavior?" Eugene asks from the back. "Since when do you care if we scare people?"

"It was your idea," Clive adds.

"I didn't think anyone was home."

The neglected garden gave me the impression she was away on a business trip or holiday. People in Groenkloof don't have unkempt gardens. They have enough money to pay for garden services. The idea was to get a feel of her environment, not to gatecrash her sleep and frighten her into oblivion. Not even I'm that low.

"We should do it again," Eugene says. "It was fun getting caught."

I jerk the wheel left and screech to a halt on the shoulder of the road.

"Hey!" Clive grips the dashboard to brace his body. "What the fuck?"

"No one is going back there." I pin the two fuckers with a stare. "Are we clear?"

Eugene shakes his head. "You're nuts, man."

"Are we clear?"

"Yeah," Clive scoffs. "I get it. No one gets to steal your idea."

It's more about Ms. Logan and less about my idea, but let him think that.

"Good." I put the truck into gear and steer it back onto the deserted road.

Now that we've conversed, I know there's a slim chance Jane Logan will ever give me the time of day. Yeah, she noticed me, but she made it clear she wasn't interested. Her body language said any advances would be unwelcome, maybe even considered unsavory. Inappropriate.

Too bad, because I'm interested. *Very* interested.

Jane

WALKING into Moyo in Melrose Arch, I catch my reflection in the coatroom mirror. Dark rings mar my eyes, and my cheeks are pale. Dorothy will notice.

Not in the mood for questions and concern, however well intended, I enter the ladies' room to apply blush and a darker lipstick. When I'm done, I study my handiwork. On the surface, it looks all right. It doesn't reflect what's inside. For over a decade, I've survived this day, waiting with each passing year for it to get better, only it never does. The ache is dormant, building to a crescendo as the months pass to blow me to pieces all over again on this date. I don't want to forget, but I can't bear to remember.

Cruel images flash through my mind's eye. The flood of pain builds like a wave. My skin goes hot even as cold sweat pearls on my forehead. Nausea makes me heave, while my throat closes up. I can't breathe. I clutch the edge of the vanity, willing my legs not to cave.

It takes a few deep breaths and a lot of determination to gain control over my emotions. My body remains uncooperative, shaking uncontrollably.

"Stop it, damn you."

I want to be strong for Dorothy, even if this is the one day she grants me weakness. The loss cuts me open and leaves me stranded, all alone, and here I am again like last year and every year before that, because of all the millions of people on Earth the only one who understands my suffering is Dorothy.

Closing my eyes, I shut out the hollow image of the woman in the mirror and focus on my breathing until my legs can carry my weight and my shivering turns to an occasional tremor. I take one last breath for good measure, straighten my shoulders, and don't meet my own eyes as I turn for the door.

Dorothy is already at our usual table, a bottle of wine open and her glass filled. My strides are brisk, like I have purpose, and my smile slips into place for the waiter who seats me.

Dorothy looks up from the menu she's been studying. "You

look like shit." She reaches over the table and cups my hand. "How are you holding up?"

"Good." I force a smile. "You?"

She purses her lips and gives a small shake of her head. This is her non-verbal language to let me know she can't speak for the fear of crying. The waiter appears at her side. Letting go of my hand, she squares her shoulders and pretends to look at the menu. She blinks three times before she lifts her head to the waiter, her composure back in place.

"My friend will have what I'm drinking," she says, "and we'll have the Mozambican crab, please." As an afterthought, she shoots me a glance. "Will that do?"

We have the crab every year, not that I care what we order. I won't be able to eat, anyway.

When the waiter leaves after serving me water and wine, she pins me with a stare. "You can't hide under your make-up from me. Didn't sleep much, did you?"

I take a sip of water. "No."

"Why don't you take the sleeping pills I told you about? My doctor will happily give you a prescription."

"You know I don't believe in that. Besides, it wasn't all nightmares. Some pranksters had a late night–or rather early morning–dip in my pool."

Her eyes grow large. "Did you call the police?"

"The guys left before they could come."

"Good lord." She fans herself with the menu. "How did they get in?"

"Over the gate."

"What about the electrified barbwire?"

"It wasn't on."

"And the alarm?"

"I forgot to activate it."

I'm not going to tell her I don't have the money to pay the security company, any longer. She'll offer to pay for it, and I don't want her charity. I don't want to feel like I owe anyone. More importantly, coming from Dorothy, it'll feel like a bribe.

"Jane! You mustn't be so forgetful. Although, I understand why you would've been distracted last night. I couldn't stop thinking about *it*. When I close my eyes, I keep on seeing Evan lying there, so peaceful, like he's sleeping in the middle of the road, and it doesn't make sense until I see the blood, so much blood, and I keep on telling myself it's not happening, it's not true. It's *not* true." She grabs my hand and squeezes my fingers. "How many times didn't I tell myself that day it wasn't true? Now, all I keep telling myself is that it *is* true, but it never gets easier. My brain understands, but my heart won't accept it."

"Dorothy, please," I whisper, looking away from her feverish stare.

This is the only day we allow ourselves to talk about what happened freely, but every year it becomes harder. Even as I want to be her shoulder and her ear, I can't cope with the memories her words conjure. The way his knee was twisted, the way his arms were bent at the elbows, facing palms-up toward the heaven... Not knowing what the helmet concealed–

"Hey." She gives my arm a gentle shake. "I ordered a wreath. I'm taking it to the roadside after lunch. Want to come?"

I'm not sure I'll survive it.

The waiter saves me from answering when he arrives with our food. My almost-mother-in-law raises her glass in a toast. When I clink mine to hers, she says, "To Evan."

"To Evan," I echo.

"He lives in our hearts forever."

He does. He took up all the space, and now there's nothing left for anyone. Maybe that's part of the problem of everything that's wrong in our lives.

We can't let go.

Brian

LEANING ON THE TRUCK, I scan the kids filing through the school gate. Thanks to the uniform, they all look more or less the same. It takes a while before my gaze finds Sam. Her golden-blonde braid hangs over her shoulder. The belt of the dress is stretched to the last hole, showing what I call her baby fat. I make a mental note to pay more attention to her diet. She's no longer a baby.

She pushes through the crowd, her head bent and her eyes downcast as she makes her way down the road to where I'm parked. Immediately, I go rigid.

I straighten when she stops in front of me, scrutinizing her face. "Hey, piglet."

"Hey."

Grabbing her chin, I tilt her face up for a better view. "What's wrong?"

"Nothing."

I cross my arms and lean back on the truck. "I guess we're hanging out here until you tell me."

She blows out a breath and thrusts her schoolbag at me. "Let's just go."

I open the door and dump the bag on the seat, but I don't budge.

"Brian," she says, dragging my name out in a way that tells me she's irritated.

Feigning ignorance, I say, "What?"

Another sigh. "Fine." She crosses her arms, mirroring my stance. "Victor threw my lunch in the dirt."

"He did what?"

"He grabbed my lunchbox and threw my sandwiches on the ground, and then he grinded them into the sand with his shoe."

I go mad. I swear to God I see my baby sister's face through a veil of red. "Why?"

"He said I don't need lunch, because I'm fat enough."

That's it. I'm going to teach that little motherfucking bully a lesson. I'm already halfway to the gate when Sam catches the sleeve of my T-shirt.

"Brian! What are you going to do?"

I stop and turn to her. "Nothing you have to worry about. Victor and I are going to have a word, that's all. Go back to the truck."

She doesn't move, just stands there rocking on the balls of her feet. "You're going to embarrass me."

"Of course not." I give her braid a gentle pluck. "Go wait in the truck."

"You sure?" She narrows her eyes. "You're not going to punch him or something?"

Crossing my fingers, I put them over my heart. "Cross my heart. We're just going to have a man-to-man talk."

"Okay," she says, still eyeing me suspiciously. "No hitting."

Not for now, but I'll tan his ass the next time he says a word or lays a finger on my sister or her property. I've got to get her out of this juvenile shithole and into a private school.

Of course, she doesn't go back to the truck, but stays next to the fence to make sure I keep my word. I spot the fucker easily enough, his spiky, bleached hair standing out like a beacon in the herd. When he sees me, he pushes through the gate and tries to split, but I've got him by the back of his shirt before he's made it two steps.

Gripping the nape of his stringy neck, I fling him around. His eyes are big, and his arms flail wildly.

I bring my head down to his ear, speaking softly enough for only him to hear. "Listen here, you little shit. The next time you touch anything that belongs to my sister, I'll break your spaghetti string arm. And if you ever insult her again, I'll break your fucking neck. Got it?"

"Yeah. Yeah, I've got it. Sorry."

The scumbag is twelve, having flunked a couple of years, but I have no problem putting the fear of God into him to teach him a lesson. I push him in Sam's direction and let him go with a shove.

"Apologize to her, not to me."

He stumbles three steps toward her. "I'm sorry."

"Tomorrow," I say, "you're bringing her lunch, and it better be something delicious, like tuna mayonnaise with gherkins."

He makes a face.

"I don't hear you."

"Okay, okay."

"Good. Now get out of here."

He's a good hundred meters away before he throws back over his shoulder, "Fuck you. I'm telling my dad."

In a few strides I'm next to him. He scarcely has time to get a fright before I grip his arm. "Let's do it, sucker." I fish my phone from my pocket. "What's his number? Let's call him now. I'd like to know what he thinks of his son picking fights with girls."

The kid goes red. His dad would whip his ass. I know Daniel well enough to know he'll lay into Victor with a belt for wasting good food, which is why I'm not going to tattletale on him, but the threat works.

"No," he says, hanging his head. "I don't want to call my dad."

"Tomorrow." I point my finger in his face. "Tuna and gherkins."

"Yeah, I got it."

He hurries away, his head hanging between his shoulders.

When I get back to the truck, Sam waits inside like I'd asked.

She flashes me a grin when I start the engine. "Thanks."

"You're welcome."

Leaning my arm over the back of her seat, I turn to face her. "You've got to defend yourself. Always. If your opponent is bigger or stronger, you've got to fight with words."

She crinkles her nose. "Like how?"

"The next time Victor touches something that's yours, speaks to you, or even comes near you, you tell him to stop looking for attention just because he has a crush on you."

Her lips quirk, and her brow lifts. "That'll work?"

"Like a charm." I start the engine. "I promise."

For the rest of the way, she tells me about school and her teachers, barely taking a breath between sentences, until we get home. I park in the street instead of pulling into the driveway, because I have to get back to work after lunch. I'm hoping to get in a shift before my five o'clock class. I don't have to come all the way from town to drive Sam. Her school is only a kilometer away from the house, and she's got a key and a mobile phone to call if there's a problem, but you never know what lurks on the streets.

Deactivating the alarm and unlocking the back door, I'm hit by the silence. One of *those* days. While Sam goes to change out of her school uniform, I go look for my mom in her bedroom. The fact that the curtains are drawn means they haven't been opened all day. The bed is unmade.

"Mom?"

Going back through the kitchen, I head for the living room, which also serves as my bedroom. Still dressed in her flannel pajamas, Mom is splayed out on the sofa bed, her face in the cushions and a burnt-out cigarette in her hand. A small heap of ash lies on the carpet. Tucking my hands under her armpits, I pull her into a sitting position.

"Brian?" she asks with a slurring tongue. "Is that you?"

I take the bud from her fingers and leave it in the ashtray. "You mustn't smoke in the house. One of these days, you'll set it on fire."

"Sorry." She pats my cheek. "You're a good boy."

"Come on."

I hoist her to her feet and help her to her room before fetching a glass of water from the kitchen.

"Drink that."

She sits on the edge of the bed, her shoulders stooped, looking lost, looking broken. I hate this look on her, and, yet, I understand.

"No more drinking, okay? Sam's home."

She lifts her red-rimmed eyes to me and gives me a weak smile.

"I have to go to work. I'll be home to cook dinner."

"You're a good boy, Brian."

I hover another moment before I make my way to the back door, opening curtains as I go. Alcohol is her coping mechanism, and who am I to judge? I don't want this for her, but sometimes life deals you a shit hand, and we all have a breaking point. She didn't hold out long. I hope to God I will.

Jane

As if Friday morning's pool escapade wasn't enough, I wake early on Saturday to the sound of a lawnmower. It's loud, like it's coming from right outside my window. Pushing up on my elbows, I rub my eyes and check the time on my alarm clock. Six in the morning.

Bloody hell.

I kick the sheets aside and swing my legs from the bed. Making my way across the room, I bump my toe on the corner of the dresser and hop around for two beats before I make it to the window. *No way.* The guy who broke into my pool, the cocky one with the blond hair, is mowing my lawn.

Gaping, I take in the scene. He's shirtless, wearing torn jeans and Jesus sandals. His muscles bulge as he maneuvers a lawnmower through the overgrown grass. The electric cable is thrown over his shoulder. It leads back to the plug point on the deck. He wipes his brow even as the late October sun has barely been up for an hour. Half of the lawn, the side farthest from the house, has already been mowed. Five stuffed garden trash bags rest against the wall.

For the love of God.

He jumped the gate again, with his lawnmower, because I don't own one. Francois took ours when he moved. The young man moves meticulously, cutting a straight line along the length of the pool. Whatever he thinks he's doing, I'm not going to give him the pleasure of a reaction. Pretending a stranger in a dirty pair of jeans is not mowing my lawn, I grab my exercise gear and dress in the bathroom. After brushing my teeth and washing my face, I pull a cap over my unruly curls, strap my phone to my arm, and walk out onto the deck.

He cuts the mower when he sees me. Leaning on the handle bar with his elbows, he looks at me. Just looks. His lips aren't smiling, but his eyes are.

I lock the door and cross the lawn, pressing the remote to open the pedestrian gate.

"Good morning," I say as impersonally as I can. He may be a nuisance, but I do have manners.

For a minute, he looks floored, but then a smile cracks up his face, exposing that single dimple. I pretend not to notice that he ogles my ass. The only thing preventing me from not calling him out on it is that he's staring at me with genuine admiration, the kind a trainer would have for an athlete. It softens my heart a fraction, but I don't stop to talk to him. My morning run is sacred. He's already ruined my sleep, not that I can blame all of it on him. I'm not going to let him ruin my exercise.

Slamming the gate behind me, I take to the road. A beaten-up Toyota pickup is parked on the curb, the back crammed with a rake, spade, weed eater, and several other gardening tools. Hoping to God he'd be gone when I get back, I choose the steepest road going up the hill.

The neighborhood is quiet, and the air is still. I pop in my earphones and turn up the volume. Energy pumps through me. The road is covered in lilac confetti from the Jacarandas that are in bloom. Their massive trunks line the sidewalk, their branches embracing at the top to form a purple tunnel. Despite the freak heatwave bathing Pretoria in temperatures of thirty degrees Celsius up to midnight, the smell of spring hangs heavy in the air, and somewhere in the mix is the odor of a freshly mowed lawn.

I take a moment to appreciate the beauty and serenity. I'm a mess after my anniversary lunch with Evan's mom. The rest of the day will be hard, but I'll get over it. I always do. In a way, it's a relief to be alone and not having to face Francois' hostile stare or forced sympathy expressed with, 'I know it's hard for you today, darling'. The anniversary of Evan's death has always been uncomfortable between us. Yet, after sharing a marriage and a child, I'm surprised he hasn't sent me a text to say he hoped I was coping. It makes the pretense of his care about my feelings in this regard stand out starkly, and although I'm glad the charade is over, it makes me feel even more betrayed.

Not wanting to overthink it, I let the beat of my trainers on the tar set a steady rhythm that lulls me like a mantra into a deep state of meditation. Bit by bit, my disillusionment and frustrated anger dissipate until there's only the sadness. The sadness I can handle. It's familiar. It's a way of living.

By the time I've done the full round, I'm better. More normal. Ready to face reality. My T-shirt is wet with perspiration, and my leg muscles burn in protest. I slow as I near the house. The truck is still there. The lawnmower and garbage bags are on the back, and the weed eater is gone. The noise coming from behind my wall tells me the guy is cutting the edges around the flowerbeds.

This time, he doesn't stop when I enter the garden. He merely acknowledges me with a nod, as if he's giving me permission to enter my own domain. He's wearing protective goggles, and his arms flex as he angles the machine over the grass edges. Not sparing him a second glance, I go back inside, lock the door, and head to the kitchen for a glass of water. When I've caught my breath, I put the ingredients for my Saturday breakfast on the counter. Cooking is, after running, my best cure. I cook when I'm sad, stressed, tired, or happy. It's an outlet I find soothing, a passion in which I can pour my emotions until I find calm.

Switching on the central sound system on the wall, I choose a lively compilation and set to work.

An hour later, a spread of peri-peri chicken livers, fried tomatoes, crispy bacon strips, pork sausages, mushrooms sautéed with garlic, and scrambled eggs are set out on the hot tray. I'm squeezing the oranges, waiting for the rye bread basted with olive oil and pesto to toast under the grill, when I look up and see him through the window. He's turning the earth, pulling out weeds under the rose bushes. He steps on the spade and stretches his back. In the harsh glare of the mid-morning sun, his skin shines with perspiration. Leaving the spade buried in the soil, he walks to the garden tap and cups his hand to drink. When he straightens and wipes the back of his hand across his forehead, he leaves a streak of dirt.

A twinge of compassion sparks in my chest. Standing there watching him, I make a rash, unwise decision.

2

Brian

The princess pushes the sliding door open with her hip and comes outside, carrying a loaded tray that she deposits on the garden table. The food smells divine, and I'm starving. I lock my jaw before I salivate on her fancy paved garden path, but the drool has more to do with the way her T-shirt clings to her tits than the breakfast. Her breasts are on the smaller side, exactly how I prefer, not that I'm fussy about features when a woman does it for me. And she definitely does it.

She sits down and, meeting my eyes, pulls up a chair with her foot. It's the last thing I expected, but I'm glad she's not chasing me off her property, or worse, pushing a bill in my hand. Treating me like a servant, ignoring that I'm a person and disregarding whatever feelings I may have, is what most people of her status would do. She inclines her head, her brow climbing a fraction as she waits for me to decide. My hesitation only lasts a second.

Dropping the shears to the ground, I wash up under the tap and pull on my T-shirt before accepting the silent invitation.

She puts an empty plate in front of me. "Help yourself."

I look into her eyes with a directness that'll have most girls blush or look away, but she holds my stare with a steady gaze.

"Would you like me to dish up for you?" she asks with a quirk of her lips.

My staring amuses her. Not exactly the reaction I'm after, but she's paying me attention, and I'll settle for any attention she's willing to give.

"Hello?" she says, reminding me she's still waiting for an answer.

"I'm good."

I pick up her plate and reach for the chicken livers. "A bit of everything?" The plate is warm, a surprising luxury I appreciate, as I loathe eating my food cold.

She doesn't object that I'm taking over. "Please."

With great care, I arrange the food on her plate and serve her a glass of juice. She watches me silently until I've done the same for myself. Only when I've taken the first gulp of juice–fuck, this tastes good–does she speak.

Her voice is a husky and feminine mixture, decadently sexy and sweet at the same time. "You didn't have to." She motions at the garden. "A verbal excuse would've been sufficient, but your apology is accepted."

I wave at the food. "You didn't have to. A verbal thank you would've been enough, but the breakfast is welcome, none the less."

She breaks her toast into tiny pieces, scoops a bite of liver onto one, and pops it in her mouth. When she's finished swallowing, she asks, "Why did you do it?"

My gaze is glued to her mouth. She makes eating look gracious. My aversion to eating noises–the slurps, chews, and swallows– makes me seldom eat with anyone other than Sam or my mother.

Tearing my stare away from her mouth, I say, "We were just

cooling down. I didn't want to scare you, but with the state of the garden I thought the house was unoccupied."

"My husband took the garden tools when he recently moved out," she says, "and I can't afford a service."

Her honesty catches me by surprise. I like that she doesn't try to make excuses.

"Is that why the electric fence doesn't work?" Worry ripples over me. It's too damn easy to get inside.

"How did you know it wasn't working?"

"We didn't. I threw the floor mat from the truck over the barbwire."

"Mm." She eats a few more bites, regarding me with a contemplating look. "Where do you live?"

It's my turn not to make excuses. "Harryville."

"I see."

Meaning she's put two and two together. People from my neighborhood don't have pools. She's still looking at me, but not with judgment or pity. What I see in her face is closer to puzzlement, like she's trying to figure out what I was doing in Groenkloof at two o'clock on a Friday morning.

Stalking you.

With the heat warming my groin at the thought, I glance away before she catches my intent and sends me on my way, because her food is fucking amazing and I love being near her, hearing her voice, and seeing her from so close-up I can discern the flecks of gray in her blue eyes. I can smell her deodorant mixed with the faint perfume of feminine sweat, and it turns me on beyond anything. I better think of ice baths in Siberia, lest my dick gives away the effect she has on me. My gaze falls on dismantled exercise equipment lying in a corner of the deck.

"That yours?"

"It was a birthday gift, but my husband–" She catches herself. "We didn't get around to setting it up before my ex-husband left."

Going over there, I crouch down to examine the squat rack and pull up bar. "You lift?"

"It's just for strength training."

I scan the bags of nuts and bolts. "I can set it up, if you like."

"You've done enough, but thank you."

Straightening, I turn to face her. She's propped her feet on the seat I've left, her delicate ankles showing where the elastic of her leggings has moved up. I can picture myself in that seat with her feet in my lap. It's irrational, but it feels more right than anything in my life.

"It's a small job. It won't take more than an hour."

"Are you sure?"

"I wouldn't have offered if I weren't."

"All right, then. Thank you, I guess."

"If you give me your number I can call when I'm free."

When I walk back to my seat, she moves her feet away. A ping of regret catches in my chest. A hip-hop song filters through the open door. There's the music, the meal, and her, and I can easily imagine this being paradise–my woman, and a perfect spring morning. Except, she's not my woman, and the world is not a perfect place. She's at ease with me, but she's still not interested. Not in *that* way. She's just a kind woman offering a hungry guy food.

"More?" She nudges the mushrooms my way.

"Do you mind if I ask you a personal question?"

"Maybe. It depends on the question."

"Why this song?"

"Why not?"

"I didn't think it would be something you'd listen to."

Her smile is charming. "You mean something *older* people would listen to."

"That's not what I meant. You strike me as a classical girl."

"I have a daughter."

"Ah. Teenager?"

36

"Early teens. *That* was your personal question?"

"No. I was going to ask why you don't move if you can't afford the security or a garden service."

A deep sigh escapes her lush lips. She looks over her shoulder at the house. "This is my daughter's home. This is where she grew up." She pauses, chewing her lip as she seems to think. "No." She gives me a guilty smile. "That's half the truth. The real reason is this is my dream, my ideal home. It's where I feel safe. I suppose it makes me feel good that I've accomplished at least one dream without buggering it up." Her smile turns weak. "The truthful answer to your question is that living here reminds me that I'm not a complete failure."

She's complicated, this perfect woman, and she's suffered some pain, including her divorce. Maybe she still loves her ex-husband. I want to ask who gave up first and why, but that's too personal for a second encounter. I don't want to scare her with the intensity of my interest. Whatever the case, her husband is a fool. If she were mine, I'd never let her go.

"A house doesn't define you," I say. "Neither do a few mistakes or disappointments in life. Wherever you live, whatever the roof over your head is made of, you'll be the same person you are right now." I wink. "I'm sure you're not that bad."

She puts on a happy face, but it's the kind that's just for show. "You don't know me."

"I don't have to know you to know you're too hard on yourself."

"Wow." She utters an embarrassed laugh. "How did we go from breakfast to psychoanalysis?"

"Life is too short for idle conversations. You've got to say what you mean and mean what you say."

"Very philosophical."

"Don't do that."

She blinks at my chastising tone. "Do what?"

"Pretend it doesn't matter. Agree or disagree with a validating argument, but don't make light of the subject just because you're uncomfortable discussing yourself."

Instead of taking offense, she considers my words with a sense of polished calm. "You're right," she says after a while, surprising me yet again with her admittance. "I *am* uncomfortable talking about myself, and I wholeheartedly agree with your sentiment of not wasting time with words."

The fact that she's not only treating me as a human being, but also as an adult with a worthy opinion forces my respect. She could've told me to fuck off.

Gathering our plates, I stack them with the dishes on the hot tray. "Do you always cook like this for yourself?"

"I find cooking therapeutic."

She lays a hand on my arm when I get to my feet. "I can do that."

Her fingers are warm on my skin, the diameter of her reach small.

"Yes, you can, but since I'm here I'll carry this for you."

Without waiting for her consent, I carry the heavy tray into the house. She skitters around a dining room table, showing me through a door. The house is as stunning inside as outside. The mixture of slate and stone mirrors the exterior. The wooden floors are a whitewashed gray, matching the slate and what looks like volcanic rock. Ethnic rugs and artifacts add a degree of warmth to the otherwise stark lines of the modern structure. The lounge and dining room that exit onto the deck is one, large room, divided by a central fireplace. A black chimney hangs over the open fire pit and fluffy cushions are scattered on the built-in benches circling the pit. Suspended from the ceiling by four chains, a wooden platform serves as a kind of swing or daybed. The bolts will allow movement. A padded cushion covers the whole expanse of the wood like a thin mattress. The ornaments are scarce, but the colorful vases and giant glass sculpture of a water lily look priceless. No wonder she's reluctant to leave here.

I'm not refined in interior decorating, but it's obvious she poured her heart into it.

The lounge gives access to the kitchen, which is an explosion of dirty bowls and cooking utensils. The floors are the same hardwood as in the lounge and dining area, and the cupboards are painted a solid gray to compliment the color scheme. White ceilings and skirtings add a measure of dimension. The mason in me has to stop to admire the engraved borders around each cupboard door. The handles are chunky crystal knobs, exposing the copper screws that fix them to the doors.

"It's magnificent, isn't it?" she asks, catching me snooping.

I find an empty spot next to the sink to deposit the tray. "How long did it take?"

"Two years for the building, and another year for the interior detail."

The area is one of the more established ones in the upper-class suburbs of Pretoria. There are no new plots for building. They would've had to knock down whatever house was here before. I can't help the awe from sounding in my voice. "Who's the architect?"

Her lips curve into a graceful smile. "My husband. Sorry, make that ex-husband."

Irrational jealousy beats in my heart. Not only is he white-collar, but he's also got talent, and she still reserves smiles for him, even in his absence, which makes it worse. If you show affection in someone's absence, it's got to be real.

She moves to the sink and starts rinsing the plates, her hip a mere inch from mine. It allows me time to study her. Wisps of hair feather over her temple. Her skin is white, the pores almost invisible, like smooth porcelain. The only color on her cheeks is a faint post-exercise blush, which is a gentle pink rather than a blotchy red. Even in this, she's perfect. Inhuman.

"Here." She hands me a plate dripping with water and uses her foot to open the dishwasher.

For the next few minutes, she rinses while I pack the dishwasher with only the sounds of our labor filling the space. I want to stay like this for eternity, trapped in the illusion of a joyful domestic act on a perfect spring morning when she's got baggage, and I've got a business card with nothing but an email address.

"Thank you," she says when we're done, handing me a kitchen towel with dainty embroidery to dry my hands.

She leans against the counter, watching me with crossed arms. "Do you work or study?"

Her interest warms me, a pathetic glow detonating inside my ribs. "Both."

"Oh?" Her eyes spark with platonic curiosity. "What do you do, if I may ask?"

"You may."

I hand the towel back, standing so close she has to arch her neck to meet my eyes. If the inappropriate proximity of my stance registers in her mind, she doesn't show it.

Resisting an urge to wipe those wisps of hair behind her ear, I say, "I'm a bricklayer, and I do some carpentry on the side."

"To pay for your studies?"

The money barely covers it, but it keeps a roof over our heads and food on the table. Instead of an answer, I give her something between a nod and a smile.

"What are you studying?" she asks.

"Communication."

"What's your major?"

"Advertising."

"Get out of here." She swats my arm with the towel. "That's what I do. Which university?"

"TUKS."

"Me, too! I graduated with Peterson. Is he still there?"

"Retired last year. Which agency?"

"Orion."

I whistle through my teeth. They're the most sought-after in the country. "What position?"

"Senior executive."

She must be earning a packet. Even so, it still won't be enough for the upkeep of this place. She'd need to be the CEO to afford the maintenance of the house alone.

"Which accounts?" I ask, my interest piqued.

"Bakers, Monroe, and Protea, mainly."

Those are some of the biggest companies, especially Monroe. "How did you end up there?"

"One of the partners is a family friend."

That figures. You don't get in without knowing someone.

She checks her watch, setting my heart beating. I'm not ready to leave her, but I've got no claim on staying.

"I have a lunch date, so I better get ready."

At the word *date* my insides start to simmer. If I have no right on her time, I have even less of a say in whom she sees, but the possessive male inside me disagrees. I'm hovering over her, reluctant to set her free. She tries to move forward and almost bumps into my chest. Flashing me a questioning look, she's all innocence, like she doesn't realize that soon I'm going to rip off her clothes and take her with all the filthy intentions floating around in my imagination. Hands, lips, teeth, and cock, I'm going to lay into her with everything I've got. I'm going to make her mine. I'll leave the marks to prove it, too. There's little I don't get if I put my mind to it.

"Come on," she says. "I'll walk you out."

She sails around me, smooth like a boat, and I don't have a choice but to follow. By the time I've gathered my phone and tools, she's leaning on the open gate, obviously eager to see me go, but her polite manners dictate that she walks me to my truck.

When I've chucked everything on the back, she says, "No more trespassing, okay?" It's an order, not a request.

Fishing my phone from my pocket, I hold it out to her. "In that case, I'll need your number so I don't have to jump the gate."

Her look immediately turns suspicious.

"For when I'll be back to install the gym equipment," I say in a placating tone.

After a moment's silent battle that wages in her eyes, she takes my phone and punches in her number. I read what she's typed when she hands it back to me. Jane Logan. I'm not blind to the fact that she's not asking for my name or number in return, but I offer it anyway.

"Brian Michaels," I say, extending a hand. "I'll text you my number."

She accepts with a firm shake.

I can't resist giving her fingers a gentle squeeze before I let go. "It was a pleasure to meet you, Jane."

I'm in the truck and winding down the window, and she's still standing barefoot on the pavement.

I lean an arm on the door and start the engine. "I'll wait until you're inside."

She turns without arguing, and I have the pleasure of studying her until the gate closes on her tight ass.

Jane

LUNCH WITH LORETTA on the day after the anniversary of Evan's death is as much an institution as lunch with Dorothy on the day. I love Dorothy. She's the only person who accepts me for who I am. With Francois, there were parts of me I couldn't show, like the part that mourned Evan. With Dorothy, there's unconditional acceptance. She'll never judge me, even if I screw up. However, talking about Evan with her drains me, and I need Loretta's levelheaded personality, judgmental or not, to restore my inner balance.

After Brian has left, I clean the kitchen, have a shower, and pull on a lilac dress with matching sandals. Our reservation is at Parrots in Kyalami. I'm early, but Loretta's even earlier, already occupying a booth at the back.

"You look gorgeous," she says when I slip onto the circular bench.

"Thank you." I eye her brightly colored, off-shoulder dress. "So do you."

"New collection. I'll set some dresses aside for you."

I have no intention of letting her talk me into buying more clothes, but if I voice it we'll argue until she believes I'm convinced I need a new wardrobe.

"How was it?" Her phone vibrates on the tabletop. She holds up a finger and checks the screen. "Excuse me." Her gaze shuts me out, turning inward. Her tone is clipped as she swipes to answer. "Yes?" Her lips thin as she listens. "Don't unpack the autumn collection until the sale starts. The snow decorations are for December, not before." A short silence follows as she assumedly waits for a reply. "I don't care if it's summer over Christmas. It's figurative. Snow and Christmas go together. Use your common sense, for once." She ends the call and gives the phone her middle finger. "For God's sake. Do I have to spoon-feed her everything?"

Loretta owns a fashion boutique on the high-end scale of the market. She always seems to be running at full-speed, and she always seems angry. Unlike me, she thrives on stress.

"So," she glances at her phone as the screen lights up with a notification, her eyes scanning the message with efficient speed, "tell me. How was it?"

"The same as every year–sad."

She lifts a brow and waits.

"Devastating," I admit with a sigh.

"That's it? Didn't Dorothy tell you?"

"Tell me what?"

"Benjamin's in town."

"What?"

My insides freeze and shatter. The noise of breaking crystal rings in my ears. How could Dorothy not tell me?

"Sorry." Loretta doesn't look apologetic. "I thought you should know."

"Thanks for telling me."

"It's a big city. It's not like you risk running into him on the street."

"Still..."

"Yeah, she should've said something. I can't imagine why she didn't."

"How did you find out?"

"One of Ralph's clients invited him to a company event. He saw the name on the invitation."

"He didn't accept, did he?" I ask in horror.

"Of course not."

Thank God. Ralph wouldn't have declined out of consideration for me, but he would've done it for his wife, because I'm her friend.

My voice is strained. "How long?"

"I don't know. Maybe," she leans over the table, "this is an opportunity to put your ghosts to rest."

"No." My tone doesn't leave room for arguing. "I'm not speaking to him."

"Suit yourself." She brushes the subject off with a shrug, and starts to butter a roll. "Francois looks happy. He came over for dinner with Debs. Nice girl. They suit each other."

I can't help the pang of betrayal that tightens my stomach. "You invited him?"

She pauses with the roll halfway to her mouth. "He's Ralph's best friend. It's not going to change because of your divorce."

"I know. It doesn't make it easier."

Lowering the bread to her side plate, she sighs. "I love you, and you're my friend, but I'm not going to lie to you."

"Okay, just don't rub it in."

"Get over it. Just because Francois fell in love with someone else doesn't mean your life is over. You should go out and meet people."

"It's only been a month."

"So?" She picks up the bread again and takes a huge bite.

"If you were in my shoes, you would've looked at it differently."

"No, I wouldn't. I'd be out there getting the shit banged out of me. I sure as hell wouldn't have lunch with my dead fiancé's mother, let alone be her friend."

Loretta hates Dorothy, which is why I can never have them in the same room. I only have myself to blame. Loretta is the only person except for Francois I confided in after Evan died.

Her phone lights up again. This time, she scoops it off the table. "I was thinking…" She reads the text on her screen before facing me again. "Why not organize a barbecue with you, Francois and Debs, and our neighbors at our place, just to get the awkwardness between the two of you out of the way? Once you've been together in a social setup the ice will be broken. Then you won't have to worry about attending Abby's graduation or wedding in ten years to come as a divorced couple who don't speak to each other."

Debbie is a nice person, a *very* nice person, which makes my friend's diminutive name for my ex-husband's new girlfriend, the woman he left me for, harder to stomach. "No thanks."

Loretta's smile is forgiving. "You'll let me know when you're ready. I'm sorry, but my shop assistant isn't handling the Christmas fucking snow crisis at the store. I have to go." She moves out of the booth, grabbing her bag from the bench. "I'll reschedule."

With an air kiss and a wave, she's gone.

Remaining in my seat, I reflect on her words. She's right, of course. Instead of avoiding Francois and Debbie, I should get over the hurt and betrayal and see things for what they are. The sooner I make peace with the situation, the sooner I'll heal. Until then, I can't be friends with Francois, let alone with *Debs*. This is why I appreciate Loretta's friendship. She won't lie to me to make me feel better. She forces me to look at the bigger picture.

Debbie is great. She's kind to my daughter, and she's crazy about Francois. That's why he loves her, why their blow-up-in-fireworks kind of love won over our stable and unlustful friendship. I knew that kind of love, too. The love I had for Evan was a once in a lifetime kind of love, the explosive kind. What I had for Francois was something entirely different, a love that grew over the years from friendship. My mother always told me if I wanted my marriage to last, I had to marry my best friend, not the guy who sets off the fireworks. I guess she was wrong. Friendship isn't enough for a man, after all. How can I deny Francois the love that turns your knees weak, messes with your head, and makes your heart leap with lust? Because he promised to always be there for me. Because he took advantage of me when I was weak with grief, making love to me without a condom, despite my protests. He slipped into my dorm room and stretched out on top of me, naked, cupping my face as I kept on saying we shouldn't through my tears, slowly sinking his cock into me, whispering promises about taking away my pain and loving me forever.

Forever lasted twelve years.

Stop it.

I didn't want Francois. I was just too weak to fight him. I knew he had a crush on me, but I only had eyes for Evan, the wild biker who was too old for me, the one my mother warned me about. How happy she was when Francois and I announced our engagement. A short two months later, when I started to show, she must've suspected we weren't marrying for love. At least, I wasn't. That's when she told me a marriage needs friendship, not fireworks.

"Will you dine alone, ma'am?" the waiter asks next to me.

I'm so tired, like I'm back in that single bed with the creaking bedsprings and Francois' weight on top of me. Like I'm pushing and pulling at the same time, throwing my future into a fatal gear. Even if I turn my face away, his breath spills hot and unwelcome over my cheek, his panting singular in its release. He comes too quickly, not getting me off, and swallows his sounds like what he's doing is dirty. Then he kisses me, his wet tongue parting my lips like his cock invaded the one part of me that only Evan had touched, a part that still belonged to Evan. I can almost forgive him for everything, even for fucking me while my fiancé was being laid out in a coffin and I was spaced out on tranquilizers, but not for the victorious glint in his eyes when he pulled out of me, letting his semen drip onto my sheets. That's why I'm hurt, why I feel the betrayal to my bones. He stole what belonged to Evan and promised me care in return. When he broke his promise, he diminished what he took. I gave away something sacred for an empty promise and unfulfilling fuck.

"Ma'am?"

Not having even the energy to answer, I put a bill on the table and leave. Where's Loretta's levelheaded judgment when I need it?

I wait until I'm home before I call Dorothy. This is a conversation I can only have in the privacy and safe comfort of my home.

"I know you're busy," I say when she picks up. *But this can't wait.*

Dorothy works as a handwriting expert at the High Court. Her job is hectic, but she always takes my calls.

"I'm never too busy for you."

"Why didn't you tell me?"

She goes quiet. After a drawn-out silence, she says, "I couldn't tell you on the anniversary of Evan's death. It would've only upset you more."

"That's for me to decide."

"How did you find out?"

"Loretta told me."

"Jane…" She sighs. "Maybe you should see him."

"I can't believe you said that."

"What happened, this war between the two of you, it's as much my fault as his."

"It's not a war, and it's not your fault, so don't look for ways of earning redemption."

"I was hoping–"

"Dorothy, stop. I don't want to see him."

"All right," she says slowly.

"Do I need to worry?"

"Not if you're adamant about not seeing him, because he said the same thing about you."

"Good. That's one thing we agree on."

"I love you, Jane, but…"

My voice comes out harsher and more bitter than I intended. "But?"

"He's still my son."

"I'm only too aware of the fact. That's why we did what we did."

"Oh, Jane. If I could turn back time–"

"You'd do exactly the same. As you said, he's your son. You love him."

"He's all I have left." She adds hastily, "Except for you."

"But blood is thicker than water."

"That's not what I said."

"You didn't have to."

"Jane," her voice starts shaking, "you're like a daughter to me, the daughter I never had."

"That's not true. We're friends. We share cocktails, hairdressers, and Thai masseurs."

"Oh, God." She giggles. "That was an amazing holiday."

"See? Who lies on a beach in Thailand and gets drunk on Sex On The Beach with her daughter?"

"We needed to let our hair down."

"Is he staying with you?"

She turns quiet again.

"I'm not going to get upset, Dorothy. I just want to know." *If I shouldn't come over.*

"He's staying with me, but I'm not seeing much of him. He's awfully busy."

Too much information. "Enjoy your family time."

"I love you, Jane."

"Ditto."

I hang up with a numbness in my body. My heart is pounding and my brain is aching, but I don't feel hunger, thirst, or heat. I spend the rest of the afternoon cooking and baking to pass the time. I should be working, seeing that my presentation is on Monday, but I can't focus on work-related thoughts. Abby loves beef olives, so I set out preparing the stuffing and marinating the meat for tomorrow night's dinner. I prepare sweet peppers, aubergines, red onions, and cherry tomatoes for an antipasta starter and bake cheesecake for dessert. Francois was right when he said the older I get, the more I'm like my mother. I'm not happy unless I feed people. By the time the blueberry sauce for the cake is done, I feel considerably better. My life might be in tatters and my idea of a stable home for Abby shattered, but I still have my family, my friends, my health, a good job, and my home. I have a lot to be thankful for. I'm done moping. I'll get over this. All I need is time.

Brian

MOM AND SAM are dancing to a tune on the radio in the kitchen when I get home.

"Hey," Mom says with an out-of-breath laugh, pushing the hair from her sweaty face.

She's pretty when she's happy. Her cheeks are flushed, and her olive skin glows. Her eyes shine like moonstones, more blue than green, just like Sam's.

I hug her before kissing the top of Sam's head. "What are you girls up to?"

Sam purses her lips together to suppress a grin as she motions at the table. "Working on my science project."

On the table lies a tangle of sticky tape, drinking straws, and pieces of a plastic milk bottle. The creation looks wilted.

"What's it supposed to be?" I touch one of the floppy ears and the whole thing comes off.

"That *was* my space shuttle," Sam says with her hands on her hips.

Mom breaks into laughter. Carefree. Sober.

I love these rare moments. Sitting my butt down in the chair, I pull the *thing* closer. "Better make it look like one, then."

Mom switches on the kettle while I cut through the tape with my knife, dismantling the pieces.

"Get some foil," I instruct Sam.

In no time, we have a perfect resemblance of a space shuttle. When Sam carries it to her room, Mom leans in the door and lights a cigarette.

"What's up?" she asks, studying me.

"Why do you think something's up?"

"I know you too well. You're brooding over something."

I push back the chair and stretch my legs. "I met someone."

"Ah." She takes a drag and blows the smoke over her shoulder. "Did this someone *meet* you, too?"

"Not yet. Not like I want her to, but she will."

"It sounds serious. I'm happy for you." Her eyes take on a wistful look.

She's had her share of shit. My dad left just after the accident, before he knew she was pregnant with Sam. Even when she told him, it wasn't enough to bring him back. I wish to God she'd meet someone else. She's young and pretty enough.

"You should try it," I say carefully, gauging her reaction. "Go out. Meet someone. Have fun."

Her posture turns stiff. It's as if my words turned her into a salt pillar. The smoke coiling into the air is the only movement. When she eventually manages a smile, it's tremulous. "I'm okay. I'm happy where I am."

We both know it's a lie. She can't set a foot beyond the peeling stairs of our back porch. It's always bothered me, but today is extra bad. The worry gnaws into my chest, carving deep lines into my heart. Maybe it's having been in Jane's beautiful home, having had a glimpse at perfect, having stepped out of my ugly comfort zone, or maybe it's the way Mom looked earlier when I walked through the door, making me want more of that for her.

Desperation makes me say, "They're gone, you know," not before I've stolen a glance at the corridor to make sure Sam's out of earshot.

"I know." Her smile is sad. "You did the right thing."

I've only told her once. I never meant to repeat my violent secret, but it's paramount she understands.

Her hand trembles as she brings the cigarette to her mouth. She takes a last drag before killing the bud under her heel and coming back inside to dump it in the trashcan. A sinking feeling settles over me when she opens the cupboard and reaches for the gin.

Goddamn.

All I do is ruin everything with my fucking big mouth.

I get the tonic from the fridge and unscrew the cap before filling up her glass.

"Thanks." She shoots me a grateful look.

"You're welcome."

She settles at the table with her drink, humming to the tune on the radio.

Pulling the sweaty T-shirt over my head, I head for the door. "I'll cook. I just need to take a shower, first."

"I can take care of it. Sam can help."

I squeeze her shoulder as I pass. "You can put up your feet."

Her eyes follow me to the door, but she doesn't answer. She's already zoned out.

Jane

DEBBIE LIVES in a two-bedroom townhouse in Centurion. I only found out after the divorce that Francois has been paying for it for over a year. I park in the street and ring the bell on the intercom. Abby rushes through the gate. Her hair is done in a French braid, and she's wearing a new orange T-shirt with Guess written in glitter. Abby is like a crow. She loves everything that shines.

"Mom!" She hugs me hard.

"Hey." I kiss her cheek. "Wow, you look nice."

She turns in a circle, her arms spread out. "Do you like it? Debs did my hair, and she bought me the T-shirt. We went shopping, yesterday. We had carrot cake and facials at Pink."

Everything inside me protests, not only to the hairdo, the clothes, and the spa visit, but also the role Debbie is taking in Abby's life.

I sound more critical than I mean. "You're too young for a facial."

"Mom," she says, dragging out the 'o' and rolling her eyes.

"Hello, Jane."

I drag my attention away from my daughter, turning it toward the sound of the voice.

Francois is leaning in the pedestrian gate, his hands in the pockets of his slacks. "Why don't you come inside? We need to talk."

Before I can answer, he strolls down the garden path that cuts through the tiny but pristine garden to the house. Abby skips along.

I don't have a choice but to follow. Debbie stands in the open door, dressed in shorts and a tank top. From the way her nipples press out from the fabric, she's not wearing a bra. Her breasts are perfect–firm and round, much bigger than mine. Her dark skin glows. She wears heavy eyeliner and dark eyeshadow. It suits her, enhancing her exotic features. Debbie is a struggling poet now that she's a kept woman and no longer working as a secretary, or that's how Francois introduces her to everyone. She's only ever published one poem in a magazine, but I suppose that qualifies her for the title.

"Hi, Jane," she says in a bright voice, shaking her dreadlocks over her shoulder. "Come on in."

Francois enters first, and I sheepishly follow. We stand crowded in the tiny entrance–Francois, Debbie, Abby, and me.

Debbie goes on tiptoes, draping an arm around Francois' shoulders and dragging her fingers through the hair scraping his collar. "Would you like something to drink?"

I'm about to decline, but Francois says, "Coffee, please."

I don't miss the flash of warmth in his eyes as he looks down at her, dragging her closer with an arm around her waist and kissing her temple before letting her go.

Uncomfortable is too mild a word for what I feel. Loser is more like it. It's as if they're rubbing their affection in my face, and I'm still too raw to deal with it. The only thing I can do is put on an act, pretending I don't notice.

"Come help me," Debbie says to Abby, and it irks me that my daughter obliges without as much as an argument, when I can't get her to set the table at home.

"Let's have a seat," Francois says when we're alone.

He leads me to their small lounge. The ugly part of me would've liked to find fault with Debbie, but everything is clean and tidy.

He takes a seat on the couch and indicates the single chair opposite the coffee table.

"I don't have much time," I lie, glancing at my watch. "I have work to finish."

"The Monroe presentation?" he asks, reminding me of how intimately we've been involved until a month ago. Yet, now it seems like a lifetime has passed with him so stiff and cold, like there's a world instead of a coffee table between us.

"Yes," I admit reluctantly, wishing I could bring up something else that he isn't familiar with, something that will prove I've moved on, that my life is my own and not part of his.

He leans forward, resting his elbows on his knees. "We need to talk."

"So you said."

He has custody of Abby every second weekend. I'm not giving him more. I need my weekends with her as much as he does.

Inhaling deeply, he regards me with a steady gaze. "I'm taking back the house."

3

Jane

A cold weight settles in my stomach. I try to swallow, but my throat won't cooperate. I must've misunderstood. We got married out of community of property, and since I didn't work when we bought the property in Groenkloof, the house was put in Francois' name. Still, he's not a spiteful or unreasonable man. The house was never his dream. It's mine. It's the only place I can see myself grow old, where I visualize grandchildren running in the yard and Christmas lunches on the deck. I can't imagine him being this cruel. Our divorce went smoothly, because we easily agreed about the splitting of custody and property. The investments and savings went to Francois. The house was supposed to remain mine. All I'm waiting for is the transfer deed. I signed the divorce papers without the transfer of property in place, because I trust Francois. I *trusted* him to be fair.

"You promised you wouldn't do this," I say when I manage to speak again.

"I know." His gaze is unfaltering, unapologetic. "We need the space."

"Why *my* house?" Francois designed that house for *me*. He did it the way *I* wanted. I supervised the laying of every brick and floorboard. "Why not buy or build something new?"

He doesn't answer.

"Debbie wants to live in Groenkloof, doesn't she?" And there are no empty plots up for the taking.

Again, no answer, which confirms my assumption.

Groenkloof is a green, hilly, privileged neighborhood overflowing with purple Jacaranda trees, but there are other fancy neighborhoods springing up all over the place, like the new golf estate properties that are in fashion.

"Why not Waterkloof?" It's right next door, and there are properties becoming available as the mansions grow too big for older people who prefer to move into retirement villages.

"I can't afford to start from scratch." His tone is firm, not open for negotiation. "It'll cost too much, and as I said, we need the space. You don't."

"You're only two people, just like Abby and me."

He keeps on looking at me with the quiet intensity I know so well, the demeanor he adopts when we're heading for a fight. This is part of what drove me nuts about him. He never talks to me. When we disagree, he grows quiet, turns his back on me, and walks away. There's something else, though, because there's also a glint of compassion in his eyes. He's not walking away. He's sitting there staring, waiting for me to catch on to something.

Oh my God.

It hits me like a ball of snow in the face. "Debbie's pregnant."

He doesn't have to confirm my deduction. The truth is splayed all over his face. Pride, warmth, excitement...all the emotions he didn't show when we found out I was expecting Abby. The protective way he held Debbie earlier in the entrance and the secretive look they shared now make sense.

His voice is level. "It's not like I'm throwing you out. You have three months to find a new place."

My lips part in shock.

He lowers his head, staring at his hands. "Debbie wants to start the nursery before she's too far into the pregnancy." He rubs his fingers together and adds softly, "You never know. The baby can come early."

The calculation falls into place in my head. I've barely dealt with the fact that my husband kept a mistress for over a year before asking me for a divorce. I'm not sure I'm ready for more. Although, I should've known.

Cursing my own ignorance, I ask, "How far is she along?"

"Four months."

That means she was three months pregnant when our divorce went through. The knife twists a little deeper, the cut bleeding a little more. "Is that why you left me?"

"No." The word sounds sure and strong. "It would've happened regardless."

"Did you know when you asked me for a divorce?"

There's a longer hesitation before he answers. "Yes."

He knew she was pregnant when he asked me for a divorce, and he didn't tell me. I shoot him a beseeching look, because I don't understand the man I thought I knew.

"Why?"

"Why what, Jane?"

"Why didn't you tell me? Were you planning on taking back the house all along?"

"No," he says with irritation. "I didn't plan on taking back the house at the time, but Debs and I discussed it since. It makes more sense, this way. You don't need all that space. I doubt you can afford it. The reason I didn't tell you about the pregnancy wasn't to hide a ploy to take the house. It was because I didn't want to put extra stress on Debs in her fragile state."

I gape at him, trying to digest the two facts he's just told me.

I have to give up my home.

Debbie is pregnant.

This is not the time or place for this discussion, not with Abby and Debbie a few paces away in the kitchen. As if on cue, Debbie appears in the doorway with a tray, Abby short on her heels with a cake. Francois jumps to his feet to take the tray from his pregnant girlfriend, and it dawns on me why he once again chose to tell me now, here, and not in private. This way, I don't get to show I'm upset or make a fuss. Selfishly, he picked the worst moment so he doesn't have to deal with my feelings.

Debbie kneels on a cushion in front of the coffee table and picks up a knife. "Carrot cake?" She gives me a bright smile. "I baked it myself."

"Thanks, but I…" I want out. I need air. I need to think of an excuse. "I've got dinner in the oven." The oven is programmed to shut down, but technically the dinner is in the oven. It's not a lie.

"Mom," Abby exclaims as Debbie's face falls. "She baked it especially for you."

"I'm sorry." I jump to my feet. "Maybe I can take a piece to go?"

"Sure." Debbie's voice is deflated.

Francois doesn't look at me as he offers her a hand and helps her to her feet, his arm going around her shoulders. She glances up at him, and I see what their wordless look communicates.

I'm trying so hard, she says.

I know, he replies.

"Do you have everything, Abby?" I ask.

She stomps past me into the hallway. Her footsteps fall hard on the wooden stairs.

"Walk me to my car," I say to Francois.

When Debbie takes a step forward, I say, "Do you mind giving us a moment? I need a word with Francois about Abby."

"Abby concerns Debs, too," Francois says stubbornly.

Fair enough. I suppose she's part of Abby's life, and it's in everyone's interest, especially Abby and the unborn baby's, that we all get along. Taking a deep breath, I say, "Congratulations, Debbie. Francois told me."

A flush darkens her cheeks. "Thank you."

I turn back to Francois. "We need to talk about how we're going to break the news to Abby."

"She already knows."

"What?"

Francois and I saw a child psychologist about how to best convey the news about our breakup to Abby, and he and Debbie told her about the baby without talking to me first?

"She took it well," Debbie says quickly.

"In the future, I expect you to have these discussions with me before involving my daughter."

"She's my daughter, too," Francois says, his posture as stiff as a lamppost.

Abby comes down the stairs, and for now the subject is closed. While Francois helps Abby with her bag, Debbie disappears into the kitchen. She returns with a piece of cake shrink-wrapped on a plate, which she hands to me before we make our way to the car. Abby slams the door of the car unnecessarily hard.

At home, my daughter dumps her bag in the entrance and goes straight to the fridge. I leave the cake on the counter and lean in the door as she goes through the contents, eventually deciding on a bottle of water. The atmosphere smolders with tension.

Unscrewing the cap, Abby regards me from the other side of the room. "I hope you weren't rude because of the baby, because that'll just be mean."

"Of course not. It came as a surprise, that's all."

"Is it because Debs is black? 'Cause that'll make you a racist."

"Abby! It's got nothing to do with any of that. The news has, well, other implications, things I have to deal with, and it's difficult."

"You mean giving up the house."

My God. If Francois already told her this, too, he had no intention of ever giving me a choice.

"I didn't know you knew."

"I know you love this house, but you can still visit as often as you like."

I'm not going to correct her misassumption. Francois and Debbie need to build a new life and reconstruct their own family. There will be no place for me here.

"Can you at least try to get on with Debs for Dad's sake?" she asks, leaving the water on the counter and yanking open the cutlery drawer. With a fistful of knives, forks, and spoons in hand, she marches to the eating nook and, surprisingly, starts setting the table. "This is hard enough for me as it is."

Abby's too young to understand the feelings I'm wrestling with, and she's crazy about her father, but bloody hell, since when did I turn into the villain in all of this? I don't want to be the bitter, disgruntled ex-wife.

"You're right." I take the glasses from the cupboard–my beautiful, backlit, glass door cupboard–and ignore the pang of pain that pinches my chest as I finish the setting of the table. "There's no reason why we can't be friendly."

I'm not saying friends. It'll take a lot of time before I'll be able to forgive Debbie for cheating with Francois when she's been a guest at my dinner table so many times in this very house. Abby's smile makes up for all the hurt festering in the cavity between my ribs as she takes the promise I halfheartedly offer.

When Abby's in bed, I call Dorothy to tell her the news about the house, omitting the part about Debbie's pregnancy. As always, she offers me the sympathetic ear I need, but it's Brian's words that bring my solace. A home doesn't have to define me.

Brian

AFTER DINNER, I wash the dishes before making us each a cup of extra strong Rooibos tea and settling on the sofa bed with Sam and Mom, who are watching a romantic comedy. This is our Sunday evening downtime, a family tradition, and for once Mom doesn't have a glass in her hand. It's good to hear them laugh. It's good to be here, together. It makes it easier to pretend we don't have problems that won't go away, such as earning enough money to give Sam a better future, or the fact that Mom can't step out of the house.

The movie not being a good enough distraction to keep my mind from darker thoughts, I type *Jane Logan* in the internet search engine on my phone. A few subjects come up. Some are aliases. She's not on Facebook or any of the other social media sites. An article toward the end of the second page makes me pause. My thighs bunch in a mixture of excitement at hitting the jackpot and dread at what I'll find. The girl in the photo is definitely Jane, albeit a younger one. Her hair is long and sleek, her face chubbier, but no less gorgeous. The headline reads, *Judge's son dies in crash after fallout with fiancée.* I scan the subtext. *Evan James, oldest son of Judge and Mrs. Richard James, dies in a motorcycle accident after an argument with his fiancée. Their wedding was scheduled to take place next week.* The date confirms the article was published twelve years ago. I quickly read the rest of the text, which explains how Evan James took off in a rage and crashed his bike after a party at his parents' house that ended in a fight with Jane Logan, his future wife. Family witnesses said the couple argued about her infidelity, but no names were mentioned. Miss Logan refused to comment. There's not much more to the article, but it was clearly the scandal of the year.

The rest of my search is futile, except for Jane's name popping up here and there in media articles about her clients and an obituary for each of her parents. The Logans were locals from Camps Bay, Cape Town. I dump the phone on the table, trying to put her out of my mind, but it's futile. Jane Logan already rules my thoughts. I wait until the movie's finished before ordering Sam to go brush her teeth.

She comes out of the bathroom in her pajamas, rubbing her eyes. "I want to sleep with Mom, tonight."

She often sleeps in my Mom's bed, but I always look at my mother for approval. Mom won't smoke in the room with Sam there. She also won't drink. If she knows she's not going to resist, Jasmine will tell Sam no. A slight nod of Mom's head says it's going to be one of her better nights.

After I've tucked Sam in, Mom kisses her forehead. "Sleep tight, my angel."

Sam grabs her hand. "Aren't you coming?"

Mom's smile is reassuring. "After my shower." She pulls the blanket up to Sam's chin. "Sweet dreams."

On her way out, she pats me on the shoulder.

I sit down on the edge of the bed, making the tired bedsprings creak. "Want a story?"

"Of course, silly."

"Hey." I place a hand over my heart, faking a wounded expression. "Why would you call me silly?"

She giggles. "You tell me a story every night."

I drop my hand and the mocking façade. "I'm just checking."

"For what?"

"The day you don't want a story, it'll mean you're all grown up."

She punches my arm. "You really are silly. You can *see* when someone's grown up."

"Not always, Sam. You might be all grown up before either of us realize."

Shit, that fills me with dread. For now, I can lock her up at night and protect her, but how am I supposed to protect her when she starts going out on dates?

Her yawn propels me into action. "Do you know the story about the slime man?"

"Slime man?" She wrinkles her nose. "Yuk."

"Once upon a time, there was this green slime dude."

"As in the squishy stuff?"

"Yeah, the kind that goes as flat as a pancake when it hits a wall."

"Where are his eyes and mouth?"

"What?"

"If he's as flat as a pancake, where are his eyes and mouth?"

"He's only flat when he hits a wall, otherwise he looks like you or me, except that he's green and slimy."

"Slippery?"

"Yeah, slimy."

"Slimy can also mean sly, so you need to say he's slippery."

"Slippery can also mean difficult to catch, so shut up, Miss Wise-ass, and let me tell the story."

She crosses her arms on top of the blanket in a defiant gesture, but keeps quiet.

For the next five minutes, I make up shit as I go until Sam's eyelashes start to flutter, not even the gore of Slime Man enough to fight the pull of sleep. I finish with the same line as always, "And he lived happily ever after," and kiss her cheek before I turn off the light.

God knows, I want happily ever after for Sam. And for Mom. No one deserves it more than Mom, but we are what life made us. Reality isn't a fairy tale. The best I can do for my sister is make the fairy tale last as long as possible.

Outside, perched on the wall in the darkness of the porch, I dial Jane.

"Brian?"

Surprise laces her tone, but I suspect it's not the good kind. It doesn't matter. It's heaven to hear her voice. The way she perfectly projects her sounds, a dead giveaway of a private school tuition, ripples through my ear until the fine hairs in my neck stand on end.

"Am I interrupting something?" I ask.

"We finished dinner, but I was about to go to bed."

"I won't keep you. I just wanted to know which afternoon this week I can set up your gym."

"I'll be working late every day, and then I have to help my daughter with homework."

"How about after homework?"

"It's the evening rush–dinner, getting the washing done, and everyone to bed."

"How about the weekend?"

"I have my daughter for the weekend. I prefer to spend time with her."

"The weekend after, then."

"Brian." There are objections, and something like fear in her tone, the kind one feels for lacking control. "You don't have to do this."

"I said I would, and I don't break my word."

Her sigh is only a soft sound, but it's as if the air brushes over me. My cock takes notice, and my balls draw tight. This woman has the ability of touching me without laying a finger on my body.

"All right, then." Her voice is uncertain. "Saturday in two weeks."

Not giving her time to change her mind, I seal the deal. "I'll be there."

I end the call with a buzz in my veins and a throbbing in my chest. What Jane does to me is no fairy tale. It's as hard as reality gets. It's raw, naked, sinful lust. She's old enough to be my mother, but lust knows no manners or rules.

What stirs in my body is off-limits.

It's taboo.

If I gave a shit about what's socially acceptable I won't go back. The problem is I don't. If it makes me foolish, so be it. In a perfect world, I'd control my impulses and take a hike. In my shithole of a universe, I'm seeing my Jane Logan hangover for what it is.

Fixation.

I'm accepting the path I'm about to take for what it is. Inevitable.

———

JANE TOLD me to install the gym equipment in two weeks. She didn't say I couldn't go back before, and the reason I'll be heading over there later is for a reason much more important than a squat rack. First, I pop into Tron's security store after my last Monday class at varsity. The place is in the main street of Harryville's cranky shopping area. His light is the only one still on at seven. Other businesses close at five.

Tron looks up from a newspaper as I push open the door. He looks like a bald gorilla with a tractor tire around his waist. His arms are the size of tree trunks. Too much beer and sitting in that chair all day gave him the wobbling three layers that constitute his chin. A tussle of black hair peeks from the collar of his khaki shirt. His arms are covered with the same dark hair. So are his stomach and back. I had the unfortunate experience of witnessing it with my own eyes on our first and last fishing trip together. Appearances aside, he's mostly a good guy, and he lets me do odd jobs in exchange for equipment.

He rolls a toothpick from one corner of his mouth to the other. "Whazup? How's your ma?"

"Same old." I scan the second-hand security cameras on the dusty shelf. "Got any motion detectors?"

He throws a thumb over his shoulder at the storeroom. "Back there. As good as new."

Going through the storeroom, I gather what I need and pack it out on the counter.

Tron scans the goods with a practiced eye. "Thought you already had all of this shit at the house."

"It's for someone else." I take a used paper bag from the hook on the counter and dump the items inside. "I'm free on Saturday. Need any jobs done?"

Glancing inside the bag, he scratches his head. "The fence needs fixing. Some idiot cut the barbwire trying to get in. Can you believe it?" His stomach shakes as he laughs. "Trying to break into a security store. Must be a fucking butthead."

"Did you catch him?"

"Al did."

Al is a vicious Pit Bull that lives in the back.

"Did you lay charges?"

"Are you kidding me? The prisons are overflowing with murderers. Who's going to come out here to arrest a thief? Nah. Dealt with it myself."

Concern makes me go still, the bag dangling from my fingers. "How?"

"Called the neighborhood watch. We gave him a good hiding. He won't come back here no more."

"If you say so." I have my doubts. He may come back with his buddies, and then we'll have a bigger problem.

He throws his hands in the air. "What else do you want me to do? Give him a medal? A pat on the head? These assholes understand only one language, and that's their own."

Lowering my head, I blow out slowly through my nose. I know what he means better than anyone. Still, Tron's putting himself in danger. He's no match for the agile fence cutters trolling our neighborhood.

"Next time, call me."

"Yeah." He spits out the toothpick. "Join the neighborhood watch, and maybe I will."

"Anything else needs fixing?"

"The toilet is leaking, and the outside drain is blocked."

"Got it." I hold up the bag. "Thanks."

The door shuts on his scowl.

. . .

AFTER FIXING dinner and washing up, I leave Mom to help Sam with her homework and get Clive to babysit. He's not happy, but is quickly swayed when I mention there's leftover apple pie from our Sunday lunch. I bake a mean pie, and Clive knows it.

At that time, it doesn't take long to drive to Jane's house. Peak hour is over, and our neighborhoods aren't far apart, at least not in geographical distance. As for the rest, worlds apart may not be enough to cut it. A well-maintained, three-bedroom house with an average garden and decent security in Harryville goes for five hundred grand, these days. The same will go for seven million in Groenkloof. Nothing spells out the tracks that separate us better than numbers. I'm not even thinking about the property prices in Cape Town where Jane's late parents used to live. Add another two zeros to the Groenkloof figure, and the maths will give you Camps Bay.

Coming down the hill, I have a good view of Jane's house before the high walls obscures everything beyond. The lights are on. She's awake. Most people consider the hour late. A doorbell ringing at this time of night is associated with bad news—death, illness, or trouble. So as not to scare her, I send a text to let her know I'm paying her a visit.

She answers the gate intercom immediately. "Brian!" She sounds tousled and out of breath, as if she ran for the intercom. "What are you doing here?"

"I brought security equipment."

"What?"

"You can't stay here without an alarm."

"It's eight o'clock on a Monday night."

"Thanks for the update, princess, but I know that."

"It's *late*."

"There's two ways of doing this. One, you open the gate. Two, I let myself in. Whatever your choice, I'm not leaving until my work here is done."

She heaves a labored sigh. "You're impossible."

"Thanks."

"I don't appreciate being blackmailed," she says on a huff, but the gate clicks open.

Hauling my toolbox and the bag from Tron's store from the truck, I make my way to the front door and stop dead when it's flung open. A child-version of Jane stands in the frame, wearing pajamas with an ice cream print. The resemblance is striking. They share the same midnight blue eyes and curly, moonlight hair.

Throwing myself back into motion, I resume my stride and hold out a hand. "You must be Jane's daughter."

She catches my fingers in a strong grip. "Who are you?"

Before I can reply, Jane rounds the corner, her socks slipping on the smoothly polished wooden floor in her haste. I forget what I was going to say. I forget my reason for pitching uninvited at an unreasonable hour. I forget my name and everything I've ever believed and wanted. Jane is dressed in shorty pajamas. The shorts are cut so high if she turns around I'll see the seam of her ass. The tank top isn't tight, but her nipples are two dark, embossed imprints on the peach-colored fabric. There's no guesswork to the size and shape of her tits. They're firm handfuls with a downward slant, topped with those perky nipples. There's something about that dip in her breasts and how they sway that makes me harder than stone and hotter than crazy. Her toned legs are bare, except for the chunky socks that only Jane can make look sexy. Uncool. Having these thoughts in front of a kid isn't where I want to go, but Jane's got me by the balls, and judging from the void in my over-heated brain, she's the pussycat who caught my tongue.

"Hey," Jane exclaims, saving me from speaking. "This is a surprise."

Her eyes are chastising me, but she's too polite to tell me to fuck off in front of her daughter.

"Um, this is my daughter, Abigail." Jane presses a palm against the back of her neck. "Abby, this is Brian."

"Hi, Abigail. May I call you Abby?" I crouch to put us on eye level. "You must be about the same age as my sister."

"I'm twelve."

"Sam's nine, but she's almost as tall as you."

"Go brush your teeth, honey. I'll be there in a minute to say goodnight."

Abby looks between her mother and me. "What's he doing here?"

"He's not staying. He's just–"

"Going to install these security tools." I straighten and jostle the bag.

Jane gives me a narrowed look. She can't back out now, unless she makes up excuses to her daughter about why I won't be securing their house, after all.

"Are you from the security company?" Abby asks.

"We met the other day." Jane places her hands on Abby's shoulders and wheels her around. "Go on. Off with you."

While Jane carts Abby off to the bathroom, I lock the door behind me. Then I set to work. I'm drilling a hole in the kitchen wall when I feel her behind me. Turning my neck an inch, I spot her insanely cute, socked feet. I swivel slowly to face her.

Jane is standing in the center of the room, her arms crossed. She's pulled on a sweater. "I didn't ask you to do this."

Biting a screw between my teeth, I turn back to the task at hand. "You didn't have to."

Her legs appear next to me, so close they almost brush the denim of my jeans. Her perfume smells of grapefruit and lemon–fresh, expensive, and edible.

"I can't pay for it."

The urge to slide my palm up her calf is magnetic. Barely resisting, I bite down hard on the piece of metal between my teeth and will my growing erection down. "I know."

"Then why are you doing it?"

I take my time to position and tighten the screw, fighting the upsurge of heat her proximity unleashes in my chest. It's a good and bad kind of heat, making me want to cuddle and fuck her simultaneously.

When the task is done and my voice under control, I dare to look at her again. "You can't stay here alone with no security. It's not top-level, but at least you'll have a visual of who's at your gate, plus an alarm will warn you if anyone breaches the property, breaks a window, or opens a door."

"There's no point."

"There's no point in your safety?"

"You're wasting your time." She stares at her toes. "My ex is taking back the house."

Shit. From the way her voice wavers, this is a sore point.

"When?"

"I have to be out in three months."

"Then I'll move the equipment to your new home. I'm not leaving you here without an alarm. End of discussion."

She shifts her weight. "The equipment must cost a fortune. It doesn't feel right not repaying you."

"Don't sweat." I wave the screwdriver at the bits and pieces unpacked on the floor. "I don't pay for it. A friend has a store. I do odd jobs in exchange for whatever I need." I continue working, feeling her gaze on me.

"What did you have to do for this?"

"What *will* I do for this, you mean. This and that."

"This and that."

"Mm-mm."

"Gardening?"

"Nope."

"What then?"

"Repairing a fence, unblocking a drain, and fixing a leaking toilet. Happy?"

"Yes and no."

I stop to look at her again. "Confused much?"

"I feel guilty."

"Don't. Your safety has no price."

I work in silence for a few minutes before she speaks again.

"Why?"

"It's a dangerous city, Jane."

"Why are you doing it for *me*?"

"Because I know how easy it is to get in here."

"Then I insist on paying it back."

I can't help but grin. "You'll fix Tron's toilet, fence, and drain?"

"No, but I thought–"

"I don't want money."

"What do you want?"

"A thank you will do nicely, and maybe a cup of tea."

"Of course."

She's about to turn when I catch her wrist. Her skin is white under my darker tone. The contrast is feminine, fragile, and seductive. I want her to know how I'm seeing her–as a woman I want. I want to give her ample warning of what's to come, that I intend to seduce, fight, and manipulate until I have my way with her. Slowly, I drag my thumb over the soft skin of her wrist. Her pulse is a flutter under the pad of my finger. The tempo speeds up under my stare, and a flush blooms over her cheeks. Awareness creeps into her distant eyes, and for the first time she looks at me like I want her to. She looks at me like I'm a man. She pulls, testing my hold, and I close my fingers tighter.

"Brian, I–"

"Mom?"

We both turn our heads toward Abby who stands in the door.

"I'm ready for bed."

I have no choice but to let her go.

Jane clears her throat. "I'll be right there, honey."

"Good night, Brian."

"Night, Abby. It was nice to meet you."

"Likewise."

With a glance over her shoulder, Jane hurries from the room.

She stays away for a long time–on purpose, I suppose–and when she returns my job is done. While she hands me a cup of tea and a plate loaded with chocolate fudge brownies, I give her a remote and run her through the basics of the alarm signals and panic button, which will activate a signal on the security app on my phone–I don't tell her this part–and speed dial an emergency service from hers.

"Any problems," I explain, "and all you have to do is push this button."

"Wow." She pushes the hair from her face. "Thank you."

"You're welcome. Thanks for the tea. The brownies were delicious."

I'd love to hang around longer, but she needs to be up early for her run, and I can't expect Clive to wait forever.

I rinse my cup and pack it in the dishwasher before heading for the door. "Sweet dreams, princess."

She doesn't answer as I see myself out.

Jane

TOBY IS A GREAT BOSS. I love that man to bits. He's like a father to me, but he's also a close friend of Francois', which is how I got a cushy job in a high-ranking firm without any experience. I proved myself since I started, gradually working my way up to the bigger accounts, thanks to Toby's mentorship. This weekend, he played golf with Francois and had dinner at Francois and Debbie's place. His assistant told me. Yet, he greets me with a warm smile as I rush through the boardroom door, just in time as usual, and I'm grateful he's not taking sides.

"Morning, sugar." Toby adjusts his safari hat. Paired with a British-cut linen suit, it's his signature style. "Looking good."

I straighten my jacket. "Thanks."

Most of the senior crew are already there–Priscilla from Art, Mable from Copy, and Beatrix from Production. The junior guys from Research, Media, and Public Relations trail in after me.

Toby folds his feet on the desk, showing off crocodile leather. "Show us what you've got."

I shiver at the sight of the shoes. "Poor crocs, Toby."

He shrugs. "You know my motto. I only wear them if I ate them."

I make a face. "You *ate* them?"

"Well, not these ones specifically," he wiggles the pointy toes, "but I had crocodile at Carnivores. A bit fatty for my taste."

"That's despicable," Mable says. "Don't let our clients find out what a carnivore you are."

"Says Miss Vegetarian who only wears leather shoes and jackets that come from cows she doesn't eat." Toby winks.

Alex from Legal enters. "Can we not discuss our ethics at the office? This is a laic company."

Bernard from finance follows short on his heels.

"We're not talking religion," Priscilla says.

Alex takes a seat next to me. "Religion, ethics, veganism… All the same thing–firepower for a discrimination lawsuit."

Toby rubs his palms together. "Let's get the show on the road. I've got a ten o'clock scheduled."

I open the presentation I emailed to everyone this morning and start going through the points. It's next year's advertising and PR plan for the Monroe account, our biggest client. A creative learning program aimed at pre-school children, it's the oldest and best-known system in the country. It's a brand our grandparents grew up with. Their program involves flash cards, board games, picture books, and family activities. Their mascot is Freddy, the fish. Everyone knows Freddy. Everyone loves Freddy, but Freddy is losing popularity in the competitive market of electronic games, which means Monroe is losing profit. They want a new approach, a wider reach, and a brand revival. I worked hard on my proposal, but as I talk the team through the roadshow involving readings from Freddy at libraries, toy stores, and bookshops, the corners of Toby's mouth draw down, and he drops his feet to the floor.

To his credit, he waits until I'm finished before he says, "Ain't gonna cut it, sugar."

"Why not?" I ask with no small amount of exasperation.

"Too costly, too time consuming, too hands-on."

"Too hands-on?"

"We'll have to hire people to wear a fish costume in which they're going to sweat in the middle of summer."

"Potential lawsuits for heat exhaustion," Alex interjects.

"We'll have to fabricate hundreds of fish costumes," Toby continues, "not to mention the logistics of coordinating with the stores country-wide."

"Yes, it involves a lot of work, but it'll give the results Monroe's after. Kids love Freddy. They'll visit the stores in hordes for a live performance. The stores will sell plenty of Freddy products, Monroe will make its margin, we'll get our commission, and everyone will be happy."

"We don't have the manpower."

I look around the table for support, but everyone stares at me with sealed lips.

"We'll outsource," I say.

"Too costly," Bernard says.

"That's relative. Look at the profits we can make." I open my budget projection.

Bernard has studied it in advance. He doesn't need to look at it to agree with Toby. "Nope. Too risky. You can't say for sure it'll work."

"Oh, come on. Where's your guts? No risk, no gain, right?"

Toby purses his lips. "Not what the client wants."

"How can you say? We haven't run it past them."

"I know them, Jane, for much longer than you. I know Mr.

Monroe, and I knew his father. I can tell you now, this isn't what he wants."

Pressing the back of my fingers against my lips, I suppress a sigh. "What then?"

"Innovation. Think outside of the box. Think keeping up with the times. Definitely don't think roadshow. That's old school." Toby pats me on the shoulder and gets to his feet. "Keep on working. You have another month."

One by one, the people file out of the room until only my laptop screen with two months' worth of pitching stares back at me. Lowering my forehead to the table, I blow out a long breath. Looks like I'm starting from scratch.

BETWEEN WORKING ON THE PROPOSAL, household chores, hunting for a place to rent, and driving Abby to modern dancing and tennis practice when I'm not helping her with homework, I almost forget about Brian. To say he doesn't pop into my mind from time to time is a lie. What happened on Monday night? Did I misinterpret the heated look in his eyes? Did the way he touch me mean something, or was it a fragment of my needy imagination?

Whenever these questions whirr through my mind, I chastise myself. I shouldn't even be asking them. What am I thinking? I can't think about him like that. I'm not going to perve over someone I don't know, someone with a sister my daughter's age, for Christ's sake. I'm *not* going to notice him in *that* way, because it'll make our very superficial relationship awkward. I'm not going to turn into an old, sodden fool, mistaking a random touch for something deeper, darker, something I buried with Evan. I don't want to wake that dragon inside of me, because when she lifts herself from the ashes, she'll be ravenous. It was hard to put her to rest when Evan passed away. I don't want to suffer through the burning need only for that wanton desire to become a madness eating into my heart and brain. There's no man like Evan, and there will never be. When he died, he left me broken with a starving dragon clawing in my chest. Part of it was emotional, and part of it was physical. The mental grief merged with the physical longing, until I couldn't distinguish one from the other. All that was left was hell and an eternity of suffering in it.

The law of energy is simple. For every action there is a reaction equal in force. The higher you fly, the harder you fall. The unparalleled highs of being fucked by a man who knows what he's doing leave you wanting with a devastating need when all that skilled, obsessive, abundant loving is gone. Francois rescued me from the dark hole I was tumbling into by giving me a purpose to live–Abby. It didn't take the hurt or yearning away, but every year I cemented a new layer of life over the ache, burying that dragon who'll settle for nothing less than the fire that burns your soul naked until you're stripped to your most exquisite passions. I'm not waking that dragon I feel stirring in my belly. It scares me more than anything, even more than losing my husband and home. When Brian has installed the gym equipment, he can't come back. I'll make it clear. *He can't come back.* This is the mantra I repeat when I catch myself wondering about that touch.

By the second week, I've convinced myself I imagined his interest. I'm such a fool. It's embarrassing. It's just a phase. The divorce. Psychologically, I've suppressed my needs, and with the tie between Francois and me severed, all these Freudian issues are surfacing in my psyche. Phew. That makes me feel a whole lot better, so much so that it's not awkward when Brian is there when I return from my Saturday morning run two weeks later. The squat rack is already set up, tools splayed out over the deck.

I stop next to him with my hands on my hips to catch my breath. "Broke in, again?"

"Good morning to you, too."

"How did you get through all the security wizardry you installed?"

"It doesn't apply to me."

"So, you can walk in whenever you want."

"Only when you're not here to open the gate. I couldn't wait. I needed to get an early start. I've got somewhere to be later." Wiping his hands on a cloth, he studies my face. "This is your cue to say thank you."

"Thank you," I parrot. "Will it take long to finish the pull up bar?"

"A few minutes."

"In that case, I'm going for a quick shower."

It's as hot as it gets in summer. Sweat is trickling down my back, and my skin is sticky. I don't feel the need to lock the door behind me this time as I rinse down quickly and dress in a cool summer's dress and sandals. Brian is securing the last screw when I come back outside.

"I appreciate you doing this."

He crosses his arms and takes a step back to study his work before he lavishes all of his attention on me with a smile.

Shit, that dimple is trouble.

"Do you know how to use it?" he asks.

"Of course, I do."

He looks between me and the top bar. "You'll need a step."

"I'll have to buy one."

"Let's try it out. Come here." He points at the space in front of him. "I'll give you a hand."

Stepping around him, I go on tiptoes and lift my arms. I won't reach, even if I jump.

"Ready?" he asks. "Grab hold of the bar when I lift you."

When his hands close around my ribs, what we are, were, and will be changes forever. Our banter, conversations, and the air we share will never be the same. The battle I've been fighting for the past two weeks is lost. I become wholly and irrevocably aware of him as a *man*. The awareness hits me like a meteorite–his strong grip, his hard body, his unusual height, his sexual vitality, and his masculine dominance. The impulses catch me off-guard, not giving me time to hide my reaction to his touch. Embarrassingly, my body freezes. Inwardly, I cringe.

Please, don't let him notice.

It's futile. He knows. The minute I tense, so does he. His hold on me grows marginally tighter, but I feel it where it matters. I feel it in the lurch of my heart and the somersault of my stomach. I feel his quick intake of breath rather than hear it, because I'm suddenly in tune with his energy, his every vibe. It's as if we've entered the same wavelength where words are mundane and senses tell all. We're suspended in our bubble of sexual awareness in time, locked in the act of him lifting me off my feet. Even when my hands grip the bar, he doesn't let go. It's a minute, a second, or hours. Our mutual awareness is thick. It darkens the air and fills my lungs until all I breathe is him.

Slowly, he lowers me back to my feet. Our bodies aren't touching, but he's standing close. His heat burns through my thin dress, and his quickened breath envelopes my naked shoulders. Goosebumps break out over my arms and legs. His fingers are still locked around my ribcage. He cups my body like it's something he doesn't want to let go, and it feels right, like his touch belongs there.

Wrong. This is a thousand shades of jaded. I should say something to break the pending disaster, something to pretend our cognizance hasn't shifted. I should at least give him a way out.

"Brian, I'm–"

"Shh."

He brings a hand around and presses two fingers on my lips.

Blood zings in my ears. My heartbeat pounds like a pendulum. The sensations coursing through me are deafening. My breasts tighten, my nipples harden, and my lower body tingles with heat. Symptoms I haven't felt in twelve years, not since Evan, rush bone-deep through my body and surface on my skin. My skin turns hypersensitive, contracting and rippling as he slides his hand from my mouth to my neck, caressing me with the back of his fingers. At the physical sign of how he affects me, a soft groan vibrates in his chest. Gently, he turns me to face him. What I see in his eyes thrills and scares me. His lust is the dangerous brand, the type that can make your fantasies come true and ruin you. I know where this is going even before he starts walking me backward to the house and into the kitchen, but I'm powerless to stop it. He's cut the chains that held the dragon, and now it's too late. I'm lost in the moment, past conscious thought or self-control. When my backside hits the counter, he leans his weight against me, lowering his forehead to mine and caging me in between his arms. When the thick, hard heat of his erection presses against my stomach, I lose another battle even before it starts.

4

Brian

I'm pushing teacups and saucers aside. The distressed sound of splintering porcelain as bone china hits the floor fills the space. It's not the brusque noise of a cheap mug breaking, but expensive and refined, like private tuition, Catholic schools, and good girls.

Jane regards me with huge eyes. Her chest moves rapidly, but no sound, not even a puff of air, escapes her lips. She braces her hands on the counter at her back, her perfect oyster-pink nails turning white on the cloudy apple marble. Colors, sounds, and scents imprint on my mind. My senses are in overdrive. She watches me as I put a step between us, giving myself the space I desperately need to hold onto my control. No parts of us are touching any longer, but her heat soaks through my shirt and jean-covered groin, scorching me. With her neck craned up and my head lowered, our gazes are locked. It's important that I read her reaction. If she doesn't want this, if there's as much as a shadow of doubt in her eyes, I'll stop. I'll scrape the barrel of my control, but

I'll stop. I'm so tuned to her body, I don't need words. I feel every ripple of sexual tension that pools in the air around us, every ounce of throbbing need, every murky, sticky gram of guilt.

My palms make contact first, two hands closing around the small diameter of her waist. Splaying my fingers, I trace the definition of her ribs through her dress. She knows what I'm doing. My cock is hard, stabbing against her flesh.

The tightening of my hands is the only warning she gets before I lift her onto the counter. My eyes never leave hers as I brace my hands on her knees, pushing the fabric of her dress up, inch by slow inch. Her breathing spikes as my thumbs brush over the insides of her legs. I stop just before her pussy to gather more control. Fuck, my dick is about to blow just thinking about the sight that awaits. Bunching the dress in my fists, I push the fabric over her hips. When the dress is hitched up around her middle, I'm still holding her eyes, not only communicating my intention, but also prolonging the sacred wait. I want to make this last. She's staring at me like she's watching a show, like my eyes command and hers follow. I drag the sweet agony out as long as I can, and only when I'm close to snapping do I drop my gaze to the center of her legs.

She's wearing white panties. The silk clings to her pussy, outlining the shape of what's hidden beneath. Hooking a finger into the elastic, I pull the fabric aside slowly, as if I'm unwrapping a long-awaited gift. A dusting of golden hair covers her pussy lips, but not enough to hide the little pearl that peeps from between her folds. I'm glad she doesn't shave. I prefer a woman to a girl. She's pink and ripe and ready all over, her flesh engorged and glistening with arousal.

I yank on the elastic. "Hold this."

She obeys instantly, pulling the fabric aside to give me access and free my hands. Arranging her heels on the edge of the counter, I push her thighs open as far as they'll go and lower my head between her legs. Before I take her in my mouth, I use her trimmed pussy hair as leverage to pull her wide open, exposing her slit, her arousal, and her clit. She's perfect, like I knew she'd be. She doesn't protest as I take in my fill, the visual alone enough to make me ejaculate. When her thighs start trembling from the strain of the position, I yank harder on her pubic hair, inviting a low moan. Only then do I taste her, pushing my tongue flat against the underside of her pussy and dragging it up her slit. She starts shaking when I reach her clit, her whimpers as elegant as the fragile breaking of the priceless china. God, she's addictive. I lick her like candy, down and up, a little bit deeper, while keeping her stretched. She cries out louder when I nip my way back to her clit, this time securing the hard nub between the gentle vice of my teeth so I can flick my tongue sideways over the bundle of nerves.

She clamps her thighs around my face. The elastic of her underwear snaps as she lets go to find purchase on the counter behind her, leaning on her elbows. Her ass lifts off the surface as I start sucking before running my teeth over her clit. She yelps and jerks. A string of soft curses fall from her lips, making the moment dirty in the best kind of way.

I pull back to study my work. Her skin is wet, red, and pulsing, her clit swollen to twice the size of earlier. The urge to slam my cock into her is so overpowering that my hand goes to my zipper of its own accord, but this isn't about my dick. It's about her pleasure. It's not difficult to get back on track when she's laying on her kitchen counter, legs and pussy splayed, all for me to play with. That's exactly what I do. I tease, suck, bite, and lick until she begs me, until she squirms and pleads, pushing herself deeper into my mouth.

I want to watch, so she won't come in my mouth. Not this time. Stretching her pussy open, I flatten two fingers over her clit and rub until I find the spot that makes her back lift off the counter and her knees slam together. A loud moan leaves her chest as her pussy contracts and she comes under my fingers. I feel her tighten and spasm on the outside. I can only imagine the grip she'll have on my cock on the inside. I'm hypnotized. I can't stop, and I can't look away. Even when she fights me, I keep on touching her, stimulating her, until there's not an aftershock left in her body.

When the impact of the orgasm is over, I straighten between her legs. The sight is stunning. She's a beautiful, upper-class lady in a passionate mess. Her face is flushed, but her make-up is in place. Her slender feet and pink-painted toenails belong on the cover of a fashion magazine, especially in those strappy sandals. These two parts, the top and bottom, form a stark contrast with the crumpled dress and eaten-out pussy in the middle. The skin is blotchy where I've pulled her pubic hair and bitten her. Together, it makes a perfect picture. My perfect, unobtainable, fuckable princess.

She doesn't close her legs to hide from me, and the voyeur in me can't get enough. The addict in me needs to slip a finger inside that plump pussy. I need to feel her tight warmth to torture myself with images of how hard she'll squeeze my cock. The pervert in me needs to sink two fingers into her ass, because the sex-craved bastard in me needs to feed on her screams. It's the optimist in me that yearns for something deeper, something that goes beyond a fuck. But it's the realist in me that reacts when she opens her eyes and stares at me soberly.

Her expression says it all.

Grabbing fistfuls of her dress, she starts dragging it over her hips. I lock my fingers around her wrists and pin them next to her face, preventing her from covering herself up. I'm leaning between her spread legs, my cock pressing against the wet, naked folds of her cunt.

Our faces inches apart, I say, "Don't you dare. Don't you fucking feel guilty."

She doesn't fight my hold. The submission slightly calms me, but not enough to let her go.

"You knew it was going to happen, Jane. The minute I saw you, it was a foregone conclusion."

Her eyes tighten, and her lips thin. "That I'll be easy?"

"If you were easy, I'd be inside your pussy right now with my cum dripping from your ass."

Her hands ball into fists, and her nostrils flare, but still she doesn't try to throw me off.

"You're vulgar."

"That's why you like me, princess. It's gets you off."

"It's got nothing to do with your filthy mouth."

"No?" I drag my nose along the elegant curve of her jaw. "Only my tongue?"

She doesn't answer.

"Tell me how hard you came, princess."

"You know the answer."

"Tell me, anyway."

Her stare is brave, defiant, and soft, all at the same time. "The hardest ever."

The admittance catches me off guard, enough to let go of her wrists. My fingers left white imprints on her skin. I've squeezed too hard. It's easy to forget my strength, especially with someone so fragile, someone so intoxicating who makes me forget everything else.

Taking one, dainty wrist into my hand at a time, I kiss the marks, rubbing my thumbs over the area to stimulate the circulation. Her wrists are impossibly small, smooth, and white in my calloused, oil-stained hands. The contrast is a visual reminder that we don't belong, that our planets don't turn in the same orbits. Fuck that. I'll defy reality, dreams, and the very laws of nature. I want Jane too badly to do otherwise.

She remains quiet through my administrations, even when I slide my hands down her sides and over her hips, catching her underwear and pulling the elastic into the crack of her ass so I can admire the perfect, white globes.

"It's my fault," she says. "I'm the adult here."

I itch to bring my palm down on these ass cheeks for the words she's uttered. Instead, I twist the crotch of the panties around my forefinger, drawing the elastic tighter against her asshole and over her clit. She whimpers, but lets me.

"If by that you're insinuating I'm not an adult, I can rectify the situation to prove otherwise."

"That's not what I meant."

I give another twist, stretching the fabric to breaking point, and start flicking the elastic from left to right over her clit. A high-pitched sound leaves her lips.

"What did you mean, Jane?"

Flick, flick, flick.

My right hand moves under her ass, my finger drawing circles around her asshole, applying just enough pressure not to penetrate, while I drag the tightly drawn string from side to side.

She grips my shoulders. "I–I'm older, more responsible."

I press a bit harder. "Responsibility doesn't necessarily come with age. The two aren't directly related."

Her fingers dig into my muscles. "Oh, God, Brian. This is wrong."

Letting go of her ass, I bring my hand to her mouth and part her lips with my middle finger. "Suck."

She does, taking me all the way in and circling her hot little tongue around the tip. Her teeth rakes down the knuckle, but she lets go when I pull out. It's not lubricated nearly enough, but this is as much for her punishment as teaching her how wrong she is. Splaying my hand under her pussy, I move the elastic aside and test her tight little hole with the tip of my finger. She clenches, everything in her lower region growing tighter.

"Brian, please."

I don't tell her to relax or breathe out. I sink the first digit into her asshole at the same time as I start flicking her clit with my nail. Hard. She screams and pushes at my shoulders. Then softer, until she moans and her ass grips my finger.

"Don't tell me this is wrong," I say, "when your pussy is slick from my tongue and I can still taste you in my mouth. This is a long way from wrong, princess. It's only the start. From here, there's only one way to go, and that's all the way. Fingers, tongue, vibrators, and cock."

A last flick on her clit and a push into her rear, and she comes savagely. Her stomach muscles lock, and her delicate neck strains as she throws back her head, her eyes rolling in their sockets. She's panting when I pull out of her ass. I caress her crack with a feather-light touch and gently rake my nails over her pussy.

"This," I plant a kiss on her clit, "is the most right thing you've done. I'm the least wrong person in your life. Don't give me excuses and guilt, and don't even think about shutting me out, because I'll fuck my way right back in, and I want to take things slow with you."

Supporting her back, I pull her to my chest. Her legs go around me automatically. It makes her pussy rub against my cock. I'm so turned on, I swear if she grinds herself on me I'll shoot my load, but I think her pretty cunt had enough for a first time. If I don't find release, I'll have a serious bout of blue balls. I'm not shy about my body or to take care of myself. Giving myself enough room without leaving the vice of her legs, I unzip my jeans and take out my cock. It's almost painful to the touch. Resting one hand on the counter next to her thigh, I fold a fist around the base and squeeze hard. It helps to not come too fast. Then I drag my fist up over the head, using the pre-cum to lubricate my shaft.

I'm holding her eyes as I start pumping. The truth is there. She's turned on in every right way. Whatever she tells herself, she can look away as little as I could. My jeans fall to my ankles, allowing me to widen my stance since I always go commando. Needing more, I start fucking my fist in all earnest. My balls climb higher, the sensitive flesh tingling with pending release. I feel no shame for my grunts or my exhibition. I like to watch, and I want her to have the liberty to do the same. From the way her gaze is glued to my crotch and her chest heaving under her dress, she likes what she sees.

It's like a thousand pins pierce the base of my spine. The pleasure is hot, near, and so intense it borders on agony. I'm going to come hard, harder than ever, all because of her. All because she's watching.

The explosion makes my vision blur. Just before I ejaculate, I pull the skin around the head back hard, giving her a prime view of the streams of cum that jets from the slit. There's a lot of juice. It goes on and on, covering the crotch of her panties and her thighs. When I'm done, my breath is gone. I have to let go of my cock to catch my weight on both my hands. My cock remains semi-erect, my balls swaying heavily between my legs as I touch our foreheads together. She doesn't touch me or speak, but that's all right. There'll be plenty of time for that. I've got the rest of my life.

It's when I zip myself up that I catch her gaze again. There's heat and confusion, and a whole lot of lust. Grabbing a roll of paper towels, I clean her off and dump it in the trashcan. Then I help her down with my hands locked firmly around her waist.

"Where's your broom?" I ask.

She gives me a puzzled look. "What?"

I motion at the broken china on the floor. "I'll clean this up."

"I can do that."

"I don't want to risk you cutting yourself."

Since she doesn't react, I start going through the kitchen, opening cupboards until I locate the cleaning utensils. In no time, the counters and floor are tidy and disinfected.

I turn to find her in a chair by the table, watching me. She's perfect. Beautiful.

"Need a drink, princess? Maybe a cup of tea?"

"Just maybe…"

"Maybe what?"

"Some time?" she asks uncertainly.

That I can understand.

Walking over, I place a soft kiss on the top of her head. "Call me if you need me."

I don't look back as I leave through the kitchen door for fear of changing my mind and not giving her one ounce of time before I fuck every hole in her body raw, but every step I take toward the gate gets heavier. A godawful sensation festers in my chest, as if I'm one of those scumbags pulling a hit and run. Given, it was only oral and my hand, but sex is sex in all its forms. Before I reach the intercom where I'll have to press the button for her to let me out, I turn on my heel and walk back to the house with fervent strides.

Jane

OH, *my God.* What have I done?

I did not just have the tongue and fingers of a man half my age on my clit and in my *ass*. Tremors run through my legs where I clamp my knees together under the kitchen table. The trembling is not only because of the physical toll those earth-shattering orgasms took, because my hands are shaking, too. I'm shocked. I'm dazed. I'm scared. What was I thinking? He's too young. I'm a sick, perverted version of Mrs. Robinson. Only, he was the one who dished out the orders. There's no doubt about who was in control. Is he even of legal age? Damn it. I could go to prison.

Shit, shit, shit.

A sick feeling burns with the guilt in my stomach. My chest tightens under an invisible vice, my breaths labored. I'm a mother, for God's sake. What kind of example am I for Abby? What if this comes out? What if Brian talks? How could I let him go so far? I'm an idiot. I'm a slut. Oh, dear God, I'm a cougar.

I can't think this through, right now. My mind and body are in turmoil. I'm a mess. What I need is to eat. Sharp, acidic hunger pains assault my stomach. My blood sugar is probably too low. It will be futile, though, because no matter how hungry I am, I won't be able to chew and swallow with the lump throbbing in my throat. Desolation swamps over me, a sudden unsettling loneliness making tears burn behind my eyes. Where did that come from? I can't explain this latter feeling, but together with the guilt it's overwhelming. No one has touched me like this except for two men. They both left me, each in a different way, and I never thought I'd let someone else touch me in this way again, least of all someone barely out of school.

The only way I know to cope when I'm not coping is to carry on with the mundane tasks of routine. Laundry. Lunch, even if I have to force down a bowl of instant soup. Clean the house.

I'm about to push to my feet when the door crashes into the wall. Startled, I freeze. Brian stalks through the frame and kicks the door shut behind him, his piercing eyes trained on me. I go weak with relief, then hot with shame.

I need him here.

I want him gone.

I can't stand for him to witness my humiliating breakdown.

The unbidden tears start flowing. Once the valves are open, I can't stop. Brian blurs in my vision. He's a talisman of strength and confidence as he closes the distance between us, making my heart race with both joy and apprehension. He slides onto the breakfast bench and pulls me onto his lap. A big, warm hand with rough skin cups my face, pressing my cheek to his chest. His T-shirt smells clean. The wall of his torso is hard like granite, but heat and a steady heartbeat give me comfort.

"I'm sorry," I sniff. "I don't know what's gotten into me."

"It's all right, princess." He strokes my back. "You're just coming down from the high of your orgasms."

The biological explanation soothes me beyond measure. My body goes slack, relaxing more against his warmth. "Why did you come back?"

His deep voice vibrates through me. "I couldn't leave you like this."

I'm pathetically grateful. After the coldness has left my bones and my shivering has stopped, he gets to his feet, bringing me with him.

"Lock your legs around my waist."

"I can walk." My protest is weak. I love that he's taking care of me.

He makes a tsk-sound and carries me to the lounge with his arms supporting my butt. My weight doesn't seem to bother him. Taking the remote from the coffee table, he sits us both down on the sofa facing the television. Then he settles me next to him so that I'm nestled under the crook of his arm. Without asking about my preferences, he scans the channels and settles on a documentary about animal life in Kenya.

Seriously?

I glance at him, but he only presses a kiss to my temple and strokes my hair.

The program is strangely calming. I'm interested, my attention quickly absorbed, without having to work my brain. In no time, I'm boneless. He seems to sense my lethargic state. On cue, he gets up and disappears into the kitchen. A short while later, he returns with a glass of wine for me and a bowl of crisps that we share.

He went through my cupboards? Secretly, I like his assertiveness. It doesn't feel invasive or bossy, because he's doing this to take care of me. My earlier loneliness, shame, and guilt make way for a warm, fuzzy feeling expanding like fluffy pink cotton candy in my chest. The wine relaxes me further, while Brian's gentle caresses make me want to purr.

I can't help but plant a kiss on his pec, just above the hard disc of his nipple. Inhaling deeply, I take in the scent that's him–pine and clean laundry.

"You're not drinking?"

He smiles down at me. "No."

I want him to stay. It's on the tip of my tongue to say so when I think better of it. I don't want to initiate something he may decline and spoil the moment. He said he had somewhere to be. I'm just happy to share this moment.

He twists a strand of hair around his finger, giving me such an affectionate look that whatever had been cotton candy before turns into mushy, gooey, deliciously sticky candy apple.

"Feeling better?"

"Yes." I snuggle closer. "Thank you. I didn't know I needed this."

His amber-brown eyes turn another ten degrees warmer, and his dimple makes its appearance. My knees turn instantly weak.

He kisses the tip of my nose. "You're welcome."

We sit like this for another hour before he switches off the television. With a broad palm on my forehead, he pushes my head back until our eyes meet. "I have to get home. Do you want me to fix you lunch before I go?"

"I'm good, but thank you," I whisper, wrapping my arms around his solid waist.

He lets me snuggle and hug him until I've had my fill before he gets to his feet.

"Call me if you need me. Anytime." His expression turns serious. "I mean it, Jane."

Suddenly shy, I fight the urge to bite my lip. "Thanks."

Placing me in front of him so that we're standing toe to toe, he runs his fingers down my sides and lets his palms rest loosely on my hips. He's staring at me with wonder and admiration, like he's looking at something precious or pretty.

"You're so goddamn perfect."

I drink in the compliment, letting it feed my self-esteem. It feels good to be appreciated. Whether it applies to internal or external qualities doesn't matter. I seem to have needed this, too.

Tension sets in his shoulders. His fingers clench on my hips. The attraction is fighting to break free. I sense he's working hard on keeping a lid on his lust, which I already know will be violent when it erupts. He spent an hour and more on putting me into a relaxed state, and getting worked up now won't serve either of us. The fact that he's not going after sex to sate his needs, but what he perceives to be good for me feels better than good. It's great.

"Thanks for today, Jane."

I echo his earlier words, saying them in the same soft tone he's used. "You're welcome."

I'm rewarded with a flash of a smile and the full impact of that dimple. His eyes are brilliant with unconcealed pleasure. My words imply I'm fine with what happened, and that makes him happy. My feelings matter to him. The knowledge fills me with a warm glow.

His jaw tightens with determination. Gently, he puts me aside and walks with purposeful steps to the door. For the full six steps it takes him, I have the advantage of the glorious view. His backside fits snugly in his jeans. His thigh muscles flex under the fabric. What will it feel like to be pinned under those powerful legs and pushed into a mattress by the weight of his body?

In the door, he turns. The once-over he gives me is heated, not hiding his feelings where my body is concerned.

"Later, princess."

He doesn't look at me again as he exits. Through the window, I watch him go. When he first left, I felt like a dirty, wanton woman. In sixty sweet minutes, Brian managed to turn that around. Where I questioned my sanity and his intentions, he left me with no reason to doubt. We shared something sacred and special.

It's our beautiful secret.

Brian

A THUNDERSTORM HANGS in the air on Sunday. The sky is a tumbled mess of purple with darkness trapped between the clouds and soil. The world is turned upside-down. It's as if I'm on the bottom of an ocean, and the foam is thundering above me. It's humid. My T-shirt sticks to my back where I'm digging a hole for Tron's fence pole. I barely register the burn of the splintered spade handle on my blisters. My mind is elsewhere. With Jane. By the unspoken law of society, our kinds don't mix. Upset the balance and you end up with this upside-down world in which someone's bound to drown. Only, I'm too happy to drown in her.

Suddenly eager to see her, I finish the work, take a shower at home, cook lunch for Sam–Mom's passed out with a hangover– and get a grumpy Clive to babysit before I drive out to Jane's house. I call her from the hands-free set in the truck, warning her of my visit.

"Oh." She sounds flustered. "Actually, I'm heading out."

My gut twists in an ugly way when I think of her meeting someone else. "Where to?" I ask, keeping my voice even.

"I'm visiting show houses."

The band of tension snaps, and my shoulders relax. "I'll come with you."

"You'll be bored."

"I'll check out the sturdiness of the structures and alarm systems." Jokingly, I add, "I'm an expert in construction and security."

Her laugh is soft. "Suit yourself. I won't mind the company. Don't say I didn't warn you, though."

In twenty minutes, I park in front of her house. Before I can exit, she walks through her gate, dressed in a pair of skinny jeans with knee-high boots and a loose blouse. The blouse hangs off one shoulder, baring smooth, peachy flesh. A designer bag swings from her hand. I don't have to look at the brand to know it's expensive. I'm so enraptured with the visual, I almost forget to get her door. She's about to flip the handle when I reach her side of the truck and lean around her to open the door.

She looks up at me with a playfulness I haven't seen in her eyes before. Her lush lips are painted pink, and her cheeks reflect the hue. In the stormy light, her hair looks more silver than blonde. A dusting of gold mars her eyelids and her shoulder, like she brushed herself with a sliver of sunshine. The enticing scent of grapefruit and lemon hits me straight in the balls.

Her smile twinkles like her eyes. "Thanks."

My voice is gruff, despite my efforts to soften it. "You're welcome."

Once inside, I buckle her up before fitting my own safety belt. "First stop?"

She pulls out her phone and checks the screen. "Garsfontein. Wait." She places a hand on my arm as I throw the truck into gear. "Shall we take my car? I have a lot of stops to make."

"No worries. You navigate. I'll drive."

We visit townhouses in security complexes, all on the east side of Pretoria. Most of the complexes are new developments, which means every house is a carbon copy of the next and there are no landscaping or trees. Coming from where she does, it must be depressing. I sense her discord throughout the visits, until we're back at her place three hours later.

"Would you like to come in for a drink?" she asks as we park. "I shouldn't take up more of your time, but I'm suffering from a terrible case of Sunday blues, and..." She bites her lip. "We need to talk."

"Sure." She can never take up too much of my time, and I'm not scared of talking.

In the kitchen, she walks circles around the counter on which I ate out her pussy, stacking plates and cake forks on a tray.

"Beer?" She finally turns to face me with flushed cheeks. "Or maybe you prefer iced tea since you're driving."

I close the distance to stop short of her, enjoying the turmoil in her eyes. Turmoil means she's aware of me.

Brushing a stray curl behind her ear, I ask, "What are you having?"

"Tea."

"That sounds good."

She almost runs to the kettle. "Will Rooibos do?"

I can watch her make tea for hours. She has this ritual about rinsing out the teapot with hot water before steeping the leaves for no more than a minute in boiled water that has slightly cooled. Then she strains the tea three times before pouring the brew into paper-thin teacups and adding a slice of lemon and a pinch of ginger to each. I like my Rooibos strongly brewed with milk and sugar, but I'll take it any way she makes it.

After serving two slices of cheesecake, she moves to pick up the tray.

"I'll get it." I pick up the heavy load and wait for her to lead the way.

We take a seat on the sofa in the lounge. She's studying me intently as I wrestle my finger through the small ear of the cup and take a sip of the tea. It's not half bad. I'm facing forward, but from the corner of my eye I see her gaze trail over me.

When she's going for a second round from my feet to my chin, I grin at her. "What?"

"Your parents must be very tall."

"My dad, yes. My mom not so much."

She lifts a hand toward my stomach, but lowers it again. "How often do you work out?"

"Every day."

"That's a lot."

"You run every day."

"How do you know that?"

"I guessed." I also watched her a few mornings, parked out of sight. I want to know her routine. I want to know everything about her.

"I love running. Can't go a day without it."

"Can't say the same about working out in the gym. It's been two years, and I still have to drag my sorry ass out of bed every morning."

"Then why do it?"

"If you want to survive, you've got to be strong and healthy." Stronger than your enemies.

She picks up her cup and takes a dainty sip, hiding her face behind it. "About that chat…"

"Can I ask you something, first?"

"What do you want to know?"

"Why is your husband taking back the house?"

She pulls her shoulders back, which makes her sit up a bit straighter. "He's starting a new family."

Damn. It can only mean one thing. "He's with someone else and having a kid with her."

"Yes."

Good riddance. He doesn't deserve Jane. I want to break his arms and legs for treating her like this while a less chivalrous part of me is happy he's out of the picture.

"Why don't you fight for it?" I ask. "It's obvious this place is important to you."

"Legally, there's not much I can do. The house is in his name."

He's not only a cheater, but also a fucker. "Did you like any of the places you saw today?"

"No." She tugs her legs under her. "It doesn't matter. I just need an affordable roof over our heads until I can figure things out."

"Have you decided which one you're taking?"

"Not yet, but I have time. Most of the townhouses we saw today are new. They're available immediately."

She sounds sure and brave, but her fingers clutch the teacup tighter. Giving up her home is harder than she lets on.

"So." Her throat moves delicately as she swallows. "We need to talk about yesterday."

If she can't say it, I will. I'm not ashamed of what we did. On the contrary. "You want to talk about me eating your pussy?"

Her cheeks light up. "Do you have to be crass about it?"

"I'm straight-forward. There's a difference."

"Whatever." She pulls at the tussles of a cushion. "It can't happen again."

I expected the reaction and I'm ready. "You enjoyed it, or am I mistaken? Should I have done it differently? If you have specific preferences when it comes to sex you only have to say so."

"No. It was good. I mean great." Her tongue trips over her words. "Not what I usually do. Not that I'm a prude."

"Then what's the problem?"

"I'm not sure what it means."

"It means I find you so hot I want to come all over your thighs again, and over your tits, and in your pussy, if you'll let me."

Her breath catches. "There you go again with your crudeness."

"Crude or not, if I put my fingers in your panties I bet they're going to come up wet. Am I right, or must I prove my point?"

The flush on her cheeks deepens. "It was a special and intimate experience, but it's not going to happen again."

"Why?"

"It was a mistake, a beautiful mistake, but one none the less."

I put the teacup down and rest my hands on my thighs lest I'm tempted to touch her while we're having this discussion about touching. "I'll definitely not describe my tongue in your vagina or my fingers in your anus as a mistake."

"Brian, please."

"Please what?"

"You're not making this easy for me."

"What is hard for you, princess? To tell me I shouldn't lay my hands or mouth on you again? Because it's going to happen, and we both know it."

"We shouldn't."

"Why not? What's holding you back?"

"For starters, I don't know what your expectations are or if I can meet them."

Fuck. If I go into detail about my expectations, she'll close the door in my face. I want everything. Every hole in her body, every minute of her time, and every ounce of her affection.

Instead of stating the truth, I ask carefully, "Do you want me to have expectations?"

"Of course not." She appears embarrassed. "I know it was nothing to you. We don't know each other, and I've only been divorced for a month. God, I'm probably on the rebound. It's just…" She waves between us. "There's no future here."

I can't disagree more, but arguing my point will drive her away. What she needs is to go slow, even if she doesn't know it herself. Fine. I'm more than ready to fall head over heels into this, fucking her first and romancing her later, but that strategy won't get me far. I need to take my time.

"Let's just enjoy the attraction," I say. "No strings. Can you do that for me?"

She stares at me with her huge, blue eyes, questions and doubts running through their depths, but she's not saying no, so I'll take that as an affirmative.

I'm going to be here for her, lock, stock, and barrel. I'm going to give her what she needs, and what she needs is an invitation to touch me, as if I'm giving her a choice.

Jane

THE LOOK in Brian's eyes intensifies, as if he's zoning in on me and only me. Everything else drops away, especially my stomach when he takes the cup from my hands and leaves it on the tray. Gently, he guides my hand to his abdomen and places my palm on the flesh that burns hot through his T-shirt. He's as hard as granite. I've been itching to touch him, but it seemed twisted. Yet, now that he's guiding my hand, slowly dragging it down over the defined muscles of his stomach, everything that felt wrong before falls into place. I'm back in the instant when I watched him leave yesterday with a deep, warm glow spreading through my chest and between my legs. Special. He makes the moment light, magical, and sacred as he encourages me to explore his body with my hand. My fingers run over the ridges that define his abs, ribs, and the V disappearing into the waistband of his jeans.

I feel him like I've never felt a man, and I don't mean literally. I feel him in every fiber of my being, as if he's flowing through my fingertips into my heart. The moment is delicately beautiful and fragile. I'm holding a soap bubble on the palm of my hand that can pop any second. It makes me feel weightless, as if I'll float to the ceiling if he lets go of my wrist. The smell of his skin is a musky kind of clean. His scent is a mix of man and fabric softener, evoking a strange blend of gentle and masculine. The way he stares at me with a warm smile as he moves my hand over the hard riffs of his abdomen, giving me permission to explore, makes this shared minute sacred. It's not lustful and animalistic, but tender and soft. This is the moment that sells me. It's the moment I decide to let go, to simply be, and let this attraction run its course. Like Brian said, it doesn't have to mean anything. It can be good if I let it. The moment can be enough.

The precise second I accept our delicate, explosive magnetism, he gives me free rein. He let's go of my wrist. Flattening my palm, I drag it over the discs of his nipples. He's leaning back against the cushions with his legs stretched out wide. His posture is relaxed, but his muscles twitch under my caress. His jaw clenches when I move back down his sternum to trace a finger over his T-shirt. He swallows when I use both hands to explore the ridges and grooves of his ribs. His neck strains when I run my hands down the V of his groin and over the waistband of his jeans to meet in the middle, cupping his erection. I've seen him naked, but I haven't felt him, and it's incomparable to anything I could've imagined. His girth is thick, but not overly so. It's more his length that's impressive.

Using the tips of my fingers, I outline the shape from his balls to the head that rests on his thigh. A hiss escapes his lips as I squeeze. I'm as wet as I'm ever going to get. My mouth waters for a taste. I want to trace him with my tongue and suck him down my throat until I can't breathe. I want to consume him with a hunger I've long forgotten, one that desperately throbs between my legs.

When I reach for the button of his jeans, he grabs my hair, jerking my head up. The bite of pain on my scalp makes my eyes water. I moan, feeling it all the way to my clit. At my verbal admission of what his roughness does to me, his brown eyes turn molten. It's as if a switch flips. He snaps back the control he gave earlier.

"Unbutton your blouse," he says in hoarse voice. "I want to see your tits."

His crass comments do turn me on. Straddling his lap, I hold his gaze as I do what he commanded. I undo the buttons of my blouse and let it fall open. His stare devours my breasts. There's nothing sinful or wrong about it. It's pure and intense, a dangerous cocktail of bottled-up passion.

Pulling my head back with a firm yank, he leans forward far enough to close his hot mouth over a lace-covered nipple. I whimper under the onslaught of his tongue. He's sucking gently, allowing the scratchy fabric to create friction on my over-sensitive nipple. A nip of his teeth makes me jerk. He bites down and stretches softly, not enough to hurt, but enough to send pangs of angst to my mind. A fraction more pressure from his jaw and it'll hurt like hell. The fear clears the haziness of my desire. Every sense comes alive with startling clarity. I'm aware of every nerve ending in my body. Another second passes with me in suspension between his teeth and mercy, and then he lets go. Cool air washes over my breast. The sensation intensifies when he blows over my nipple. The areola contracts, sending delicious goose bumps over my skin. I'm still grappling with the mind-shattering feeling as he starts licking my other nipple. I squirm with pleasure, almost allowing his skillful ministrations to derail me from my intention. When I lean back, escaping his tongue, he gives me enough of a reprieve to jerk the T-shirt from his jeans and push it up his chest. He assists me by letting go of my hair and grabbing the fabric in a fist to expose his abdomen. I fumble with the zipper like an inexperienced teenager. I'm nervous. When was the last time I was nervous around the body of a man?

Catching my wrist in his free hand, he says, "I'll get it."

I understand his concern. Under the jeans, he's commando. He wouldn't want me catching his skin in the zipper. He parts the edges of his fly and frees his cock. The skin covering his hard flesh is a flawless, tanned color, like the rest of him. The veins running down his shaft are visible, but discreet. He could've been a photoshopped model in an artist magazine. More. I want more. I want his unmarred body and all of its flaws.

"Show me more," I demand, giving voice to my desire.

He doesn't hesitate. Keeping a tight grip on the T-shirt, he lifts his ass and uses his free hand to push his jeans over his hips down to his thighs.

My breath catches. He's a perfect example of a male specimen. Everything is beautifully proportioned, from the heavy sac at the base of his length to the ridge around the ring of the head. Pre-cum leaks from the slit. Using my finger, I catch the drop. His cock jerks. I tear my gaze away from all that beautiful masculinity to measure his reaction. What I see makes me dizzy with feminine power. He gnashes his teeth and breathes heavily through his nose. He's holding back, and from the strain in his face and body it's hard for him. For a moment, our eyes lock. Time stands still as our bodies rage underneath and on top of one another. His regard simmers with something dark and profound, a message I instinctively know I need to decipher, but fail to understand. Whatever is hidden in those turbulent pools is vital. It's a key to a secret. All I need to do is reach out and snatch it, but it's like a word stuck on the tip of my tongue. My body is aware of his male power and the pleasure it promises, but my sixth sense is even more aware of this strange truth as we keep on staring at each other.

The intensity is too much. I'm the first one to look away. Even as my gut acknowledges the flag waving in the back of my mind, my desire is more powerful, outweighing everything else. Wetting my lips, I lower my head, but his words stop me.

"If you're going to suck me, take out your tits."

I let the shirt fall over my shoulders and flip the cups of my bra down to show him my nipples. I don't have big boobs, but the underwire pushes up the curves the way men like.

"No," he says. "Take it off completely. I want to see them bounce."

Heat floods my cheeks, but little arrows sting my clit, building my need. Only one man has been this honest with me about what he liked in bed. I push the thought aside. I don't want to spoil the moment by bringing someone else into it. I push the blouse from my arms and unhook the clasp of my bra. When my upper body is naked, I reach for his cock, but he stops me yet again with further instructions.

"Put your hands on my hips." He grips the base in a fist and angles his cock. "Suck me without using your hands."

Brian

FUCK, Jane's mouth is sweet. She licks from the base up my shaft, her pretty blue eyes locked on mine when her lips steal over the head. Another spurt of pre-cum heats the slit. We're not even a few seconds into this, and I'm ready to come. Biting back the ejaculation takes extreme self-control and a shitload of concentration. While she stretches her jaw and slides my cock down her throat with an ease that should alarm me, I study her face. Her twisted expression as I vandalize her mouth sends me over the edge of my control. I'm going too far too soon, but I can't stop. Palming her tits, I find her nipples and twist. It should be painful, but she moans in a way that tells me she likes the bite of pain. The sound vibrates all the way to my balls.

"Keep your hands exactly where they are," I instruct.

Threading my fingers through her hair, I cup her head gently and take over the pace. Up and down, I work my dick into the heat of her mouth slowly, pushing deeper to test her limits. When she gags, I let up, giving her room to breathe before I sink through her lips again, this time knowing how far I can go. As soon as I find a pace and depth that are within her comfort zone, I keep at it for a while, letting her lick and suck at will. Her tongue is hot, and her saliva sleek. The involuntary noises she makes as I fuck her lips make me harder. My dick is like a loaded gun, and she's got her finger on the trigger. I won't last much longer. It's going to be tough. My befuddled mind is clear enough to realize she needs a warning.

"I'm going to fuck your mouth hard. Don't panic. It'll be quick."

Tightening my hold on her head, I quicken the pace, sliding all the way to the back of her throat. Oh, fuck. This is so hot. She gags, and her eyes tear up, but she keeps her gaze fixed on mine. Her calm regard spurs me on. I move faster, making her beautiful tits bounce like I promised. The sight is too much. I push her head down with one hand and use the other to spank her breasts, first the one, then the other. They sway from the impact, her pearl-white skin immediately sporting red marks. Her scream reverberates around me, and her teeth graze the skin of my cock that is stretched to its limits. She didn't do it intentionally, but I use the excuse to spank her ass cheek hard. This time, her teeth indent my flesh, probably from shock. She didn't break skin. The delicious pain is just enough to push me over. I didn't ask if I could shoot my cum down her throat, but it's too late. It's swallow or choke.

I come for a long time, so long that I have to pull out to let her breathe. She gulps in air as the last jet of cum spills on her bottom lip and dribbles down her chin. If I had more in me, I'd mark her blushing breasts, too.

"Easy now." I wipe the hair from her face. "Breathe in slowly. That's good. Just like that."

It takes a few ragged drags before she finds her breath.

Cupping her head, I drag her face to my chest and let her rest there while I stroke her hair. The petting is my way of rewarding her for her trust and obedience, and my heart warms as she melts against me, allowing me to hold her close. After a long time, she pushes away. She doesn't say a word, but it's there in her eyes. She liked my roughness, but she thinks we shouldn't have done it. Maybe she's right. My intention was taking it slow, which is impossible with her. She pushes all my right–or wrong–buttons. I'm a demon, and my lust rules me. No matter. She'll get used to it. A revelation as clear as a turquoise sea hits me right in the chest. She's mine. I've claimed her, and I'll do anything to keep her. *Anything.* That's the part that scares me the most, because I'm not a noble man.

Regret already infuses the moment, but it's not regret for what I've done or am going to do to her, it's because I have to leave.

I pull her closer for a kiss. "I have to go."

I can read her so easily. She wants to ask where, but she doesn't.

"I have responsibilities at home," I say.

"Of course."

She lifts her thigh over my lap and settles next to me. With her tits bare and her skinny jeans outlining her crotch, she's the most fuckable thing I've seen. It takes even more willpower than holding back my climax to put my dick back in my pants and zip it up. As I get to my feet, she follows. Another second in her presence and I may be tempted to forget about Clive, Sam, and my mom.

"Stay," I say.

The single word comes out like a harsh order. She flinches. Rejection washes over her features.

"Lock the door," I tuck my T-shirt back into my jeans. "You don't have to walk me out."

I can't help but caress the soft skin of her cheek, running my thumb over her lips to catch the cum she didn't catch with her tongue. One day soon, she won't have the freedom I'm granting her now. I'll have her tied up and fucked so raw she'll pass out from multiple orgasms. All I can do is turn and head for the door, leaving my fast-growing obsession half-naked, tousled, and sexy as hell in the middle of her lounge.

Jane

I HAVEN'T FELT like a cigarette since Evan died. It's a good thing I don't have any in the house, or I might've caved. The best I can do for my shaking nerves is a glass of wine, which I carry to the bath I run after Brian leaves. I lower my body into the soothing water, letting the heat dissolve the tension in my shoulders.

What the hell are we doing? This wasn't part of the plan. I was going to tell him the incident in my kitchen was a once-off, and now we've extended that to the sofa. I don't know what has gotten into me. The attraction between us is nearly irresistible. My body hasn't felt passion like this since the love of my life passed away, and it's starved for what Brian can deliver. Still, I'm behaving irresponsibly and immaturely. I don't know him. I know precious little *about* him. Then again, why not? I'm single, and we're consenting adults. Why not give in to my wildest passions and enjoy it while it lasts? With our age difference, it's not going to develop into a relationship. It's not what Brian will be after, so why stress about it? He probably wants nothing but a good lay. And from what I've experienced so far, we like the same dark things when it comes to sex, things Evan awakened in me and I buried when I married Francois. With the newfound resolution, I feel a lot lighter, so much so that my appetite returns.

When the water cools, I dress in a warm bathrobe and fix myself a toasted cheese sandwich to gobble down with the rest of my wine. I even manage a productive work session in front of the television before I go to bed after tidying the house. That night, I dream of Brian's mouth and hands on my body until I ache for his cock with a deep-pulsing need that throbs in my core.

5

Brian

Clive is at our house when I get home on Monday from varsity. He sits at the kitchen table with a beer, shooting worthless advice at Sam who's trying to do her homework. Mom is cooking, for once. It smells like spaghetti. Grabbing a beer from the fridge, I shoo Clive outside with me so Sam can work without his interruptions.

"What's up?" I twist off the cap and sit on the wall, resting my back against a pillar.

Clive gives me a suspicious look. "What's up with *you*?"

"What do you mean?"

"You've been out all weekend, telling no one where you're going. We waited for you at the bar."

"I've been busy."

"Doing what?"

"None of your business."

"I'd say it's my business, seeing that I'm babysitting your mother and sister."

"I'd do the same for you."

"You're avoiding the question."

"You want a report on my movements? What are you? My lapdog?"

"I'm just saying. It's not like you not to hang out."

"As I said, I had stuff to do."

He leans a shoulder against the wall, scrutinizing me. "Tron said you were at the shop."

"So?"

"You took security cameras and whatnot."

I take a sip of my beer, not bothering with an answer.

"What are you cooking up, Brian?"

"Nothing."

"Who needed security shit?"

"I was doing someone a favor."

"Fine." He gives up with a huff, knowing it's fruitless to push me.

"Relax, will you? And stop checking up on me like you're my mother."

"So, it's nothing?"

"Yes."

"If you say so." He doesn't seem convinced. Pushing away from the wall, he says, "Come on."

"Where?"

"Playback. Eugene will already be there."

Clive is supposed to be my best buddy. At least, we were best buddies back in school. He's not used to me having a girlfriend or not spending my free time getting pissed with the guys. In a way, I understand his sulking mood. I've shut him out, and he feels it. Since Mom seems to be having things under control tonight, this is the least I owe him.

Chucking the last of my beer, I get to my feet. "I can't stay late. I have class early tomorrow and work in the afternoon."

"Mike's swinging by later. He'll understand if you rock up with a hangover."

I slap him on the head. "He won't, and I'm not fucking up this job. I need the pay. One beer, and then I'm out."

"Okay, okay. Keep your panties on, fuck-face."

He grins at me when I pull my keys out of my pocket.

After checking with Mom to make sure she'll be all right, I text Tron who lives up the road to tell him to keep an eye out until I'm back. Everyone knows Mom's history. Our neighborhood may be piss poor, but we watch out for each other.

Playback has a few pool tables and a big screen television mounted on the wall. It's in Hatfield, in the student area. It's happy hour. As always, the place is crowded. Eugene is at the bar, watching a cricket replay on the screen. He waves as we make our way through the tightly packed bodies and loud music. Smoking is forbidden, but the place reeks of stale cigarettes.

Eugene slaps me on the back when we make it to his spot. "Where the fuck have you been?"

I take the beer he slides my way. "Is your old man still into real estate?"

"Yeah." He squints. "Why?"

"A friend needs a place to rent."

"Who?"

"No one you'll know."

"He's being mysterious," Clive chips in.

I give him a fuck-you look and turn back to Eugene. "I'll go see him later."

"Come by tonight. He'll be home."

A noise that rises above the music on the opposite side of the room draws my attention. A bunch of guys in TUKS sweaters are cheering for the South African cricket team. In the midst of them stands a blonde girl with hair so straight it looks like it's been ironed down her back. Lindy Williams. Her dad is the wealthiest man in Pretoria North thanks to a chain of car dealerships. He's got enough money to make it in Groenkloof, but not the status.

Monkey Williams–the nickname stuck from childhood because he was such an agile tree climber–prefers to be a big, rich fish in our small, poor pond.

Lindy shakes her golden hair over her shoulder and gives a shy smile, pretending to be listening to one of the nerds instead of staring at me. I turn my back on her group, giving my full attention to Eugene, but not before he's caught on.

Eugene motions with his beer in Lindy's direction. "Her eyes are all over you."

I take a sip of my drink and make a face. It's lukewarm. "Not interested."

"Her dad's the richest man in the north," Clive says, "and she's an only child. You'll be the king of the castle if you can get her to tie the knot."

It's hard to keep the irritation from my voice. "Go for her, then."

Clive laughs. "It's not me she's got the hots for."

"Will you two assholes cut it out and let me enjoy my beer in peace?"

On second thought, I leave the can on the counter. I could ask for a cold one, but it'll go from the bartender's paycheck, and she's is a sweet kid who tries hard to pass as a punk.

"Just saying," Clive says under his breath, smothering a chuckle.

The three of us have been thick since school, but the more time passes, the more I feel myself detached from them, like they're heading somewhere I'm not. I don't have any facts to base the feeling on, because we're all in the same boat, rowing fucking hard in the same direction, which is nowhere. There just seems to be this division that gets bigger with each passing year. Sure, I'm trying to get a degree while they're working manual labor jobs like their daddies and granddaddies before them, but it doesn't make me a better man. It's more like they're content with where they are while I'm sitting on an ant heap crawling with the big red kind. Not that I know what I want, except that I'm not going down like my old man or theirs. I steal another glance at Lindy, finding her eyes on me again. Or like Monkey, for that matter.

Suddenly jittery, I get to my feet. "Come on. I'll give you guys a ride."

"What the hell?" Eugene stares at my untouched beer. "Are you the fuck serious?"

"We just got here," Clive adds.

"One game," I say over my shoulder, walking toward the pool tables.

I put down my coin and wait my turn, arms folded over my chest as I watch Eugene play the vintage pinball machine. No sooner does the pool table clear, than Lindy scrapes together her courage and walks in our direction. I position the balls, paying her no attention, but she stops right next to me, her hip touching mine.

"Hey, Brian."

I don't have a choice but to acknowledge her. "Hello, Lindy." I take a step to the side. "How have you been?"

"Great." She swirls the paper umbrella in her glass. "Studies have been hectic, though."

"Yeah. Law will do that to you."

She smiles and blushes. "You remember what I'm studying."

"Not many in our school make it to law school."

"How about you?"

"I'm good."

She glances at Clive and Eugene from under her lashes and then lowers her voice. "I was wondering…"

Ah, shit. I know what's coming, and I feel bad for hurting her ego when it has taken two of those cocktails to summon the courage to come over here.

"Well, I…" She blushes some more. "There's this movie–"

"Lindy." I take her shoulder and turn us away from my friends, sheltering her with my body to save her the humiliation of their unabashed stares. "I'm no good for you. You know that, right?"

Her blushing cheeks lose their color.

"That's to say if you were going to ask me out," I add. "Of course, I may be a pompous prick assuming something you had no intention of doing."

"No." She takes a stuttering breath and brushes her hair behind her ear. "I wasn't asking you out. I was going to tell you about this movie I saw."

"My apologies for assuming." I give her shoulder a squeeze and let go. "You're way out of my league."

"I..." She looks over her shoulder toward her group. "I just wanted to say hi. I'll catch you later."

"Enjoy the party."

She takes a step backward, almost stumbling before righting herself. "Bye."

"Bye, Lindy."

Before my last word is out, she hurries away and hides in her law boys crowd.

"Jeez, bro," Clive says when I turn back. He imitates my voice. "You're way out of my league." He raises his arms. "What was that?"

"Just letting her off gently."

It's not her fault I'm not interested in girls my age. Sometimes it feels like I've been born old.

I hand Eugene the cue. "You break."

For the next hour, I play like a donkey's ass, losing on purpose to get the hell out of here quicker. I'm not here because I want to be. I'm here to prove to Clive and Eugene that we're still on the same page.

We're wrapping it up when Mike walks in. He's the opposite of me, a young guy in an older man's soul. I swear he'll never grow up.

"How's the meat tonight?" he asks with a wink, looking around the room.

"Good, if you're a wolf in sheep's clothing," I retort.

He gives me an injured look. "That's nasty." His gaze slips to the keys in my hand. "Going already?"

"I want to be fresh on the job tomorrow."

"Speaking of which, we're invited to a piano recital."

"We?"

"The building staff. It's the inauguration of the new stage. The president of the Performing Arts Council thinks it'll be good PR, and my boss agrees with him. Unfortunately. We need butts on those seats."

I don't give a damn about the theater other than the money the job earns me.

"Is that a yes or no?" he calls after me as I push my way through the people to the door. "I need to confirm numbers."

I'm at the exit when his voice reaches me. "I'll take that as a yes, and you better bring a partner."

I throw him a good-natured finger over my shoulder before the bouncer shuts the door. In the parking lot at the back, my truck makes a stark contrast to the sleek city Toyotas and new Corsa models the other students drive. The red Alpha Spider belongs to Lindy, courtesy of her daddy.

After dropping off Clive, I drive Eugene home. It's still early enough for his old man to be up. Albert sits at the kitchen table, cleaning his pellet gun.

"I'll be damned," he says in a cigar voice. "If it ain't Clive Claassen."

"It's Brian, Dad," Eugene says, moving toward the kettle.

"Brian. Yeah." Albert kicks a chair toward me. "Sit down. Have you eaten? Katrina," he bellows in the direction of the doorway.

"Leave Mrs. Prinsloo." His wife will be in bed, her hair in curlers. "I'll grab a bite at home."

"Tea?" Eugene asks from the sink.

"Thanks." I take the seat Albert has offered. "I need a favor."

Albert lifts his eyes to me, not stopping to shove the pipe cleaner down the barrel of the gun. "What kind of favor?"

"A friend needs a place to rent."

He mumbles under his breath. "There's a lot going around here."

"Not around here. North-east, maybe."

He chuckles and whistles through his teeth. "East? So, this friend's got money. Not my territory."

"I was thinking toward the dam."

From the places we saw yesterday, I deduced Jane doesn't have the budget. If she can't afford a garden service or security company, finding something agreeable out east isn't feasible.

"Those plots are big," Albert says.

Eugene puts a cup of tea in front of Albert.

"What about a granny flat on one of those plots or a small house in a safety complex? Safety is a must."

Eugene shoots me a questioning look. "Who are you scouting for?"

"A friend you don't know." I turn back to the old man. "Can you look into it for me?"

He picks up the mug and slurps the tea. I grit my teeth, fighting the impulse to say something that will evoke his anger or to walk away from the noise I can't handle. When he draws another long, noisy sip and smacks his lips, I push my chair away from the table, getting ready to leave. This is as much as I can handle. Eugene is oblivious to my vixen insides. I've never told anyone about my misophonia.

"I'll see what's available." Albert puts the gun on the table and fixes me with a stare. "What's in it for me?"

"Commission from the rent?"

"Nah." He leans back in his chair. "An eye for an eye."

"What do you want?"

He throws a thumb toward the window. "Help with driving the junk to the scrapyard. I need a truck."

Eugene rolls his eyes. Katrina probably put pressure on Albert to get rid of the junk. Both Eugene and I know a trip to the junkyard won't make a difference, but neither of us comment.

"How's Saturday?"

"Good." He pushes to his feet and pats my shoulder. "Don't be late now, Clive. You're just like that no-good father of yours. Can't read a clock."

"Dad," Eugene says, drawing out the word.

Before Eugene can correct his father, I cut him short. "I'll be on time."

Albert gathers his gun and ammunition, and shuffles from the room.

With the old man gone, Eugene loads a tray with the tea he takes his mom every night. "Care to tell me what's going on?"

"Just doing a friend a favor."

"That's what you keep on saying."

There's hurt in his voice and the same look in his eyes I'd seen earlier in Clive's. He's upset that I'm hiding something from him. Tough luck. Jane is not up for discussion with anyone. She's nobody's business but mine.

He picks up the tray. "See you on Saturday, I guess."

"Yeah," I say as he leaves the room.

The gap between us has just become another inch wider.

Jane

THE OFFICE IS in uproar when I arrive on Tuesday morning. Erica, our receptionist, called in sick, and our recruitment company is still looking for a temp to stand in for the week. The assistants take turns to man the front desk and phone, which leaves my small team a member short for a few hours. Everyone is running behind schedule. On top of that, my Bakers client wants an emergency promotion to boost the relaunch of a cookie range that isn't performing as well as anticipated. This adds another chunk of stress to my day. I'm barely meeting my deadlines as it is.

By lunchtime, I'm mentally and physically exhausted. There's no time to go out and get something to eat, and with my assistant in reception, I can't send her to pick up something healthy from Woollies. I should've packed lunch, but I crashed into bed early last night, preparing nothing more than Abby's snack for school, and despite being up before sunrise, I ran late this morning due to Abby's hair crisis. I had to help her fix it no less than four times before she settled for a ponytail. The emergency stock of cereal bars and dried figs in my drawer will have to do. I've just removed the wrapper of a Snacker when Candice, my assistant, dials to inform me I have a visitor downstairs.

I frown. Pulling up my agenda on my phone, I double-check that I have no appointments. Maybe it's a proof delivery from the printer. With an inward sigh, I abandon my untouched Snacker, pull my jacket straight, and make my way downstairs. In the foyer, I come to an abrupt halt. Brian is standing in the middle of the floor, scanning the surroundings. My core heats with a rush of warmth before it hits my cheeks. Dressed in ripped jeans and a tight T-shirt, he's mouthwateringly delicious. His dark blond hair is messy. The sun filtering through the windows catches the highlights. When he spots me, he smiles, exposing his dimple. His hands are tucked into his back pockets, stretching the jeans over his narrow hips. Even through the thick material, the long length of his cock is visible where it bulges beneath his zipper and rests against his inner thigh. I swallow, catching Candice's eyes. There's a question as well as admiration in her gaze as she drags it from Brian to me.

"Hi," I say, recovering quickly from my shock.

He does that thing where he zones in on me, making the room and everyone else in it disappear.

His voice is smooth and husky when he replies. "Hey."

Taking his arm, I lead him to the small boardroom off the side. I don't talk until the door is closed, but we're visible through the glass walls.

"What are you doing here?"

He cocks his head. "Not happy to see me?"

I shouldn't have told him where I work. I don't mix business and pleasure, and Brian falls into the latter category.

"Brian, I'm really busy."

He assesses my body, taking his time in doing so. "You look stunning."

Unable to stop myself from fiddling, I touch the hem of my jacket. "Thanks, but that doesn't answer my question. Why are you here?"

"Are you losing weight?"

I stare at him in confusion. "What?"

He motions at my waist. "I swear your stomach is getting flatter. When was the last time you ate?"

"Last night, but–"

"No breakfast?"

"I didn't have time."

"Did you go for a run?"

"Of course."

"You ran without refueling your body?"

"This morning was an exception."

He takes a step toward me, standing too close for what's considered socially acceptable. "Did something happen?"

I want to tell him he has no place coming to my office, but the genuine concern in his voice weakens my resolve. "Nothing serious. Abby had a bad hair day."

His face muscles slacken.

"I'm sorry, Brian, but I have to get back to work. I'm drowning in deadlines."

"Health comes first."

Taking my hand, he pulls me toward the door.

"What are you doing?" I ask through my teeth, glancing around to see if anyone is watching.

"I'm going to feed you."

"Brian, please."

I dig in my heels, but I'm no match for his strength. He simply drags me along. If I don't want to cause a scene, I have to follow.

"My bag," I say meekly when he heads for the exit.

He smiles back at me from over his shoulder. "I've got this." As we pass the reception desk, he says to Candice, "She'll be back by two."

Her stare follows us into the parking where Brian bundles me into his truck. It's as hot as a summer's day in Pretoria can be and hotter. After the air-conditioned interior of the office, the pressing heat feels worse. The inside of the vehicle is an oven. I peel off my jacket, sweat already making the dress stick to my back. He reaches over me and unwinds the window, flashing me one of his irresistible smiles. The hot wind doesn't do much to cool me down.

I wipe the hair from my face, pressing it flat on top of my head to prevent it from blowing into my eyes as he pulls off. "Where are we going?"

He glances at me. A smile flirts with his lips. When we've cleared the hill after Centurion, he puts his hand on my thigh. The contact makes a shiver race over my skin. His middle finger brushes under the hem of my dress, drawing circles on my inner thigh. The touch is precariously close to the crotch of my panties. A flick of his finger and he'll stroke my clit. I bite down on my lip, trying to focus on the road to get an idea of what his plans are, but my core is swelling and getting slick. He doesn't go any further, seemingly content to do nothing but tease, unless he's unaware of the effect he has on me.

At the mall, he pulls in at the Naturo drive-through and orders two vegetarian pitta breads, a fruit salad, and lemon water. I do have to eat, and I'm starving. Instead of questioning him again, I sit back and wait to see where he takes us. He drives toward Midrand. Where the office parks and housing development end, he takes an unfinished road and parks. We're surrounded by tall Highveld grass. The plateau stretches to the horizon from where the skyline of the Dainfern Golf Estate is visible. The cars traversing the highway are audible, but otherwise it's peaceful. The breeze moves the grass, the rustling sound serene. Grabbing the food parcels, he comes around and opens my door. It'll be difficult to navigate the field in my heels, and I can't go barefoot. Though the grass looks deceivingly soft, the polls are hard enough to cut your soles. I'm still contemplating the problem when he scoops me up and carries me to the shade of an Acacia tree. He lowers me to my feet and stomps on a few polls until the hard stalks are flat and harmless. Taking off his T-shirt, he spreads it out over the grass and guides me down.

We eat in silence. The food is good and wholesome, and I start to relax despite my work stress. When I attack the fruit salad, Brian angles his body away from me. When he doesn't move by the time I'm halfway done, I lay a hand on his back. The muscles contract under my palm.

"Brian? Is everything all right?"

He tenses further.

"What's going on?" I ask, suddenly alarmed.

"You done?" he asks, eyeing me from over his shoulder with a wince.

"Yes. Why?"

He turns back to me slowly. "It's a thing I've got with eating noises."

"Eating noises?"

He pulls a blade of grass from the poll. "A phobia, I guess."

"A phobia? With eating noises?"

"It's noisy chewing or drinking, and talking with a mouth full of food. I can't stand it. It's like dragging nails down a blackboard."

"I'm sorry. Did I chew noisily?"

"No." He offers me a weak smile. "You eat very ladylike, actually. Don't mind me. It's not your fault. It's the crunch of the apple."

I smile. "The crunch of the apple, huh?"

He shrugs.

"I'll pay more attention."

"No," he says quickly. "Please, don't. As I said, it's my problem."

"How are you dealing with it?"

He gives me a sheepish look. "Avoidance."

I offer him the half of the salad, but he shakes his head.

Putting the container aside, I ask, "That's your solution? You avoid eating with people?"

"Can you think of a better one?"

"Hypnosis?"

His laugh is scruff. "Been there, done that."

"It didn't work."

"No."

"What about your family?"

"They know my *tics*. They pay special attention."

"You ate breakfast and drank tea with me. You must've been irritated out of your mind."

"You're the exception, Jane." A flash of a smile curves his lips. "Unless you eat apple."

"How about when I suck cock?"

He goes still, his expression shocked, but it only lasts a second before his cheekbones darken. His eyes take on that dangerous, lustful look.

When he reaches for his zipper, it's my turn to be shocked.

He pulls out his cock. "Come here and show me. I'll tell you what your sucking noises do to me."

We're sheltered by the tall grass. If another vehicle approaches on the deserted road, we'll see it long before it arrives. I don't hesitate. I pull my dress up to my hips so I can straddle him and grab his cock in my hands. This time, he doesn't stop me from touching him.

He leans back against the tree. "Give me all you've got, princess."

I do. I suck him deep and move my hands where my mouth doesn't reach. It takes five seconds before he takes over, fucking my lips with a fast pace. My saliva coats his cock as he pushes to the back of my throat. I flatten my tongue to make space for him. He pulls out before plunging back in, quickly finding his rhythm. My jaw is stretched to the point of aching. I can't control the noises. He takes my mouth roughly, forcing me to utter gurgling sounds.

"Yes," he hisses, grabbing my hair and tilting my head for our eyes to meet. "This is what your cock sucking noises do to me."

His balls contract under my palms. A tremor runs through his body. His neck muscles strain so hard the tendons and veins pop out. With a roar, he comes down my throat, not easing his hold until I've swallowed every drop. Only when I've licked him clean does he release me, his shoulders slumping against the trunk.

"Fuck, Jane." He stares at me from hooded eyes, his chest rising and falling. "Fuck, fuck."

His weakness and pleasure make me feel like I haven't in years–wanted, beautiful.

"I guess that gives blowjobs a green light," I tease, wiping away the wetness that coats my chin.

There's no humor in his gaze as he keeps his heated stare fixed on me. "Stand up on your knees."

"What?"

"I'm going to take care of you."

My insides go up in smoke. I love that he cares about my needs. When I'm on my knees, he pushes his hands up under my dress to grab my hips. I almost combust with anticipation. The way he holds my eyes as he pulls down my panties as far as they'll go is so hot.

"Do you want to unzip my dress?" I know how much he likes looking at my breasts.

"No. If someone comes I want you covered."

I appreciate his consideration, too.

"Are you ready, Jane?"

"Yes." I'm wet and needy. I ache to find release.

Fastening one hand on my hip, he slips the other down my leg and up my inner thigh. I jerk when his fingers reach my core. His touch is light as he drags one finger through my soaked folds. I don't need to tell him how turned on I am.

"Now," he says at the same time as he plunges his finger deep inside.

The effect is shocking, surprising, pleasuring, and judging by the satisfied look on his face as I arch my back and cry out, exactly what he was aiming for. He runs circles over my clit with his thumb and curls his middle finger inside, hitting a spot that makes my hips move of their own accord. I whimper when he starts moving his hand as harshly as he's penetrated me, fucking me deep and hard with his finger. The rhythm is grueling. I have to grip the tree to stabilize myself. The bark digs into my palms. Spots dance in my vision as he fucks me until I can't take anymore.

Pleasure starts to coil in my abdomen just as he adds a second finger. His pace turns even more relentless. Every time he hits my pussy with the heel of his palm, the breath leaves my lungs with a hitch. There are the noises I'm making, and the sound of his hand slapping my flesh. It's dirty and erotic, right here in the open between the innocent bird song and swaying grass.

"Come for me, Jane, only for me."

He must've read my expression, because his words are perfectly timed. My orgasm erupts, my inner walls contracting around his fingers. Pleasure floods my body. The pressure of his thumb on my clit prolongs the aftershocks that tingle down my spine. When I have nothing left to give and my legs feel like jelly, he pulls out to cup my sex gently. The warmth of his hand is soothing. It's as if he's calming the storm he caused. I rest my head on his shoulder, wanting nothing more than to curl up in his lap, but he's already straightening my underwear.

He kisses the shell of my ear. "We have to go."

"I know."

My lunch hour will long be over. Toby isn't worried about our comings and goings as long as the job gets done, but Candice will be wondering what's taking me so long.

With my breathing more or less back to normal, I sit back. Brian's hands are on my ass, squeezing gently.

The act is playful but his tone serious when he says, "You sound delicious when you come. Every sound you make, every cry, every gasp when I push into your pussy are mine. These noises belong to me and me alone."

Heat creeps into my face at his bluntness. When I don't immediately answer, his palm comes down hard on my ass, making me jump and cry out in surprise. The sting hurts, but in a good way. The darkness I've hidden deep inside threatens to surface. I want more. The dragon opens an eye and lifts her head.

"Say it," he says, his voice urgent.

I know the game. I played it with Evan. Men like Brian need control. They want to own the situation, because they don't share well.

Playing by the rules, I give him the right answer. "Yours."

He all but jumps on me, grabbing my head between his broad palms and plundering my mouth as if it's the end of the world. He steals my breath and feeds me his until I know nothing but his lips and his will. I'm gulping in air when he finally lets me go.

Brushing a tender touch over my cheeks, he says, "We need to fix you up, or everyone will know what you've been doing."

Damn, and I don't have my bag.

Brian helps me to my feet, his cock already semi-hard through his open fly. Undisturbed by his nakedness, he pulls down my dress and drags his fingers through my hair. He takes his time to *fix* me while I itch to touch him again. I suppress the urge. If I do, we'll get back even later. Finally satisfied, he adjusts his cock and zips himself up. He gathers the garbage and lifts me over his shoulder like a bag of marbles, carrying me back through the field to the truck. Once he's buckled first my seatbelt and then his own, he throws the truck into gear and drives us back to the office.

He insists on walking me in, but luckily there's no one in reception. Instead of going straight to my office, I visit the Production Department. The detour gives me an excuse when Candice questions me.

"Where have you been?" she asks with a glint of suspicion.

"I had a quick bite to eat with Brian."

She checks her watch. "I wouldn't call an hour and a half quick."

"I've been to Production since I got back."

"*That* was Brian? Holy smokes. What's he to you?"

"None of your business," I tease, but she won't let me off the hook.

"Friend or more than friends?"

"We're in the same business."

"He's in advertising?"

"Studying to be."

"You'd like me to believe this was a business meeting?"

"Exactly." That may not be what it was, but that's what I'd like her to believe. Candice has too big a mouth to trust her with the truth.

She makes a sound under her breath, which gives me the opportunity to escape to my desk.

The game we're playing has gone too far. I'm completely trapped in the web. It's too late to walk away. Even if I want to, I won't be able to stay away from Brian. It's a beautiful, fragile, and addictive game.

It's a dangerous game. No one can ever know, but I trust Brian. I trust him to keep our secret.

Brian

I'M mindful of when Jane's daughter is home, which is why I stay away the following weekend, even if it damn well kills me. The stolen hour and some minutes at her office aren't enough. I'll go out of my mind if I don't see her soon. At least the Saturday chore of helping Albert drive his trash to the junkyard occupies me. Albert drives with me in the truck, and Eugene follows in his dad's Chevy to help with the offloading.

As usual, we return with more junk than what we've driven away. Albert could never resist a piece of metal, no matter if it's a rusted gutter pipe or twisted roll of barbwire. To him, everything seems usable. None of it ever gets recycled. The items he saves from the scrapyard gathers more rust until the next time Katrina has a fit and forces him to throw it away. Then he returns with an even bigger heap of new garbage, and so the cycle continues.

We've barely offloaded all the shit in his yard when Monkey pulls up. He parks on the curb and gets out of the Corvette with some difficulty. Folding his arms over the top of the door, he yells, "Hey, Brian, come over here."

Wiping the sweat from my brow with a sleeve, I shoot him a wary look. Monkey is knee-deep in the mafia and has fingers in all the gang pies, which is why I stay away from him.

Eugene jabs me in the ribs with a pole. "Are you deaf? Monkey called you."

"I heard."

He nudges me again. "Do you have a death wish? Go over there, already."

Albert watches from the porch, smoking his pipe, but he's wise enough not to say anything.

My tread is hesitant when I make my way over to the man who rules our neighborhood from his castle in the north. Keeping my emotions concealed, I clean my hand on my jeans and offer him a handshake.

"What's up, Mr. Williams?"

He glances up and down the street before he faces me again.

"Good to see you, son." His smile is fake.

I'm in no mood for chitchat, not even for Monkey. "What can I do for you?"

"How's your mom holding up?"

"Good."

"Good." He nods. "Sam?"

"She's good."

"Good."

We stand there, nodding and not speaking for a while.

Finally, he says, "Lindy is my life, my whole life."

Ah, fuck. "She's a great girl."

"She is, isn't she? Any man who has a chance with her should consider himself lucky."

I steel myself for what's coming.

Monkey leans over the door, putting our noses inches apart. "For some reason, Lindy's taken a liking to you. Here's what's going to happen. You're going to ask her out and treat her nicely. If you put your paws on her before you've put a ring on her finger, you're dead."

"Mr. Williams…" I rest my hands on my hips, staring at the ground. "I'm just another piece of scum." I lift my eyes to his. "You know Lindy deserves better."

"She does, but Lindy gets what Lindy wants, and what she wants is you."

I inhale deeply. "I'm afraid that's not going to happen."

He scrunches up his face, every wrinkle a rigid line of anger. "Why's that, boy?"

"I'm taken."

His eyes widen, and then he laughs. "You're taken."

"Yes, sir."

"By who?"

"Can't say."

Grabbing my collar in a fist, he gets into my face. "I suggest you think this over very carefully. Take a couple of weeks. Hell, take

126

four. When you've realized your mistake, you call my Lindy and make damn sure she's happy." He lets go with a shove. "Well, then, you have a nice day, now." He pats my neck and nods in Albert's direction. "Say hi to Katrina for me."

Without another word, he worms his way back into his convertible and pulls off with fumes pumping from the double exhausts.

When the car disappears around the corner, Eugene walks up.

"What did he want?"

"Nothing." I kick an empty can and return to my truck to finish the offloading.

Katrina puts a jug of Kool-Aid and glasses on the garden table just as we finish. She says her greetings and scurries back inside to fetch a jar of homemade apricot jam for my mom.

"I've got someplace for you to look at," Albert says as I swallow down the last of the artificial drink.

"Where?"

"North-east. It's a cottage on a plot."

"Can we go now?"

"The owner said to come around any time. They're home all weekend."

Albert and I drive out toward Silverton and follow the road to the Roodeplaat Dam. The properties are huge and lush. It's not Groenkloof, but it's better than the grassless yards in the cookie cutter complexes out east.

The cottage is a stone structure situated not far from the main house on a property owned by a German couple, both of them general practitioners. I immediately like what I see. There are only two bedrooms, but they are spacious. The lounge is huge, too, with a view of the dam. There's a fireplace in every room, including the kitchen, and a shady deck with a built-in barbecue that overlooks the valley. The landscaping incorporates the naturally rocky terrain and crassulaceae, leaving no gardening work. The property is fenced off with electrified barbwire. It's a fifteen-minute drive from Silverton. With no traffic, it'll take Jane no more than thirty minutes to drive to work. The money sounds fair. It's way less than the rent of the new townhouses we saw during show day, and the place has a lot more character. I can picture Jane living here.

After promising to bring Jane over for a visit, I thank the owners and drop Albert off at home. Then I head over to our place to check on Mom. I promised to take Sam to the municipal swimming pool. On the way, my head swims with images of another pool on a different night, the event that changed my life. Scrap that. My life changed the day the dandy showed me a photo of Jane in Oscars.

Jane

THE TRUCK I know all too well is parked in the street when I get home from carpooling Abby and her friend to their dance class on Thursday. Brian gets out and comes over to the passenger side of my car when I pull up to my gate. *Sweet Lord*. He's wearing a sports T-shirt and rugby shorts. The stretch fabric shows off every perfectly defined chest and abdominal muscle. His arms are big without being bulgingly huge, and those legs… His thighs and calves contract with every step. His whole comportment exudes power and strength. I can't help my elation when he opens the door and slides in beside me.

"Hey, princess." He runs the back of his fingers along my jaw and down my neck, ending at the neckline of my dress.

It's almost six. Most people will be home from work. I'm not close friends with my neighbors, but it doesn't mean they're not watching. Aware of the risk we're taking, I push the remote to open the gate and roller door, and pull into the garage. When the door closes behind us, the light comes on, basking us in its yellow glow.

I turn off the ignition and turn to him. "Have you been waiting long?"

"A while."

"I dropped Abby off at her dancing lesson."

He brushes a finger over the curve of my breast. "You don't owe me an explanation."

"It's an apology for making you sit outside."

"We didn't have a date. No apology needed."

"We should be careful when Abby's here."

"How long do we have?"

"Forty-five minutes. Abby's friend's mom will drive her home."

In the dim light, his eyes are so dark they seem black. The intensity with which he watches me makes me squirm, and when his fingertip grazes my nipple, my body jerks. I'm so aware of him, the light touch feels like an electric shock.

"I'm surprised you didn't jump the gate," I say with a smile, trying to conceal the dangerous effect he has on me, but he's not fooled.

"I didn't jump the gate, because you're exactly where I wanted you."

"In my car?" I ask with an awkward laugh. Nothing he does is predictable.

"In your car," he agrees.

"Why?"

He retracts his hand. "Take off your dress."

"What?"

"If I have to repeat myself, we'll add a spanking to your pleasure."

My blood pressure jumps to a number that has to be a health hazard. I haven't been spanked since Evan. My sex clenches at the thought of Brian's hand on my ass while he makes me come.

"I'm sorry," I whisper, my voice throaty, "but I'm not getting naked in my car."

His voice drops an octave. "I'm going to start counting. If

you're not undressing when I get to three, you're not going to sit comfortably on this beautiful ass tonight. Do as you're told, and I won't leave marks."

That's all it takes for me to reach for the zipper. I push the sleeves down my arms and lift my hips to wiggle out of the dress. Brian folds it carefully before putting it on the backseat. His breath is coming faster when he looks at me. I'm wearing white underwear with stockings and suspenders. Honestly? I thought about him when I dressed this morning. Secretively, I've been hoping he'd get a glimpse at the seductive lace. The way his eyes smolder and his jaw clenches makes it worth the effort. His hard-on is tenting the shorts, but he doesn't try to hide the effect I have on him. It's as if he wants me know, as if he's paying me a visual compliment.

"Take off the bra and panties," he says, "but keep the stockings and heels."

I do as he says, abandoning the scraps of fabric on the floorboard.

"Climb over."

I want to ask what he means, but he's already out of the car and walking to my door. Obeying, I climb over to the passenger seat while he slips into mine.

"Push the seat back and put it down. All the way."

When I've complied, he twirls a finger at me. "Turn over onto your stomach."

It's not comfortable. I have to bend my knees on the seat and hug the seatback, which pushes my ass in the air. "We'll be more comfortable in the house."

"Have you ever made out in a car?"

Biting my lip, I contemplate my answer. That part of my life is sacred, but I don't want to lie to him. I don't want untruths to come into what's about to happen.

"Yes," I say after a hesitation. That's where Evan took my virginity.

"That's why we're doing this here. I want you to think about every other time you've fucked in a car, because when I'm done, doing it with me is the only time you'll remember."

His self-assurance is the medicine I need to surrender my control. I don't care where I am or what he does. All that matters is my release and pleasing him. He's in charge, and I trust him to understand my needs in order to not abuse them.

He turns sideways in his seat and curls his fingers around the back of my neck. After squeezing gently, he smooths his palm down my spine and over my ass to the juncture of my legs. With a shove, he pushes my thighs apart, putting me on display in the most vulnerable way.

His voice is gruff. "I've been dreaming about you like this."

Fingers pressed together, he drags the edge of his palm through my slit. My insides clench, and my back arches when he continues the path to part my ass cheeks.

He leans over and kisses the shell of my ear. "How hard do you like it to hurt?"

Familiar anticipation mixes with apprehension, making me shake. "Not enough to leave bruises."

"How's your tolerance?"

"On the short side."

"Okay, princess. Here we go."

Thwack.

His palm connects with my left cheek. The pain stings, heating my skin. If I was wet before, now I'm soaking. He caresses the spot with a slow rub before moving to the other cheek, warning me of where the blow is going to fall by smoothing his hand over the under-curve.

Smack.

It hurts. I grind my hips down in reflex to escape the next blow, but he slides a palm between the seat and my stomach, using my pussy as leverage to lift me. He brushes a hand over the right cheek. Oh, God.

Thwack-thwack.

I moan, pushing into his hand. His fingers find my clit, pinching softly. When he starts playing with me, I almost come, but his deft fingers know how to keep me on the edge while he spanks me into a state of frenzied need. Pinching my clit hard, he holds it while a succession of smacks rain down over my ass and thighs. When he lets go of my clit, I cry out at the sudden blinding pain as the blood flow returns. My senses are heightened, and everything I feel is centered on the spot between my legs. He pinches, then rubs, cutting off the blood flow and massaging away the pain enough times to make me throb with such an ache I'm going to die if I don't come. Pain becomes pleasure and pleasure becomes pain until all I know is extreme pleasure. I don't even realize he's stopped spanking me until his touch abandons my clit.

My lower region glows with heat. Wetness coats my folds. My inner walls spasm with need.

"Now," I mumble into the headrest. "I need to come now."

There's a shuffling of clothes, and then Brian's naked thighs straddle mine, our knees pressed together. There's not enough space for the two of us between the dashboard and the seat. The weight of his body pins me down. The long length of his cock rests on my lower back. He drags his erection through my crack. Down, up.

"Brian, please."

One hand pushes between the seat and my stomach, lifting me an inch. He catches his weight on the other next to my face.

His tone is guttural. "If we go further, you know what's going to happen, right?"

My euphoric state doesn't leave room for coherence. The need to find release is too overwhelming. I can't focus on anything else, let alone the question, which takes up too many words.

"If I stop, we go inside, and I make you come with my mouth," he says when I don't answer. "If we stay, you come on my cock." He gives me a moment to let his words sink in. "What'll it be, princess?"

I understand. If we go into the house, he'll have time to gather his control. If I push him now, he's going to fuck me the way I want him to. I need more than his fingers and his tongue.

"Here," I say.

His breath catches on a grunt. "Jane."

My name is an appeal. He's giving me a second chance. I don't need to think it through. I'm way beyond that. All I can manage is a small shake of my head.

For a moment, he rests his forehead against the back of my head. Two, three seconds pass. I'm not sure what he's waiting for, but time seems sacred. Another second passes before he moves. The broad head of his cock pushes between my legs and nudges my opening.

"You're the first woman I fuck without a condom. You don't have to worry about STDs."

I barely have time to think of a reply before he spears into me. In one thrust, he buries himself up to his balls. He's not wide enough to hurt me, but his length is uncomfortable. A dull ache flowers deep inside as he starts pounding into me. He groans with every shove, hammering a harsh rhythm of pain-filled pleasure into my core. Then he changes his angle, and all the pain is gone. All that is left is detonating pleasure. He jerks out of me just as my orgasm explodes. Warm spurts of liquid land on my back and ass as my release races through my body. It's the kind of release I feel all the way to my soul, because he's tying more than my body to him. He's conquering me in a way I'm not sure he realizes. The woman in me needs the man in him, and not only on a physical level. I need his strength, protection, and comfort as I need his cock as deep as it can go, and then some more. I want to be consumed by him, in every sense. I want to be exclusive. I want to be the only one. I want him to defy deceit and betrayal. I want him to be what no other man could be for me yet.

I want him not to leave me.

For once, I want to be enough.

Brian

LEAVING Jane like this is the hardest thing to do. It seems to be all I'm doing, giving her orgasms before walking out on her. It's not my style, but Abby will be home soon, in less than ten minutes, to be exact.

Retrieving my clothes from the floor, I clean Jane's back and ass with my T-shirt and watch her dress. Her movements are efficient and fluent despite the hard way in which I took her. I've fucked enough women to know she'll be tired and not just a little bit sore. I want nothing more than to fix her dinner, run her a bath, and hold her while she falls asleep. Even as I'm thinking these things, she's turning so I can zip up her dress. My fingers linger on her neck, moving through the soft curls of her hair. There's a console and gearshift and a thousand other things between us, but I put my arms around her shoulders and drag her back to my chest. The best I can give her for now is a kiss on the head.

She moves out of my embrace and turns in her seat. Flipping down the visor mirror, she wipes mascara from under her eyes. Her tone is apologetic when she looks at me. "You have to go."

I cup her cheek. "I want you to look at a place that's for rent."

Her smile is huge and warm. It's such a sincere expression, my heart melts on the spot.

"You looked for a place for me?"

"Of course. When are you free? I'd like for you to see it in the day."

Her smile turns mischievous. "Daylight will change my opinion?"

"The view might."

"Brian." Her tone is surprised, laced with appreciation. "Thanks for doing that."

A glance at my watch confirms I have five minutes to get my naked ass out of here. Yanking on my clothes, I press the issue. I'm anxious for her to settle this. She can't be at ease, not knowing where she's going to stay. "Tomorrow?"

"I'd have to check my schedule with Toby."

I pause with my hand on the door handle. "Toby?"

"My boss."

"Call me." A kiss on the lips, and I'm out.

It's dark outside when the roller door lifts. She must have a button in the garage to control the pedestrian gate, because it clicks open just as I reach it. I'm in my truck in five seconds flat. I'm turning the corner when a latest model Jeep comes from the opposite direction. The Jeep slows as it nears, and when it passes me, I recognize Abby in the passenger seat. Both Abby and the driver have their heads turned toward me.

Shit. I hope this isn't going to cause questions for Jane. With a bit of luck, Abby won't even remember me.

My thoughts on the drive home are troubled. I've just fucked the woman of my wet dreams. I had my dick so deep in her she'll still feel it tomorrow. I should be elated, but all I feel is disappointment. In myself. I'm a piece of shit. Jane deserves better. Taking her like that–in a car, for God's sake–was low. It wasn't my intention, not until I posed the question and saw the truth in her eyes. She'd done it. It was there in the way her lashes lifted and dropped, shuttering her expression. It was alive in the air for the duration of her hesitation to reply. It was the way her voice caught when she finally said it. Whoever she'd done it with meant a lot to her, and suddenly I couldn't stand the thought. My jealousy turned into an ugly monster. If I couldn't make Jane's first time with a man who wasn't me undone, I wanted her to remember *me*, not him.

6

Jane

On Friday I get away from work to visit the place Brian told me about. He meets me there with the rental agent, an older man with a hole in his jersey and tobacco-stained teeth who introduces himself as Albert Prinsloo. The couple who owns the property is there, too. They live in the main house a small distance from the cottage.

"We travel a lot," Hilda, the wife, says, "so you'll often have the place to yourself."

"What about security?" The serenity is beautiful, but the plot is remote.

"There's a neighborhood watch," Brian says, proving he's one step ahead of me. "You have to call in every night at eight, no matter where you are. If you fail to make roll-call, armed reservists will drop by to check out the house."

"There's also the six-foot, electrified, barbwire fence," her husband, Gustaf, says, "as well as our security company. There's a panic button on the remote that opens the gate. Any problems and armed response will here in less than five minutes."

"Five minutes?" I look around the stretch of nature. "We're at least a fifteen-minute drive outside of the city."

"We have a community security company a couple of miles from here, servicing only the farms in this area."

Albert gives me a measuring look. From the way his face pulls into a scowl, I must be coming up short.

"Better get a gun," the elderly man says, "just in case."

"A gun?" I look back at Brian, but it's Hilda who speaks.

"We've been living here for five years without any issues."

She offers me a smile, but there's something hesitant about it. Maybe she's freaked out by Albert's remark, although most farmers and plot owners have guns. I'm not sure she'd be shocked by that.

"What do you think?" Gustaf asks. "We're traveling to Namibia next week, and we'd like to draw up the contract before we leave if you're interested."

I'd like to show the place to Abby, but I'm sure she'll love it. What's there not to like? It's paradise. On top of that, the rent is much lower than what I budgeted for.

"Fine," I say, feeling excited about a home for the first time since Francois dropped the bomb about the house. "I'll take it."

We shake hands on the deal. Gustaf agrees to finalize the contract with Albert in the next few days. Since the cottage is standing empty, the previous lessees having relocated to Cape Town, I can move in on the first of next month. That suits me. The sooner I can make a new start, the better.

Hilda and Gustaf walk us to our cars while we exchange telephone numbers and email addresses.

"Which removal company are you going to use?" Hilda asks.

Before I can formulate a reply, Brian answers. "I'll take care of it."

Hilda blinks. She looks between us. "I see." When she speaks again, her voice is much cooler. "I just wanted to remind you to inform them the road here is gravel. It can be an issue for some of the bigger trucks."

Brian's look is level. "That's considerate." He moves to my side, leaving only an inch of space.

"Right, then." Hilda's gaze drops to our hips that are almost touching. "If there's nothing else…"

Gustaf regards us with a curious light in his eyes. His attention, too, is drawn to our close stance. I cringe inwardly at the judgment that thickens the air. Albert seems smug. Only Brian acts unaffected.

"Nothing else for the moment," he says, facing Hilda with a direct stare that makes her look away.

After an awkward greeting, Hilda and Gustaf excuse themselves. As they walk down the dirt road toward the main house, Albert chuckles.

He spits tobacco and opens his car door. Leaning his arms on the top, he studies me with a squinted eye. "What's he to you?"

I straighten my spine. "Excuse me?"

"I'll see you tonight," Brian says in a clipped tone, rudely dismissing the agent.

Albert taps the door twice and gets inside with his smirk intact. Brian stares after him as he takes off, not turning back to me until there's nothing but a trail of dust on the road.

When he finally looks at me, his face is tight. He advances, backing me up against my car door.

"What am I to you, princess?"

The sunbaked metal burns my skin through my dress. "What do you mean?"

"What would you have said if I'd given you the chance to answer?"

I regard him dumbly. I don't have an answer. What are we? Acquaintances? Friends? I'd liked to say the latter, but our age gap doesn't allow for platonic relations, not by public standard. He's barely out of school. I could be his mother. No matter how I sugarcoat it, I'm an older woman fucking a much younger man. By social perception, I'm the one taking advantage. That'll make him the victim.

"Say it," he urges, parting my legs with his knee. "Tell me what I am."

"I don't know," I whisper.

Brian is many things, but he's not a victim. I have no idea how to introduce him to my family and friends without embarrassing him or myself.

He grinds his thigh on my sex. "Is this what I am?"

"What do you want from me, Brian? What do you want me to say?"

"The truth." He cups my face, searching my eyes. "Always the truth."

Taking a moment, I reflect on the truth.

"A secret," I say after a while. "You're my secret."

I can't help leaning forward, finding comfort in the broadness of his very hard, very young chest. *Don't think about his age.* If I do, I'll have to walk away, and I'm not sure I have the strength. Not now. For once, I want to be selfish, taking what I need. What Brian gives me is exactly what I need.

From the way he sighs as he pulls me tight against him, I gave the wrong answer. I strain my neck to look up at him. His expression is shuttered.

"Brian…"

"Talk to me," he encourages when I trail off.

"You had no right to make a decision on my behalf."

His hands smooth down my arms. "What decision?"

"The move."

He frowns. "What about the move?"

"You said you'd take care of it."

"What's wrong with that?"

"We didn't discuss it, and it could give people the wrong idea."

"Are you worried about what people think?"

"Not particularly, but *this*…" I place my hand on his chest. "Our situation is delicate."

His jaw clenches. "What's delicate about it?"

Taking a deep breath, I fix my gaze on the thorn trees that mark the landscape. They're stark and brutal in their beauty. Uncompromising. Unapologetic. With butter-green, new leaves unfolding, they're inviting to the touch, but only a fool would risk it.

When I look back at Brian, I suck in a breath. Even the ghost of a smile on his lips, which is closer to sad than happy, shows off his dimple. He's so beautiful it hurts to look at him. Desire takes up every square inch of the space between us, but I don't want to look too deeply, because what I'll see will hurt.

There's a challenge in his voice. "What's delicate, Jane?"

"How old are you?"

He stares at me unblinkingly. The beat of my heart marks the seconds that pass.

"Twenty?" I ask.

His voice is flat. "It's irrelevant."

"How can your age be irrelevant?"

"I've been old forever. It's not the number of years that matter."

"Please tell me you're at least in your twenties."

"Fine. I'm twenty. Since that issue is sorted, is there anything else you need to get off your chest? You better do so now, because I'm not going to run away because of a judgmental look from a couple of hypocrites."

"You can't take over aspects of my life, Brian."

"You think making this move easier on you is taking over your life?"

"That's not the issue. It's speaking on my behalf, without my consent."

"Then give it to me." His hands roam over my body, coming to a stop on my hips. "Say yes, because whether you want it or not, I'm taking care of moving your furniture."

"Why?" I battle to understand his intention. I'm a temporary fuck. The acknowledgement hurts, but if I can't examine what lies under the surface of our desire, the least I can do for my self-preservation is not bury my head in the sand. "You don't have any obligations toward me."

His gaze travels over my face. "I've got the time and means. It'll save you the money, for one."

"I don't want you to think I'm taking advantage."

His fingers tighten on my skin. "The thought has never crossed my mind."

"All right, then," I say slowly, knowing when I've been beaten. "I gratefully accept the offer. Just don't assume again."

His smile is broader, his dimple deeper. "Believe me, I never assume when it comes to you."

I check my watch. "I better get back to work."

He holds onto me as if he wants to fight the fact, but after a moment, he sets me free. "You go ahead. I'll follow so you don't have to drive in my dust."

He plants a chaste kiss on my lips, staring at my mouth for another second before walking off briskly and getting into his truck without looking back.

I'm not sure what just happened, but we're not on the same square as yesterday. Whatever game we're playing, our chips have moved. The stakes are higher.

FRANCOIS CALLS to ask if I can pick up Abby from school and drop her off at their place since he'll be in a meeting all afternoon. I was planning on leaving the office at a decent time anyway to have cocktails with Loretta. Normally, with Abby at her dad's, I would've worked late, but Loretta and I have both been too busy to reschedule our lunch date. If we don't make an effort, we'll never see each other.

We meet at a trendy bar in the financial district of Sandton where the yuppies hang out. It's a place to network or get picked up. The décor strives for shabby chic, but turns out kitsch, instead. The cocktails are overpriced. I'm not crazy about the place, but I didn't have a better suggestion.

"I ordered daiquiris," Loretta says when I take a barstool at the cocktail table. "You look different."

"I haven't changed anything."

"I'm not talking about your hair or clothes. You look less stressed. Happier."

"Francois is taking back the house."

"I know. He told us. I'm sorry, Janie. Letting go of your home must be a bitch. I know how much the place means to you."

"I found a place to rent."

"You did? Where?"

"Toward the Roodeplaat Dam."

Her lips part. "That's miles out of town."

"There are smallholdings closer to Silverton."

"I don't see you on a smallholding. You're a city girl, not a country woman."

Actually, I prefer the countryside. "It's better than any of the townhouses I've seen so far."

Her phone vibrates on the table. For a change, she doesn't look at it. "How did you find this place? You don't know anyone out there."

"A friend."

"I'm your only friend."

"That's not true. I have friends at the office."

"Who is it then?"

"You don't know him."

"*Him?* Was it Toby? Alex?"

"No."

"Who then? I know everyone at your office." She tilts her head, scrutinizing me. "You got laid."

A waiter puts a frozen strawberry daiquiri in front of each of us.

"Stop it." I grab my drink and take a big sip.

"Out with it." She kicks my foot. "When? Where? Who? How?"

Loretta has been my confidant since university. I've never held anything from her, but I'm not keen on talking about Brian behind his back as if he's a piece of meat. I'm not going to degrade him by discussing his sexual skills.

"Out with it. Where did you meet?"

My phone rings, saving me from an answer. I wouldn't normally take a call when I'm out with a friend, but it could be Abby.

"Excuse me." I take the phone from my purse and check the screen. Brian.

Rejecting the call, I slip the phone back into my purse. "How did the Christmas decorations go?"

Before she can answer, the ringtone sounds again.

"I'm sorry, but I have to take this. I'll be right back." Hopping from the barstool, I walk out onto the balcony and find a quieter corner.

"Where are you?" Brian asks when I answer.

"Out."

"I know. Out where?"

He can't know unless… "Are you at my house?"

"Yes."

Despite myself, a shiver like a ghost sensation of the pleasure he's capable of delivering runs over my skin.

"Where are you?" he repeats.

Glancing over my shoulder, I meet Loretta's curious eyes through the glass. I lower my voice. "Brian, that's none of your business."

A moment of silence passes. Even if he says nothing, his disagreement is palpable.

"I want to make sure you're safe," he finally says.

"I am. I appreciate your concern, but I've been taking care of myself for a long time."

"You haven't."

"Excuse me?"

"You're not taking care of yourself."

Leaning my arms on the rail, I lower my head to hush our conversation. I doubt the people at the nearest table can hear with the background chatter, but I'm not taking any chances.

"I don't have time for this conversation. I have to get back to my friend."

"Friend?" He doesn't even try to sound nonchalant. His tone is uneasy. "You're out with *one* someone?"

I bite back a smile. "Are you jealous, Brian Michaels?"

"As hell."

My heart softens at his admittance. I should tell him who I'm out with isn't his concern, but I feel a need to soothe him. "It's a she."

"What's her name?"

"Don't you trust me?"

"I do. I just want to know everything there is to know about you."

"Like who I spend my Friday evenings with?"

"Yeah, and everything else, down to the color of your panties."

"I'm being rude to my friend. I have to go."

"Then hurry up and tell me."

I'm smiling so hard my face muscles ache. It's been a while since anyone has been this invested in me.

"Loretta, and it's green." Somehow, relenting with Brian always feels good.

"What are you and Loretta doing?"

"Having cocktails. Catching up."

"That wasn't so hard, was it?" he coos.

"Goodbye, Brian."

"I'm not done, yet."

"Don't make me hang up on you. I don't want to be that woman."

"Loretta has all night with you. I'm just asking for one more minute."

Relenting is also easy with Brian. "What else do you want to know?"

"Describe your underwear."

I look over my shoulder. Loretta is typing on her phone. "It's chiffon with a lace trimming."

"Chiffon," he muses. "Is that see-through?"

"Yes."

"Do your nipples and pussy hair show?"

My cheeks heat. I lower my voice another octave. "Yes."

"Don't ever shave. I love the hair between your legs."

"Brian." It's meant to be a reprimand, but it sounds more like a breathless gasp.

"What are you wearing on top of that sinful underwear?"

"A dress."

"Describe it."

"It's white and sleeveless."

"Does your underwear show?"

"No."

"Good."

"Can I go now?"

"Yes, I'll let you go."

I imagine him sitting in his truck in the dark outside my gate. "What about you? What are your plans for tonight?"

"My plans are wearing fuck-me underwear and drinking cocktails with Loretta."

A laugh bubbles from my throat. "You're impossible."

He groans. "I bet my plans are turning every male head in the room, even as we speak."

I chuckle. "Is that a compliment?"

"No. The hard-on in my pants is."

A full-body flush warms my insides. "You haven't answered my question. Are you spending the night in your truck on my pavement? The neighbors may get suspicious."

I'm not even half joking. It won't be long before someone questions the presence of the truck parked frequently in front of the house. Maybe it's a good thing I'm moving to the middle of nowhere.

"Since you're taken," he says, "I'll meet up with some friends at a bar in Hatfield. Call me if you get bored and want to join us."

"I won't."

"Of course you won't."

There's a smile in his voice but a bite in his words I don't get. When I glance back, I'm just in time to see Loretta leave our table and make her way to the door.

"I'm hanging up now, Brian."

"Later, princess."

The line goes dead. I straighten, taking a big breath of night air to clear my head and cool my body.

"What's going on?" Loretta asks. "Is there a problem at home? Is it Abby?"

Turning, I smooth back my hair. "Everything's fine. Sorry about that." I don't offer an explanation. I may not feel like sharing intimate information with my friend, but I don't like lying to her.

She narrows her eyes. "You *did* get laid. It was *him*."

"Whatever has gotten into you?"

I try to sidestep her, but she reaches for my phone. "Give it here."

"No." I drop the phone in my purse and zip up the bag.

She tries to snatch the purse from me, but I'm quicker and

taller, holding it out of her reach. Our exchange attracts attention. A few heads turn our way.

She crosses her arms. "Why won't you tell me?"

"There's nothing to tell."

"Mm." She studies me for a second and then says, "All right."

All right? It's not like Loretta to give in so easily.

"Shall we get back to our table before someone snatches it?" I motion inside. "The place is getting busy."

We're barely seated when she says, "We're having a dinner party at our place next weekend. Francois and Debbie will be there."

"Oh."

"Why don't you join us? You can bring your mystery man."

Ah ha. This is her strategy. Instead of shifting the focus to *my mystery man*, I keep it on the real reason why I won't accept the invitation. "Thanks, but I'm not ready to have dinner with Francois and Debbie."

"You have to get over it, Janie."

"I am over it. I've accepted it. Maybe it *is* for the best. I'm just not ready to socialize with them. Someday, but not next weekend."

She blows out a puff of air that lifts her fringe. "Let me know when you're ready. Until then, I'll keep on pushing, because that's what you need to heal."

In time, I'll be able to forgive.

Time is supposed to heal everything, but it didn't heal the pain of Evan's death. I give a mental start. Oh, my God. I haven't thought about Evan for days, not until now, when he's all I usually think about after the anniversary of his death. I'm not sure if I'm upset or relieved. The deep-seated pain is still there, but it's more manageable. Is this the turning point in the lapse of time I needed to start healing, or is the tipping point meeting a certain person?

Loretta must've felt my mood shifting, because she places her hand on mine and says, "Did you confront Dorothy about Benjamin being in town?"

"She said she didn't want to upset me."

"Bullshit. She was too much of a coward to tell you. Have you considered speaking to Benjamin?"

Her question surprises me. "Of course not. Why would I do that?"

"To clear out the skeletons, give the closet a good old dusting."

"Our history doesn't need dusting. The only thing it needs is to be left in peace."

"Peace?" She snorts. "That's the last thing it'll be if you keep on walking circles around it."

I'm tired of talking about me. I'm tired of talking about my problems, because it's talking that keeps them turning in this maelstrom of emotions. I'm good with them exactly where they are–buried beneath the dirt the years piled on.

"Can we please talk about something else?"

She mixes the slush in her glass with the straw. "Abby seems happy about the baby."

"Did she tell you that?"

"Debs did."

My voice comes out harsher than intended. "Debbie?"

She cocks a shoulder. "I can't not talk to her when Francois brings her over."

"Do you talk about me?"

"Janie." She gives me her cut-it-out look.

"Do you?"

It's an unreasonable situation to put Loretta in. Can she be friends with both of us if we're not getting along?

She sighs. "She doesn't want to become your best friend. She wants you to be friendly for Abby's sake."

I can't help the anger that burns in my stomach. "It's about Abby, is it?"

"Debs loves Francois. It's only natural that she cares about his daughter."

"I don't trust her motives."

"Are you saying she doesn't really care?"

"I don't know her well enough to be a good judge of her character."

"Francois chose her. He's not an idiot or a frivolous man. It has to count for something, right?"

"Right." But men can also be led by their dicks. "Look, I'm being protective. Abby is my only child. I just need some time."

"Oh, Janie." She squeezes my hand. "Time is all you've been taking, and look where that's gotten you."

Tension aches between my shoulders. My temples start to throb. I feel a headache building. Plastering a smile on my face, I say, "Tell me about the new range. Is there anything pretty?"

She lets go of my hand, shaking her head. "I know what you're doing, but I'll play along for now."

I raise my palms. "What?"

"I've put aside a business suit. I swear it was made for you. You must try it on."

For the next hour, I let her lull me with fashion talk. When the waiter comes around, I refuse the second round. I have to drive, and the alcohol isn't helping my headache. Instead, I ask for a glass of water and gulp down a Triptan. I don't get migraines often, but when I do, it's better to kick them in the butt before they get so out of hand the only cure is a dark room and several hours of sleep. It's almost midnight before the thumping behind my left eye subsides and Loretta asks for the bill. The pill wakes me up. There'll be no sleeping for me, but friend or not, I've had as much of Loretta as I can take in one night. I prefer to relax in the solitude of my home with a book or movie, trying not to think about how much I miss Abby.

Brian

It's late. Playback is already full when I arrive. Eugene and Clive are at the pool tables, waiting their turn. I grab a beer at the bar and join them.

"Where the hell have you been?" Eugene says, eyeing me as if he's looking for clues about my whereabouts.

"I had to see Tron about watching out for my mom and Sam."

"My old man says the place you were looking for is for a woman."

"So?"

"Got something to tell us?" Clive asks.

I take a swig of my beer. "Nope."

"Good," Eugene says, "because I'd like to remind you that you're spoken for."

Clive looks between us. "By who?"

Eugene points his beer bottle toward a table at the back. Four girls are squeezed in on the bench, Lindy in the middle.

"Wait a minute." Clive grabs my beer. "What did I miss?"

I let him get away with it. I owe him at least a case for the babysitting.

"Monkey came around," Eugene says.

I punch him on the bicep. "Zip it, asshole."

He grunts, holding his arm. "Said Lindy gets what Lindy wants, and what she wants is douchebag over here." He throws a thumb in my direction.

News sure travels. He'd been out of earshot when Monkey delivered his speech. "Who told you?"

"Lindy's mom told my mom. Apparently, she went crying to her daddy after you gave her the cold shoulder last week."

"Fuck." Clive stares at me with something between envy and pity. "That's rough, man."

He doesn't have to say more. Whether I fancy Lindy or not, I don't have a choice. You don't say no to Monkey. Not if you value your bones and your life. Lindy chooses that moment to look up. Our eyes meet.

"You've been spotted." Eugene gives me a sympathetic pat on the back. "Looks like you've got your job cut out for you."

"Yeah," I say, not moving my gaze from the girls' table.

Lindy and I need to talk, and I'll have to be very tactful if I'm to wake up with ten fingers and toes tomorrow. Lindy turns pink under my blatant stare, another sign she's no match for me.

More pats from my friends send me on my way like a soldier embarking for battle. I get another two beers and carry them over to Lindy. The group falls quiet when I approach.

"Hi, Lindy. Can we talk?"

She sweeps her hair behind her ear. Her cheeks turn a darker shade of red. "Sure."

Her friends all but fall over themselves to move away. In a second, we have the table all to ourselves.

I place a beer in front of her and take the opposite bench. "Will that do or do you prefer something else?"

"A beer's perfect." She cups the bottle. "Thanks."

Taking a deep breath, I drag my hands over my face. I tried to give her the easy way out with her pride intact, but no matter how I say it, she's going to feel rejected.

"You look tired," she says, mistaking my gesture.

"I've been working a lot."

"How's it going with the job?"

I shrug. "It pays."

"I see Mike a lot in here. He looks like a nice guy."

"He's okay."

"I mean, he looks like someone who'll understand if you need to take a couple of days off to catch up with your studies or rest."

I smile. Lindy will never understand that I don't have the luxury of *taking a couple of days off*. Not if I want to pay the bills.

Encouraged by my smile, she launches into a conversation. "What are you doing for the holiday? I'm going to Margate during the December break with a few friends. We're renting a flat. Dad said I can go if I'm back for Christmas." She traces a circle around the beer bottle on the table. "We have a spare space." She meets my eyes fleetingly. "You should come. It's already paid for, so it won't cost you a cent. It's right on the beach. Rachel was supposed to come–You know Rachel, my roommate at the dorm before I moved back to my parents' house?–but we had a huge fallout." She lifts her head and flicks her hair back. "I can't believe how nasty she's turned. She's going around campus spreading all this bullshit about me, would you believe it? I mean, how's that for friendship? Even if she's mad at me, she shouldn't be petty, right?"

I don't give a fuck about her disagreement with her friend, but I make an effort at being polite. "What did you fight over?"

"She said I flirted with her boyfriend." She gets real animated, gesturing with her arms. "Patrick. That scumbag. Just because all the girls think he's handsome doesn't mean he can hit on everyone wearing a dress. You know Patrick from Economics, right?"

Actually, I don't.

"He cornered me one night outside the toilets." She makes doe-like eyes. "He said there was a spark between us. Urgh. Disgusting. I wish there'd been someone like you to rescue me."

Inwardly, I smile at her attempt to make me jealous. It might work on Clive or Eugene, or any other guy in the bar, but not on me. My feelings only stir for Ms. Logan. As Lindy drones on, I tune her out, my thoughts drifting to green underwear and a white dress. I hadn't noticed how hard I'd fallen, because I'd already fallen the day the prick in the bar had showed me her photo. I touch the shirt pocket where I keep it. I look at it during all hours of the day–while I work, eat, piss, and jack off. The image of Jane burns a hole through the fabric of my shirt, the acid of its lie eating through my skin and seeping into my heart. I can't tell Jane. I can never let her see the photo. If she knows why or how we met, she'll send me packing with a well-deserved kick on the ass, and I'm not planning on going anywhere. Jane is mine.

Lindy's giggle draws my attention back to her. "The October

Beer Festival is so much fun. You should come with me. There's an oompah band and blah blah blah..."

Her beauty is young. Developing. Her skin is flawed with a few pimples that come with puberty. It misses the character of laugh lines and mature silkiness that speak of experience.

No, I don't want to drink cheap beer with her in a tent in the middle of a mud-drenched sports field. I don't want to have an immature conversation about her grades and teachers and how much her ex-roommate irritates her. I don't want to look at her legs, still unshaped, or the soft tube of skin around her young girl waist. It's not her fault. It's not that's she's unattractive or unkind. She's everything a young student can ask for. I'm just not interested in young girls. I'm interested in no one else except Jane. Ms. Logan spoiled me for other women, and I'm a lucky bastard that she gives me the time of day.

"...as I was saying, if I get the internship with Daddy's connections–"

"Lindy."

She snaps her mouth shut at my interruption.

I lean across the table, lowering my voice. "I need you to understand something."

Her newfound self-confidence takes a dive. She's back to being shy. "Yes?"

"I'm seeing someone."

I'm trying to be gentle, but there's no easy way of saying this. The blood drains from her face. She drops her arms on the table, clutching the beer like it's a lifeline.

Her voice is a whisper. "Who?"

"It doesn't matter. You don't know her. What matters is that you speak to your dad." I keep my voice soft. "You have to tell him you're not interested in me any longer."

Her expression grows hard. "I don't believe you. You're always here alone."

"Not by choice, believe me." If I had my way, I'd have Jane by my side every minute of every hour.

She jumps to her feet. "How dare you insult me? Who do you think you are?"

"Insulting you was the last thing on my mind, but you left me no choice when you went to your dad. You have to tell him you've changed your mind. Do you understand?"

"I don't have to do anything," she hisses.

She jumps over the bench and heads for the exit. She's already outside when I catch up with her. Tears streak her cheeks.

"Lindy, I'm sorry."

I grab her arm when she tries to run.

"Let go of me!"

"Just listen. You know what your father will do if you don't get your way. He'll have me beaten into obedience."

She gives me a horrified look. "Daddy's not like that."

Oh, fuck. She really is innocent. She doesn't know half of it. "Trust me. If you like me, even just a little as a friend, tell him you've changed your mind."

She frees her arm from my grip, but she's not running any longer. Eyes downcast, she asks, "Are you really seeing someone?"

"Yes."

When she lifts her gaze back to me, there's no compassion or understanding. There's only determination. "Maybe that will change."

She storms to her car, leaving me with her words.

Never.

That will never change.

Jane

It's after one in the morning when I get home. No truck in the driveway. I laugh out loud at the disappointment that drops in my belly. Did I really expect Brian to be waiting for hours? I'm behaving like a horny teenager.

Thankfully, my headache is gone, but I'm on a buzz from the pill. All I want to do is kick off my shoes and cuddle up in bed, maybe with a movie. I doubt I'll concentrate on a book.

After pulling into the garage, I use the connecting door to enter the kitchen. I left the lights on so I didn't have to fumble around in the dark when I got back, but the setting is brighter than I remember. An uneasy feeling settles over me. My senses go on high alert. There can't be someone in the house. The alarm would've tripped. It's probably the medication messing with my mind. Just as I adjust the dim switch, a shadow falls through the scullery door.

7

Jane

A cold sweat breaks out over my skin. Flinging around to assess the danger, my gaze falls on the profile of a man. My body jerks. I barely contain a scream before I recognize him. Brian. He's shirtless, wearing torn jeans that hugs his body as if it was designed to make him look like a sex god. A sheen of perspiration emphasizes the well-cut muscles of his torso. A dishcloth is thrown over one shoulder.

Leaning back against the sink, he runs his gaze over me. "Hello, princess."

"Shit." I place a palm over my heart. "You scared me."

"I didn't mean to."

I have more to say, but it takes a moment to regain my composure. Something is different. The mess I left before going out is gone. The dirty dishes and table have been cleared, and the counters wiped down.

"What are you doing here?" I ask. "How did you get in?"

"I fixed a few things while I waited." He throws a thumb toward the sink. "Dripping tap. Hook coming out of the wall. And I got in using a key."

"A key?"

Warning bells go off in my mind. He's acting like a stalker. I don't like it, and I do. The latter confuses me.

"I took the key number when I installed the security equipment and had one made."

"You can't do that." I close the door to the garage, making sure to lock it. "This is an invasion of my privacy."

"Ask me to leave, and I will."

I part my lips, but I can't form the words. It's wrong to let him stay. It's unwise. Yet, I've never wanted something–or someone–more in my life.

He straightens, a small smile bringing out his dimple. "Shall I take that as an invitation?"

His tone is soft. Soothing. I can't make myself throw him out. My body starts to buzz with something more than the side-effect of the pill. Excitement. Anticipation. A little bit of fear. It's the good kind, the kind I discovered with Evan.

"You can't come and go as you please," I say in an effort to salvage what I can of my common sense.

"I'm careful." He takes a few steps forward. "That's why my truck is parked around the corner, and I knew Abby wouldn't be here."

After wiping his hands on the dishcloth, he hangs it neatly on the hook. I'm speechless, unable to formulate anything cognitive. My body is drawn to him like a vampire to blood. If I send him away, I'll miss out on a night filled with endless possibilities. Who knows how long what we have will last? Can I throw away this chance for the sake of sane and wise?

I already know the answer before he's leaning on the counter with his palms, studying me with his unique kind of unwavering attention, and so does he. As always with us, words fall to the wayside. I'm utterly and completely caught in his web. He can be a venomous spider, ready to devour his prey, or a praying mantis about to eat its mate. I'm entranced. Hypnotized. I can't move from my spot by the door. While he's at ease with the silence, happy to just stand there and watch me like I'm prey, I need to find something to say.

"You cleaned my kitchen."

His lips tilt in the sexiest way. "Obviously."

That damn dimple. "Why?"

He shrugs. "I knew you'd probably come home late and be tired."

His consideration makes a dent in my apprehension. No one has ever made my life easier in such a sweet way.

"Thank you."

"You're welcome," he says in that same warm tone from earlier.

He lifts something from the counter, holding it in both hands. A coil of rope. He gives a pluck, testing the stretch. He doesn't say anything. He simply holds my eyes, his gaze communicating a thousand words.

The fear I crave blooms in my chest. The chain breaks, and the dragon is free. My breath catches more at that knowledge than the sight of the rope.

He walks around the counter and stops a distance away from me. "Go to the bedroom and undress. When you're naked, lie down on the bed. Don't speak unless you have questions or requests. Otherwise, feel free to be as loud as you wish."

My heartbeat spikes. My skin pricks, every follicle humming with awareness. His intention is obvious. I want it, even if I shouldn't, but it's too late to turn back. He successfully unleashed the perverted side of me.

I take one step. Two. Dropping my purse on a chair, I walk past him to the hallway. He's barefoot. The only evidence that he's following is the snapping sound of the rope behind me.

In the bedroom, I turn to face him. I can undress for him. I can take it as hard as he wants to give. Can I let him bind me? Can I risk giving up that much control?

"Shoes first," he says, watching me with his arms crossed over his chest, the rope dangling down his side.

The single order makes it easier to comply. I kick off the one heel, then the other.

"Now the dress."

Holding his eyes, I pull the zipper down slowly. My hands tremble when I push the fabric over my arms. The linen is heavy and the silk lining smooth. The dress swooshes down my body and pools around my feet. I'm standing in front of him in only my underwear, trying to imagine what he sees. My stomach flutters with nerves. I've never put myself on display for a man, not like this. Not wearing three chiffon triangles that provide nothing but a sheer hue of green over my skin. I'm over-conscious of my hardened nipples and the dark patch between my thighs.

For long seconds, he looks at me like I'm porn. He doesn't hide the hungry look in his eyes as he unashamedly studies my breasts before dropping his gaze to the center of my legs. Draping the rope around his neck, he closes the distance. His fingers clench around the ends of the rope while his torso rises and falls with his breaths. He reaches out to circle an areola ever so slowly. My breast tightens under the light caress, my own breaths coming shallow and fast. He traces my cleavage and draws a line to my stomach, giving the action his full attention. When he reaches the lace-trimmed panties, he drags his gaze back to mine. In the soft light of the nightstand lamp, his eyes are dark and intense. The desire in his expression is so thick he must have a hard time controlling himself. His body is tense, like a tightly coiled spring, but the self-assured and calm way in which he walks around me as he completes his assessment tells me he's the master of his lust. I tremble under his scrutiny, feeling every sweep of his eyes like a physical touch.

He speaks calmly, but with authority. "On second thought, keep the underwear on. Now get onto the bed. Lie on your back and spread your legs."

I glance at the rope. "Brian, I…" I wet my dry lips. "I'm not sure about this."

He leans in close enough for my flimsily covered nipples to brush his chest. A big hand cups my face. There's so much gentleness in the touch I can't help but melt against him.

His look is warm and reassuring. His voice is a gentle whisper. "Trust me, Jane."

I stare up at him. Do I trust him? Do I have enough confidence in his intentions to let him tie me up? Once I'm secured, he can do anything to me.

He watches me closely, searching my eyes as my internal battle continues. I want to give in with my whole heart, but my brain is screaming caution. It's not what clever girls do. It's not like me to be irresponsible. I don't know him. Not really. If I'm wise, I'll say no, but the pull of my body outweighs the rationality of my mind.

I need more reassurance. "Will you untie me if I ask?"

His answer is curt. "No."

My lips part on a silent gasp.

He runs a thumb over my cheek. "I want to push you, tonight. You'll ask me to untie you long before you've reached your threshold. I want to show you how much pleasure you're capable of feeling, but you have to trust that I won't exceed your limits."

I swallow, fear and arousal sending heat to every crevice of my body. "How will you know my limits?"

"I'm good at reading signs."

"What kind of signs?"

"The size of your pupils, the focus of your eyes, the contraction of your muscles, your pulse, heart rate, and how wet you are."

"Wow." I utter an uncomfortable laugh. "You must have quite some experience."

"None that matters."

Is he saying *this* matters? Him and me? He drags his palm from my cheek to my shoulder, the earlier predator touch when he traced my nipple now something different, something gentle.

"I want to make you come harder than what you believe is possible, Jane."

"I'll be happy with coming by normal standards." He's the first man in twelve years who gave me an orgasm.

"This is for me, not you."

I blink up at him. "What do you get out of it?"

"I get off on your pleasure. The harder you come, the more intense it is for me. I can't explain it. It's more of a mental than a physical thing."

My restraint is starting to slip. "Are you going to hurt me?"

"Not unless you want me to."

"You said no talking. How do we communicate?"

"I said no talking unless you have questions or requests. While I'm working your body, I want to concentrate on the task and only that. Talking is for after, as much as you like."

I'm combusting from his words alone.

"Can you do this for me, Jane?" His voice is already praising me, encouraging me for a decision I'm about to take. "Can you trust me?"

If he was going to abuse me, he could've done so by now. Nothing stops him from overpowering me and tying me up against my will. The fact that he asks for my consent is what finally sways me.

Walking over to the bed, I do what he told me.

Brian

JANE CLIMBS onto the bed and spreads her legs for me. If I feel between those slender thighs, I'll find her wet. I already know what turns her on. Her body is willing, but her mind is uncertain. I can see it in the way she bites her lip and keep her arms pressed tightly against her sides. No one has ever gone this far with her. That's good. I like to be first. Ultimately, I will be the only one. I can prove to her how good we'll be together. Tonight, I had to ask for her trust. From here on, she'll give me her trust freely, because I'm going to work hard to earn it.

Sliding my hand down her calve, I caress her ankle before tying one end of the rope around it. Her skin is soft in contrast to the roughness of the hessian fiber. If I'd planned this in advance, I would've gotten a rope made from silk, but my impromptu decision had me improvise. I had to make do with what I had on hand. Her right ankle follows next. Rounding the bed, I gently lift her arm and tie her wrist to the bedpost. When I'm done on the other side, she's spread-eagled with enough room to bend her knees. From her wrist, the rope goes under her knee. When I pull it through the side frame of the bed's base, I force her bent knee sideways, opening up her pretty cunt. The rope reaches all the way to the other side, where I do the same. I step back to admire the picture. The flimsy green fabric doesn't hide much. It's perfect. She's perfect.

I strip fast. There's nothing I like better than the feel of her skin all over me. Her eyes widen a fraction as I climb between her legs. My cock is painfully hard and my arousal difficult to contain, but I push my own sensations on the backburner as I home in on hers. It's vital that I read her right. My princess likes it when I talk dirty. The spanking made her wet. From the way she anticipated and accepted it, she's had spankings before. She likes it a little slutty and rough. I palm one breast while tweaking the nipple of the other. She arches her back, offering me more. Flicking down the cup of her bra, I let one perfect curve spill over. The underwire pushes up her tit, plumping it for my mouth. I swear her nipple tastes sweet. The way it hardens on my tongue makes pre-cum rush to the tip of my cock. I'm greedy, so I take as much as I can fit into my mouth before letting out slowly, sucking extra hard and stretching her nipple as far as it'll go. She yelps, but a flush colors her neck. There's a red mark around her nipple when I'm done. Her breasts are gorgeous, but they're perfect with my mark on them.

It's time to start playing in all earnest. Moving the elastic of her panties aside, I find purchase in her trimmed pussy hair. A gentle tug prepares her for what's to come. Using it as leverage, I pull her pussy lips apart like that first time in her kitchen. Holding her open like this exposes her clit and the moisture that covers her slit. I can't help but steal a taste, dipping my tongue inside before circling her clit. Her hips lift off the mattress when I suck almost as hard as on her nipple. Stunning. She's got the prettiest cunt I've eaten. I take my time to look at her, long enough to make her squirm, before I grab a pillow.

"Lift your hips."

I slip the pillow under her lower back, lifting her butt and giving me access to her asshole. She tenses when I trace the tight pucker.

"Have you been fucked here?"

She shakes her head.

As I'd thought. I love tits, but I'm an ass man, and by God, Jane has the hottest ass. The globes are tight and firm, perfectly rounded. I'll never get enough of spanking and fucking her ass.

"Would you like to see how my cock sinks all the way in here?" I lick my finger and breach the ring of muscle with my fingertip.

She squeals.

"Would you like to feel me come in your ass?"

Straining her neck, she looks at me. "Do you like it?"

"I do."

"Why?"

"It's different. It's tight. I like to possess as much as I can, which makes every hole in your body a challenge."

"Will it hurt?"

"It's different for everyone. It always hurts to various degrees.

Some women like it better than others." Enough talk of anal for now. "Did your ex make you come?"

A frown pleats her brow. "What does that have to do with anything?"

"Just answer the question. Did he get you off?"

She shakes her head again.

"How do you climax? Fingers or vibrator?"

Her cheeks turn pink. "Vibrator."

"Where is it?"

"Why?"

"You trust me, remember?"

Her throat moves as she swallows. She turns her head toward the nightstand. "In the drawer."

"Lube?"

"In there, too."

Leaning over, I open the drawer and locate the items. The vibrator is a simple rabbit model with a rubber dildo and adjustable speeds. I test the switch to make sure it's charged and leave it on the bed next to the lube.

For the next few minutes, I do nothing more than run my hands over her body, covering every inch of skin. I want her relaxed and at ease. I make sure I frequently touch her nipples and pussy, keeping her primed so she doesn't fall out of a state of arousal. When her arms and legs are slack, I cover my finger with lube and start working on her ass. At first, she resists, pushing me out, but when she gets used to the sensation I manage to fit two fingers without making her tense up again. Keeping my fingers where they are, I go down on her. I fuck her pussy with my tongue and lick her clit until she writhes in the tight hold of the rope. When her moans turn to pants, I start moving my fingers. Her focus is on coming. She's close. Using the distraction, I fuck her ass gently but deep with my hand, twisting to stretch her after every pump. Her abdomen contracts a second before her pussy tightens around my tongue. She cries out softly, lifting her head to look at me. Her neck muscles strain, and her back arches. The tangy taste that's all woman, sophisticated sensuality, and dirty sex intensifies as she comes. I fuck both holes with soft pressure but a determined pace, prolonging the orgasm until her body collapses, her shoulders falling back onto the mattress. Before the euphoria wears off, I gather more of the lube that slickens her ass and carefully insert a third finger. Her channel is supple, taking me easily. It won't take much work to fit my cock. After a last few pumps and twists, I pull out slowly.

She's still catching her breath with her head thrown back and her eyes closed when I lubricate the vibrator and slip it inside her pussy, angling the bunny ears toward her clit. She moans as I thrust in and out, setting a slow rhythm. I can watch her cunt take the vibrator all night. Her pussy lips stretch around the intrusion, putting her clit on display. Beautiful. Using two fingers, I pull up the hood of her little nub. I almost come from the sight. Her feminine parts are swollen and pink. It makes me want to sink my cock into her and take her as deep as I can. I want to wring everything out of her, every ounce that's bottled up inside her gorgeously toned body until her limbs are boneless and her voice hoarse. The intensity of my need to take her to that dangerous point is new. I've always put a woman's pleasure first, but I've never felt a need to make it so absolute, all-consuming, and complete that when my cum drips from her ass she'll remember nothing but my name. When she thinks about sex, I'll be the one she recalls. When she craves an orgasm, I'll be the one she longs for. When she dreams about fucking, it'll be my face she sees. I want to ruin her. I want to take a place in her life–present, past, and future–that no other man can ever take.

The idea makes me feverish. Anxious. I won't rest until I've accomplished my objective. I want to kiss her, but the urgency burning in my gut won't let me. It's like I'm running a race, and I'm dead scared of losing. I'm dead scared someone else will make it over the finish line first. I give her more. Harder. The wet sound of the toy fucking her cunt turns louder and faster. So do her moans. The room smells of woman, rubber, and lube. It's intoxicating as hell. I'm sweating from arousal rather than exertion. On the contrary, the perspiration on her brow is from pure, physical output. I've taken it easy on her with the first orgasm, making it quick and effortless. The second one won't be a walk in the park, but it'll be worth it.

Gathering more lube, I slip a finger into her ass again. The passage is slick. Two, three fingers. I switch the vibrator onto a low setting. The hum of the toy penetrates the thin wall between her vagina and anus. The vibration tickles my fingers. My left hand keeps the vibrator in place while the fingers of my right hand play in her ass. When there's too little reaction from the beautiful nymph lying half-naked and trussed on the bed, I readjust the bunny ears. Spot on. Her inner thighs jerk, and her legs strain to close, but the ropes keep them open. Her asshole clenches around my fingers. She tosses, turning her head from side to side.

That's it, princess. Feel it. This is one is going to make you sweat.

I have an urge to talk her through it, but I'm too busy concentrating on the signals of her body, plus it will take away some of the surprise effect, and surprise is part of the pleasure. Instead, I keep the conversation in my head, enjoying the noises she's making. They're rawer now, less inhibited than before. I use her ass harder and speed up the vibrator. She utters a cry that sounds close to desperation, but it will be a long time yet before she comes again.

"Brian, please."

It's a request to finish her, but she's a strong, fit woman. She can take a whole lot more.

"Brian. I can't."

"You trust me, princess."

Turning the bunny ears from side to side, I tease her clit until her hips lift off the mattress. Every time I sense she's close, I remove the stimulation, letting the vibration inside keep her on the edge. We carry on like this until her abs must be sore from spasms. Her whole body is slick with perspiration from the workout I'm giving her pussy and ass. I'm making sure she'll feel it everywhere tomorrow, from her shoulders to her calves. I want her to remember me every time she moves.

"Brian. It's too much."

"You can take it."

"I can't. I can't come again."

Just to prove her wrong, I flick the vibrator onto a higher speed. Her reaction is fucking perfect. It's dizzying to watch. Her eyes grow large and then turn out of focus. Her whole upper body lifts off the bed. It's like a perverse scene from Poltergeist–a pretty, tied-up woman possessed with pleasure. She gasps, sucking in air, chasing the release that's building too slowly while my fingers fuck her stretched pucker. A little bit faster, pushing the vibrator a little bit deeper, and she clenches her teeth. A cry escapes her lips. She pants, breathing hard.

"Oh, fuck. No. Yes. Oh, God."

A slow orgasm detonates through her body, pulling her abdomen so tight the vibrator is sucked deeper and her ass squeezes my fingers hard. Perfect. It holds and holds. She gnashes her teeth, biting back a scream. Her fingers clench around the rope that binds her. I'm mesmerized. I've never seen anyone come so hard or long. When her eyes roll back in her head, it's my cue to cut the stimulation. I free the vibrator, careful not to yank and tear her overstretched skin, and give her ass a reprieve. She sinks back against the sheets, her hair damp and disheveled, but her make-up still in place. Her lips are the kind of red only a lady or whore can pull off. I want to kiss her and smear that lipstick all over her face, but my cock is about to explode. I wasn't joking when I said her pleasure gets me off. The harder she comes, the more turned on I am. Since she needs a small break before her next climax…

I crawl up her body to stand on my knees over her face. We've already established she can deep-throat. She doesn't need urging.

Staring at me with hazy eyes, she parts her red lips. I go straight for the kill. There's not enough willpower left to hold back. The fog lifts from her eyes as I push my cock so deep down her throat that my balls threaten to disappear into her hot mouth, too. One, two, three. I pull out slightly to let her breathe. One, two, three. Fuck, she's good at giving head. Her tongue is flat when I'm deep and curled when I'm shallow. She's going to make me come in no time. It'll be a new record.

"Suck me, princess."

I give her the space to do so, and when she does, it's not the wicked work of her lips and wet tongue that sends me over, but the look in her eyes. Wide. Innocent. Submissive.

Accepting.

Fuck, I'm exploding. The first jet of seed shoots down her throat before I pull out and scramble back. The rest marks her where I aim my cock–her tits, stomach, and crotch. She's a stunning picture of classy beauty and slutty perversity. Her posture is regal, even bound in rope. I made damn sure that lipstick is smeared. Her hair is a mess. Cum streaks her body and pubic hair. Her cunt and ass are well-used. She's the most beautiful sight I've seen. I take a moment to commit the image to my memory. It's one I'll see on my deathbed and take to my grave. It's the kind of image that defines a man, that makes you feel powerful and humble all at the same time.

When I've had my fill, I stretch out between her wide-open legs, keeping my weight on one hand. I use the other to pump my cock before dragging the head over her clit. I needed that climax to blow off steam. I don't want to come too quickly when I'm inside her. I keep on stimulating us both until I'm hard enough again to penetrate her. Wiping the excess cum from my cock with a corner of the sheet, I cover my sheath liberally with lube. One of the advantages of not having a thick dick is that anal is easy. My length makes up for what I lack in circumference, but the women I've fucked told me too big was more of a challenge to fit than a pleasure.

My focus goes back to Jane. She's boneless, lying back on the mattress, her head turned to the side.

"Jane."

She faces me obediently. Her eyes are back to an alert state. Her breathing is calmer.

"How are you holding up, princess?"

Her full lips tilt. "I'm good."

It'll be easier if I untie her and flip her over, but I'm too impatient. I also don't want her to start coming down from her high. I only untie her ankles and knees, leaving her legs free. Kneeling in front of her, I throw both legs over my left shoulder and grip her ankles with one hand. The other grabs her hip to keep her in place. Her ass is ready for me. My cock goes stiff at the mere thought of pushing into her rear. Holding her still, I angle my cock and press forward. Despite my preparations, the broad head strains against her pucker. I apply pressure slowly until the ring of muscle gives way.

She hisses and sucks in a breath.

"Do I need to stop?"

She inhales and exhales. "No."

I go slower, sinking in another inch.

"Spank me, Brian."

I tear my gaze, which is riveted to where my cock is spearing her ass, to her face.

"Spank me when you push deeper."

I get it. One erotic pain will ease another.

With the next thrust, I bring my palm down on her ass cheek. The cry that tears from her throat is pain mixed with ecstasy.

"Ah, yes," she whimpers. "Just like that."

I continue like this, with a spank and a shove, until I'm inches away from being buried balls-deep.

For the last stretch, I go flat-out. I drive in all the way while raining a quick succession of sharp slaps over her gorgeous globes. Her ass tightens, and her cheeks clench, but she doesn't try to get away. Her screams and my palm on her flesh fills the room like music until her hips starts grinding, driving me in and out of her ass. Grabbing her legs with both arms, I angle her body and start pounding a steady beat. She gasps and moans, saying my name and other things, but her words are too incoherent to make out what she says.

Release builds in my scrotum. I need to come so badly I'll give up my birthright, but I'm not going faster or harder. I need her orgasm first. Without it, my release will be disappointing. Pushing one hand between her legs, I find her clit. I fuck her ass raw before her orgasm starts building. She's going to need more to come. Throwing one ankle over my right shoulder, I sit back on my heels so her rear rests on my thighs. There's not enough time or hands to lubricate the vibrator, but she's so wet it slips right it. I go straight for maximum speed. When her thighs start to tremble and her ass clenches down on my cock, I give her all I've got.

My grunts and her gasps mix as I fuck the air out of her lungs. Two more seconds, and she comes. When her orgasm hits, I let go, emptying my second load for the night where it belongs–in her tight asshole.

It takes a long time to catch my bearings and breath. I almost remember too late to pull out and let my cum seep from her hole so I can watch. Like a perverted caveman, it turns me on. It's like I've marked my property. Mine. Then I let her down gently.

The sheets are tangled and wet with cum. The room reeks of decadence and pleasure. She looks tussled and ravished. With one tit falling out of her bra, her panties sitting sideways on her cunt, a vibrator stuck in her pussy, and her ass spanked red, she's a sight to behold. A piece of art raw in its beauty, stripped down to its dirtiest fantasies.

I'm in no better state. Sweat runs down my temples and back. My flaccid cock and balls are sticky with cum.

We're a mess. An awful, beautiful, arousing mess.

Jane

If Brian's fucking is amazing, there are no words to describe his aftercare, which he tells me is part and parcel of sex to him. After untying me, he checks every inch of my skin. The marks where the rope chaffed my wrists worry him to no end. He applies a soothing balm from my medicine box and massages my shoulders, back, arms, and legs. He fetches a pitcher of water from the kitchen and makes me drink two full glasses. Then he settles against the headboard and pulls me into his arms. For a long time, we sit like this while he drags his fingers through my hair, extending the heavenly massage from earlier to my scalp, as he praises me for how well I did. Like the first time we had oral sex, he holds me until I'm not only rested and relaxed, but also inexplicably happy. Only then does he lead me to the shower and washes my hair and body like I'm precious porcelain.

As he towels my hair dry, the ache of the spanking sets in. I guess the effect of the Triptan diminished the pain, and now the medication is wearing off. Seeing my discomfort, he rubs arnica gel onto my skin and makes me fetch clean sheets while he rips the sweat and sex drenched ones from the bed. He refuses to let me help and orders me to sit on the chair, which I do gingerly. When the bed is made, he lies down and brings me with him, pulling me tight against his chest. I didn't expect him to stay, but I appreciate it. I'm not in the mood for being alone. Not after what we did.

Originally, I was against putting a television in the bedroom, but Francois insisted. Now, I'm glad for it as Brian flicks through the channels while I rest my head on his chest. It's close to four in the morning. My mind battles to digest that we've been fucking for three hours while my body tells a different story. I'm battered and bruised in the best way possible. Hands down, he's the best lover I've had. It makes me curious. He's young for that kind of experience.

"Brian?"

"Princess?"

"Your sexual preferences…"

"What about them?" he asks in a lazy voice.

"How did you…?" I clear my throat. "Did someone teach you, or did you always know what you like?"

He thinks for a while. "A bit of both. My first time was a defining moment, I guess."

My lethargy evaporates. I'm intrigued. "How come?"

"She asked me to spank her. That's when I discovered it made me hard."

I can't help my curiosity. "Who was she?"

"My teacher."

My body tenses in shock.

He continues to play with my hair, unaffected by my question or reaction. "She was fifty-something, but by God she was a looker."

An arrow of jealousy pierces my heart.

"Maybe she spoiled me for girls my age," he continues, "but my guess is I've been spoiled long before she and I overstepped the line."

"How old were you?"

"Close to sixteen."

I jerk my head up to look at him. "She took advantage of you."

Smiling, he pushes my cheek back to his chest. "It's not what you think. It was me who instigated the sex."

"Why?" I don't understand. "Did you have a crush on her?"

"It was purely physical. We both acknowledged it before we fucked."

"You both took a huge risk."

"We were careful."

"You never told anyone?"

"Not until now."

"She trusted you," I say as the notion dawns on me.

He chuckles. "The fact that she gave in to my seduction would suggest so."

I want to know more, and I don't. Closing my eyes, I try to block out the picture that conjures the unfounded and unreasonable envy pinching my chest for this woman who will be fifty-something plus four years old now.

"Tell me about your first time," he says.

"Why?"

"Because I'm jealous of all the times you slept with someone other than me."

Talking about past sexual experiences with a new lover is a no-go. Everyone knows that. But for a reason I can't explain, I want to talk about it. I want him to know.

"His name was Evan." I drag my fingertips over his chest, outlining the hard ridges of his muscles. "He was too old for me, at least according to my mother. He was the brother of a university classmate, Benjamin. We met at Benjamin's birthday party."

He strokes my arm. "How old were you?"

"Twenty-five."

"That's when you had sex for the first time?"

"It's old by general standards, I know. I didn't know what I wanted to do after school, so my parents sent me to do voluntary work for two years in Africa. They were kind of hard that way. They wanted me to learn about struggling and appreciate what I had. After Africa, I needed to clear my mind from all that suffering. I backpacked for two years through Europe before settling in my father's company. I worked there as a secretary for another two years before I decided to take up studying at the ripe age of twenty-five. I guess there wasn't the time or right person before then."

"Did you fall in love?"

"It was love at first sight. He took my virginity on our first date." I glance at him. "In the back of my car, of all places." I draw a circle around the flat disk of his nipple. "He said the choice of venue was inexcusable, but he didn't apologize." I smile at the memory. "He wasn't taking chances with waiting and giving someone else an opportunity to take my virginity."

"Go on," he encourages when I lose myself to the past and fall silent.

"He was starting up his own plumbing business. Times were hard, so he temporarily moved back to his parents' place. Since my parents were in Cape Town, I stayed in a girls-only dorm on campus in Pretoria. We didn't want to be disrespectful, so we didn't make love in his room, at least not when his parents were there. We did it wherever we could—in dark corners of the campus and parked next to the river. Evan was always gentle, until one night in his old bedroom. The door was locked, and the music playing loud, despite the fact that we were alone. He got carried away and turned a bit rough. I liked it. That's when he spanked me for the first time. It made me come so hard the neighbors must've heard me scream despite the blaring music."

My insides heat at the memory while a familiar pain crumples my heart. This is the hard part, the part that still makes my chest wheeze and my ears ring.

His hand stills, his fingers clenching on my upper arm. "What happened?"

"He died."

There's a long moment of silence in which I feel him struggling with words. It's there in the way his breathing changes and his chest heaves differently. I don't want sympathy. I only want someone to share this with, and that's exactly what he gives me. He offers no pity or useless words.

He hugs me tighter and kisses the top of my head. "Go to sleep, princess. It's been a long night for you."

. . .

I'M NOT sure when I fell asleep, but I slept like the dead, because when I wake up, which feels like in no time at all, the alarm clock tells me it's past ten. Brian's side is empty, but he hasn't left. A clanging of pans comes from the kitchen, and the smell of coffee fills the air.

Stretching, I flinch. Every bone and muscle aches. It's nothing compared to how my backside hurts when I get up. I make my way with small steps to the bathroom. There's no way I'm jogging today. I relieve myself, wash my hands and face, and brush my teeth. When I throw the hand cloth I've used to dry my hands in the washing basket, I notice my green underwear. Brian must've put it there. In the bedroom, I look around. The only disorder is the unmade bed. A quick look in the nightstand drawer confirms the vibrator has been washed and returned with the lube. Heat spreads from my neck all the way to my belly.

Who was the wanton woman of last night? I've never gone that far before, although it's not difficult to follow when Brian leads. I can't believe he made me come three times. It's a first for me, and not for lack of trying. The kind of stamina he displayed comes from lots of practice or youth, or a combination of both. Not willing to linger on his practice, which surely involves other partners, I pull on a T-shirt and shorts and follow the smell of caffeine to the kitchen.

He's wearing the same yummy jeans from yesterday, and he's donned his T-shirt. His broad shoulders bunch under the fabric as he stirs something in a pot on the stove. I lean in the doorway to appreciate the view. As if sensing my presence, he turns a fraction, looking at me over his shoulder. His gaze is melting hot as he drags it over me, regarding me as if I'm a Playboy centerfold. His dark eyes soften, and his lips curve. That damn dimple. It'll be the end of me. He turns toward the counter where two bowls are waiting. The rest of the kitchen is spotless.

"Just in time for breakfast." He shoots me a look from under his eyebrows as he puts the pot on a cork plate. His voice drops an octave, going gruff and sexual in the tick of a second. "How do you feel?"

"Sore."

Alarm flashes across his face.

"In a good way," I add quickly.

He dishes oatmeal into the bowls, sprinkles it with nuts and raisins, and adds a scoop of honey.

"Come," he says, carrying the bowls to the table where two places are set. He takes a cushion from one of the chairs and places it on top of another to form a double padding on the bench. "Sit."

I do so carefully, feeling every movement. He fetches coffee, sugar, and milk before taking the seat opposite me.

"You made me breakfast." I'm touched. Evan and I never had an opportunity to sleep over, and Francois never cooked.

"I hope you don't mind that I went through your cupboards."

"Of course not. There are eggs and bacon, too, you know."

"This is a better meal for you this morning." He pours a mug of coffee.

I raise an eyebrow. "Better than protein?"

"Eggs are quickly digestible and bacon high in fat. Oatmeal will give you sustained energy for a longer time, the iron in the raisins will boost your strength, the nuts contain all the good oils and protein you need, and the honey is a natural antibiotic for your sore ass."

"Oh." I flush a little, not sure what to say.

"I know how you drink your tea, but how do you like your coffee?"

"Two sugars and milk, please."

He adds the milk and sugar, stirs, and pushes the mug toward me. "Eat up. You need it. Careful not to burn your mouth. It's hot."

I can just sit here and bask in his care and consideration all day long. I haven't felt this alive since... No, I don't want to think about Evan now. I don't want to compare a dead man with Brian when I should simply be enjoying the present moment.

"What are your plans for today?" he asks.

"Catching up with some work." I take a spoonful of oatmeal and blow on it. "How about you?"

"I'm working at the building site, but I'm free tonight." He gives me an uncertain smile. "Want to hang out?"

My heart lurches. "Sure. What did you have in mind?"

He watches me over his untouched bowl of food, his arms crossed on the table. There's a flicker of nervousness in his eyes. "How about I take you out to dinner?"

"You want to take me out to dinner?"

I expected a repeat of last night, but not going out. Somehow, I thought being seeing with me in public would be the last thing on his mind.

"Yes," he says. "I can make a reservation at Oscars."

I stare at him in surprise. The place is out of a student with a part-time job's league, but I'm not going to insult him by bringing up money. If he suggested Oscars, it's because he's thought it through and decided he can afford it. Bringing me there must be important to him. The least I can do is accept gracefully.

"Thank you. That sounds wonderful."

His face lights up. "Yes?"

I laugh. "Yes. Is it a special occasion?"

"Just dinner."

"All right, then. At what time must I be ready?"

"Seven. I'll pick you up."

After we've eaten, he gathers our crockery and loads the dishwasher. Then he takes me in an embrace, his hands resting on my ass. He stares into my eyes as he squeezes each cheek possessively.

"I'm in love with your ass, Ms. Logan."

"Just my ass?" I tease.

"Your pussy and mouth, too. And your tits."

I run my hands up his back under his T-shirt, marveling at the hardness of his muscles. "Want to come back to bed?"

"Yes, but you need to recover, and I need to get to work."

"What time are you off?"

"Not until six. I'm working a double shift."

"Where is this building site where you're working?"

"At the State Theater. It's the new extension."

"Can I pack you lunch? I can fix something quickly."

"Thanks, but I'll grab a pie from the snack stand. I'm already running late."

Reluctantly, I let him go. "I'll see you tonight."

"Later, princess."

The door closes, and I'm shut in silence, alone. The happiness I felt since last night leaves the house with him. I'm back to being me, a divorcee and single mom. If my belly wasn't so full with oatmeal, I would've thought last night was nothing but a fragment of my imagination.

I give Abby a quick call on her mobile phone to see how she's doing, and then I stretch out on a deckchair by the pool with my laptop, working on my new Freddy Fish proposal. For once, it's flowing. I'm in the middle of a paragraph when Loretta calls.

"Hi," she says, "I just wanted to check on you. Was I too hard on you last night?"

"Your honesty is one of the things I love most about you."

"Good. Then you'll say yes to morning tea at the shop."

"It's eleven, already."

"Better get your butt over here, then. I want you to try on that suit I told you about."

"Maybe another day."

"Janie."

"What?"

"I'm not taking no for an answer. If you're not coming over, I'm coming to you."

"Okay, fine." I shut my laptop with a sigh. "I'm not dressed for boutique shopping, though."

"Just come as you are."

Thirty minutes later, I walk into Loretta's store in the same T-shirt and shorts I pulled on that morning. At least I've added a long-sleeve summer shirt, underwear, and flip-flops.

Loretta's shop assistant gives me an once-over. "She's at the back."

I know my way to the office where Loretta makes deals with designers and secretly smokes. The air freshener and breath mints don't mask the odor of the cigarettes.

"There you are." Loretta waves me in and sticks her head around the door, calling to her assistant, "Bring us two Red Bulls and Vodka."

"Just tea for me," I say. "I'm driving."

She waves my comment away. "You can hang around until the alcohol's worn out of your system."

It won't help to argue, even if I have no intention of drinking hard liquor at this hour of the day.

"Here." She takes a suit from a portable clothes rail. "This was made for you." She removes the plastic cover and holds it up against my body. "White really becomes you. Go ahead. Try it on."

I'm about to turn back to the shop when she grabs my arm.

"The changing booth is occupied. You can change here."

We've been roommates. We've seen each other naked enough times, but I can't strip down to my underwear, not with Brian's handprints still on my skin.

I take the suit from her. "I'll try it on at home."

"I might have to make adjustments."

"It's my size. I'm sure it'll be fine."

The assistant enters with a tray, which she places on the desk.

"Don't be silly." Loretta undoes the single button on the jacket and slips it from the hanger. She holds it open. "Let's see how this looks."

"Anything else?" the assistant asks sourly. "Maybe some crackers and cheese to go with your drinks?"

179

Loretta ignores her sarcasm. "I'll let you know if I need anything else."

With a stiff smile, the young woman leaves.

"Come on." Loretta gives the jacket a shake. "My arms are getting tired of holding this up."

With a sigh, I concede, pushing my arms into the fabric. She grips my shoulders and turns me to face her. Her gaze runs critically over the fit.

"Mm." She buttons it up and takes a step back. "We'll have to take the arms in a bit."

"I haven't decided if I'm taking it."

"Of course you are." She grabs my hand and folds back the fabric. "You've got the perfect figure to pull off the tailored waist and–"

Her eyes are fixed on the sleeve. When I look down to see what caused her to cut her words off mid-sentence, I freeze. The red bruise around my wrist stands out like a flashing neon sign.

8

Jane

"Janie!" Loretta's gaze shoots to mine. "What's this?"

I free my arm, smoothing the fabric back in place. "It's nothing."

For the life of me, I can't think of an excuse. I pretend to look at the clothes on the rail to hide the flush I feel creeping into my cheeks. A trickle of sweat runs between my shoulder blades. It feels ten degrees hotter inside than outside where the sun is scorching. The clink-clink of the hangers as I flip through them is deafening in the silence that follows. Loretta's shock and judgment carries on the air like the smell of stale smoke and forbidden cigarettes. I pull out a red dress, holding it up to the light.

"How about this one?" I ask with my back to her.

"That's way too young for you."

My spine goes stiff. What makes me rebel? The fact that I truly love the dress, or that she implies I'm old? Or is it something totally different, something about the fact that I'm fucking a guy twenty-two years younger than me?

"I'll take it." I scramble out of the jacket and fold it over the rail. Only then do I trust my coloration to face her. "Since when are we too old to wear what we love? Where are those two university girls who didn't care about the opinions of others?"

"It's not the same, Janie. Those were the opinions of idealists. Reality is very different."

"I disagree." I have an inexplicable urge to turn back the clock, to take us to a time when we were carefree and the air wasn't stained with judgment and silence. "We don't have to conform to the norm because society says so. Why can't we wear backless red dresses and grow our hair long when we're eighty? It should come from here." I place a palm over my heart. "What we truly love and want. Not what *they* say we should be and wear."

She shakes her head slowly. "I'm in the fashion business. Rules are what make us successful. Rules are what match cuts with body shapes and styles with ages. Rules make us look respectable. Presentable. Looks are everything. It might not be fair, but that's how the world turns."

Since when has my friend become so cynical, and why am I only noticing now? Is it because I've lost my way so truly by playing fair and following the rules that I'd forgotten about the person I used to be? The person I should be. It's as if Brian hasn't only woken my dragon, but also the parts of me I've locked away. If life were a fairy tale, he'd be my wakening kiss in Sleeping Beauty.

She closes the distance and grabs my hand in both of hers. "I'm the one who said you should get laid, but I'm worried about you." Her whole face transforms into a frown. "I'm not a fool. Whoever screwed you tied you up. Why do you do this to yourself? You've always been drawn to the wrong type of guys."

"Wrong?" I pull my hand away. "Just because it's wrong in your eyes doesn't mean it's not right for me."

"Look at Evan, Janie," she exclaims. "Look what happened with Benjamin."

"I'm not talking about that."

"Fine. We're not talking about the night Evan died. Let's talk about the things he did to you."

I never should've told her. "He didn't tie me up."

"No, but he abused you."

"Never!"

"Christ, Janie. He hit you."

"He spanked me. It's not the same."

"It's violence."

"Spanking is not about violence. It's the exact opposite. It's about self-control and trust. Evan practiced a tremendous amount of self-control when he spanked me. He knew my limits, and he never went beyond them. That's why I trusted him."

"Do you hear yourself? You make it sound like it's something good. How can pain be good?"

"I don't expect you to understand. I'm not criticizing your vanilla sex life. Why are you concerned about my kink?"

"It's not normal to let a man tie you up or give you a hiding. I'm worried that you're going down that same, self-destructive road from seventeen years ago."

"Maybe, for once, I'm following my heart instead of my mind."

"Let me tell you something. Stick to your mind. It's the wiser choice."

We're talking in circles, like last night. "I can't stay. I have a lot of work to catch up with." I wiggle the red dress. "Will you put this on my account?" I give her a quick hug. "Thanks, Lottie. I'll call you."

I'm gone before she can say more.

It's only in the solitude of my car that I notice my heart is pounding and my hands are shaking. I'm upset. I'm angry with Loretta. I'm not angry about her judgment and lack of understanding. I'm angry about her lack of acceptance and support. Mostly, I'm angry with myself for not having achieved any of the things on my List. I didn't get a degree in BSc Food

Science. I didn't open a restaurant. I didn't move to the countryside. I didn't learn to speak Italian, and I've never been to Rome. When I learned I was pregnant, I married Francois and dropped out of university. I stayed home while he finished his degree. I tried to complete my BSc part-time, but we were always short of cash after Abby was born, so I did temp work to keep us afloat. When Francois finally finished his nine year-degree, he earned enough for me to stay at home and take care of Abby. We decided it would be best for her to have one parent's full-time attention, as the first few years of Francois' career was hectic. He was hardly home. As she grew and became less dependent on me, I became bored. It was Francois' idea to take up a degree in communication, specializing in advertising. That's where the big money is, these days. My dreams and bucket list fell to the wayside. It's easy to see where all those plans I had for my future derailed, but I don't have an excuse for becoming just another sheep that follows the flock. I can't blame circumstances for forgetting how to live.

On impulse, I drive to a nearby deli. After stocking up with gourmet salads, iced coffee, mineral water, and carrot cake topped with cream cheese icing, I find the building site at the theater. I park in the dirt lot and carry my purchases to where men with yellow hardhats are scurrying around in the heat of the day. I spot Brian from a distance. He's a head taller than everyone. I stop in my tracks. He's got a bag of cement thrown over his shoulder, carrying it as if it's a bag of tennis balls. That bag must weigh at least a hundred kilos. His gait is swift, but at closer inspection I see the strain his back is taking from the way his muscles flex and bunch under his sweat-drenched T-shirt. He dumps the bag on a mountain of similar bags against a half-finished wall and returns for another on the back of a truck. Backward and forward he goes, his wet T-shirt clinging to his torso and sweat dripping from his temples. It's as if a stapler pierces two neat little holes into my heart. Seeing him like this does something to me. He's literally breaking his back to pay for his studies. When I was a student, I never knew need. My parents had enough money to pay for my studies, accommodation, food, car, entertainment, and trendy clothes.

A man wearing a white hardhat and safety vest approaches me. "Sorry, ma'am. This is a restricted site."

"I'm here to see Brian Michaels."

"Michaels?" He scratches his jaw, looking me up and down. "You know him?"

I hold up the paper bag. "Lunch."

A smile tugs at his lips, but his confused frown remains as he turns toward the men, puts a forefinger and thumb in his mouth, and whistles.

As one, the men drop what they're doing and turn their heads our way. Their gazes run over me, most with curiosity and some with interest. My eyes find purchase on Brian. Surprise registers on his features. He drops the bag he's carrying, shooting up a small cloud of dust. Crap, was it wise to come here? All I seem to be doing around him is making impulsive decisions. It's not like me. For all I know, his work buddies may think I'm his mother dropping off his lunch.

The curve of his smile is slow to grow, but then his dimple appears. With long strides, he makes his way to us, his heavy work boots kicking up dirt and his powerful thigh muscles knotting under the fabric of his jeans, the same torn ones he wore when he tied me up. Heat grows in my belly at the untimely thought.

The man in the safety vest holds out a hand. "I'm Mike Joubert, by the way." His grin is friendly. "I run the show around here."

"Jane Logan," I say, shaking his hand. "Nice to meet you."

I drop his hand just as Brian stops short of us. The other workers are still staring.

"Take an early lunch break," Mike says to Brian, already walking back to the site.

I open my mouth, about to apologize for a very bad idea, when

Brian's arms come around me. Pulling me tight against his chest, he lowers his head and kisses me before I have time to contemplate the move. The kiss catches me off guard. It throws me off balance. He parts my lips with his tongue, delving inside and kissing me with long, tender strokes. His mouth is skillful, his lips molding mine with soft precision. The intensity I've come to know with Brian infuses his kiss. He kisses me as if no one else matters, as if we're alone, and for a moment I forget we're not. The act takes up all of his attention and focus.

Instead of suffusing me with the gentleness he practices, the softness of his touch has the opposite effect. A fire combusts in my body, flames leaking down my lower region. I feel it so profoundly and instantaneously, my clit swells and throbs with a need for attention. I'm helpless to his touch. It goes beyond the lust and perverse fucking of last night, promising something I equally crave. I can't help but surrender, getting carried away. I can't help but let him shape my lips, will, and desire. It's all give and no take. This is for *my* benefit, whether he meant it to be gentle warmth or scorching heat. It doesn't matter, because it's both, and more.

When he brings the tangle of our tongues to a slow halt, sucking my bottom lip softly into his mouth, I open my eyes. His are closed in concentration. He's fully emerged in the act. It's both beautiful and scary. Like him.

As he sets me free, I come back to earth, remembering we have an audience. On cue, wolf whistles permeate the air. The men are clapping and cheering as he takes my hand and leads me to the shade of a tree, but he pays them no heed.

He dusts a pile of bricks and pulls me down next to him before taking off his hardhat.

A twinkle sparks in his eyes. "Missed me already?"

I put the bag between us. "I thought you'd be hungry. I'm not the only one who needs to fuel up after last night."

Even as I say it, my cheeks heat. What happened to the self-confident, forty-something year-old woman I used to be? I'm a blushing teenager around him.

He peers inside the bag and takes out the salads. Wiping his palms on his thighs, he opens one, pulls out the fork sealed in the lid, and hands it to me.

I study him from under my lashes, trying to read his expression. "I hope I haven't caused you any trouble."

"Believe me, you're the kind of trouble I enjoy."

"Seriously, Brian. I didn't want to get you into shit with your boss."

"Eat." He motions at my salad before taking a big forkful of his own.

While we eat, I mind my chewing, and he tells me about the building project. Through the chatter, he takes charge, pulling the wrapper off my straw and unscrewing the cap of my iced coffee. I drink and eat on his prompt, our exchange flowing naturally. It's the kind of bossiness I don't mind, the kind that is done with consideration for my wellbeing. We function like a unit, seamless and effortlessly. It's different to the push and pull, hide and seek I'm used to with Francois. It's liberating.

By the time he stands and pulls me into a hug, I've lost track of time.

He kisses me lightly on the lips. "I have to get back to work. I'll see you later."

"Here." I hand him a bottle of mineral water. "Don't dehydrate. It's too hot for manual labor."

"Yes, Mom."

He meant it as a joke, but it stings. The earlier amiability vanishes. Determined not to spoil the moment, I shake it off, keeping busy with gathering our wrappers and empty cups.

"Bye, princess."

Smack.

I fling around. He did not just whack my ass in front of

everyone. A grin splits his face as he shoots me a dimpled look from over his shoulder. His expression is both playful and possessive. There's no doubt about the message in his eyes. *Hands off. She's mine.*

Brian

As AGREED, Clive waits for me when I pull into our yard, a tie hanger in his hand.

"Fucking hell." I shut the truck door and take the hanger from him. "How many ties do you have?" There must be thirty or more, not that I've ever seen him wearing one.

He shrugs. "Birthday and Christmas gifts. You know how it goes."

I actually feel sorry for the bugger. Clive has a huge family with grandparents, aunts, uncles, cousins, nieces, and nephews. On any given birthday, a crowd of forty people are crammed in on Clive's lawn around a bring-your-own-meat-and-drinks barbeque. The elements that make up the day are invariable. You can count on it like sunrise. There's always a cake, someone who has one too many, and the inevitable insult and fight that follow. And the gift tie.

"Won't hurt you to say thank you," he mumbles as he trails behind me into the house.

Mom sits at the kitchen table, smoking and listening to a soapy on the radio. Sam rushes through the door and grabs me in an anaconda hug.

"I missed you." She pouts. "Where were you?"

"Yeah." Clive snorts. "Wouldn't we all like to know?"

"Busy," I say, ignoring him.

Mom's gaze flickers to me, but she doesn't ask the questions I see in her eyes. That's not our code of conduct.

I have ten minutes to shave, shower, and change before leaving for my date with Jane. Freeing myself from Sam's embrace, I move toward the door, but she yanks on my T-shirt.

"Where are you going with all those ties?" She narrows her eyes and crosses her arms.

"None of your business, piglet." I pull her braid and kiss the top of her head.

She points a finger at Clive. "Is he sleeping over again?"

"Yep."

Clive's voice follows me down the hallway. "No fucking way, man."

"Watch your mouth around Sam," I call back.

"I'm not, Brian. I'm serious."

Slamming the door on his words, I shave my two day-old stubble and strip the dirty clothes from my body. The dirt-streaked jeans and T-shirt go straight into the washing machine. It takes less than five minutes to do the rest of my grooming. I have to open the door to let the steam out so I can see myself in the mirror. I'm not sure about the shirt. I try another one.

By the third shirt, Mom leans in the doorframe, clearing her throat.

I look at her reflection in the mirror. "What?"

A smile teases her lips. "Are you going on a date?"

"What makes you ask that?"

She motions at the shirts piling up on the floor. "They all look the same, you know."

"Thanks. That's a big help."

She utters a soft sigh and steps into the room, placing a hand on my shoulder. "No matter what you wear, you'll look handsome."

"I'm not aiming for handsome."

I try on an old button-up of my dad. I'm going for decent, although I don't have the demeanor to pull it off. The problem is the restaurant where I'm taking Jane has a dinner dress code. Shirt, tie, and jacket. I told her it's just dinner, but it's to ease my conscience. I'm not going to fuck her tonight. I'm going to make love to her and I want to do it right, with the romance and candlelight a princess deserves. Which brings me to problem two. I know how to fuck, but I haven't got a clue about romance. Hell, I'm a nervous wreck.

"I've never seen you getting like this over a girl," Mom says, pulling my attention back to her. "It must be serious."

I jerk the blue shirt off and try the white one I wore to the confirmation at the Dutch Reformed Church all eighteen-year-olds suffer through after battling through twelve years of Sunday school. It's the religious equivalent of passing matric. The fact that none of us has ever been back to church says a lot about the outdated system. Or maybe it says a lot about us.

"When are you bringing her home?" she asks, her smile widening.

I catch her gaze in the mirror again, but don't reply. That depends on Jane, and I'm not sure she'll want to visit this side of the tracks. Not that I blame her. No one who lives here wants to be here. We're here because we don't have a choice.

The white shirt is half decent. At least it's brand new. I never wore it except for that one time. Even then, I wore it open-collar. I don't have a tie to my name. I flip through Clive's ties, finding everything from cartoons to porn, but nothing fit for Oscars.

Mom takes the hanger from me, her fingers skipping deftly from tie to tie. "How about this one?" She pulls a silver one with a pink stripe from the back and holds it up in front of me in the mirror.

It's better than Goofy or Teasers tits.

"Let me get this." She turns me around and makes the tie, the ends the perfect length.

Memories of her doing Dad's ties in the mornings flash through my mind.

My voice is extra soft. "Thanks, Mom."

She pats my cheek. "It's a pleasure."

Clive shoots me a long look when I step into the lounge. He's playing Scrabble with Sam. He doesn't ask where I'm going, but there are accusations in his eyes.

"Wow," Sam says. "You look different."

I tap her nose. "Is your homework finished?" We have a no-homework-on-Sunday rule.

She bats her eyelashes. "Yes."

"Bedtime is eight, not a minute later."

"Yes." She folds her arms over her chest. Her sweater is getting too tight.

"No more snacking. Brush your teeth before you go to bed."

"Yes, boss."

I tickle her. "Goodnight, piglet. Be good."

Grabbing my black leather jacket, I kiss my mom on the cheek and give Clive a slap on the head, but he doesn't reciprocate. He simply stares at me until I'm out of the door.

Running low on cash, I stop at the ATM on the main road. I don't qualify for a credit card, yet. Tonight's bill is going to eat a huge cut into my earnings, but this is important to me. As I pull the bills out of the machine, a Corvette rounds the corner. There's only one Corvette in this neighborhood. Stuffing the bills into my pocket, I make my way to my truck with big strides. I'm opening the door when Monkey cruises by, his head turned in my direction. For a moment our eyes lock. There's no smile on his face. He lifts a hand in a salute, and then he speeds up. By the time I'm in my truck, he's gone. I should be worried about Monkey, but not tonight. Tonight, I have bigger concerns on my mind. It's Saturday evening, and Abby is with her father for the weekend, which gives Jane and me all night. I've never dated anyone. My sexual experience is broad, but it consists of a string of one-night stands.

When Jane opens the door, my jaw drops. Fucking fuck. Holy cow. She's wearing a short, red dress with matching heels. Her only accessory is a pair of solitaire diamond earrings. The lace of nude, thigh-high stocking peek out from under the hem of the dress when she moves, and she's not wearing a bra, because the dress is backless, the V reaching down so low I can guess the crack of her ass. Her hair is sleeked back, and she's applied smoky eyeshadow and black eyeliner. Her lips are bright red. She's nothing short of a goddess.

I bring the flowers I'd picked up after work from behind my back. The florist said they're Starfighters and mean prosperity. I only choose them because they smell nice.

"Oh, Brian." Her eyes twinkle. "Thank you." She takes the flowers and kisses my lips. "You're the first one to ever give me flowers. Let me put them in water and get my bag."

Satisfaction is warm in my chest, although I can't fathom why no other man would've done this for her before. She deserves to be showered in petals. I follow her sheepishly into the house, watching as she arranges the flowers in a vase before picking up a clutch bag from the kitchen counter.

She tilts her head. "My car or yours?"

Her ease and self-assurance make me hard. There's nothing sexier than a woman who's comfortable in her own skin.

"Mine." Call me old-fashioned, but I'm stuck-up that way. Plus, I want her to have a good time. I'll stay sober to drive.

She waltzes ahead of me. With the way her ass sways, I want to take her right here, and not in a vanilla way, but I'm not allowing my lust make me jump the gun again. Taking the keys from her, I lock up and set the alarm before leading her to my truck. I'm drowning in her subtle grapefruit perfume and sensuality. It's enough to make any man drunk.

"Are we going on a date?" she asks, glancing sideways at me as I start the engine.

"Yes," I say honestly, not caring if I scare her, because if she runs I'll only catch her and bring her back.

My hands are clammy on the wheel as I steer us through her classy neighborhood toward town. It's got nothing to do with the too warm evening and everything with the way my heart sits askew in my chest. I'm out of my league with Jane, but also with where I'm taking us, and I don't mean literally. I'm going down a road from where there's no turning back. I'm here to stay. Rejecting me is not an option. I only hope I'll be what she needs. I'm a good fuck, but am I good boyfriend material?

She places her palm on my arm. Her skin is white and soft against the black leather of my jacket.

"You look nice." She grins. "I never imagined seeing you in a tie."

I never imagined myself in her life, and here I am, the Sunday school shirt and Clive's Christmas tie demonstrating not only the age between us, but also the difference between our worlds.

"What did you imagine seeing me in?" I wink. "Nothing?"

"Yes." She doesn't blink an eye.

Just like that, I go hard. Her honesty is refreshing. There are no games or unspoken rules, only expectations we're not shy to verbalize.

"Since when?"

"Since you lifted me onto the pull up bar."

Innocent awareness, on her part. Not so for me. My awareness came from much earlier, long before I orchestrated our paths to cross. I've been imagining her naked since the day I first laid eyes on her photo. I pride myself on making things happen, on getting what I want, and I'm planning on seeing her naked for a long time still to come.

At the restaurant, a valet parks my truck, and the same surly maître from before sees us to our table. It's a different experience from the last time I walked through the door. This time, I'm not an outsider at the bar. I'm the lucky man who shares the most beautiful woman in the room's table. I belong, if only at her side.

Before the waiter can get her chair, I pull it out and seat her. I don't want his hands to accidently brush her arm or leg when he places her napkin. I can't stand the thought of another man's fingers near her. He hands me the wine menu when I've taken my seat.

"Wine?" I ask Jane.

"Yes, please."

Good. I want her to drink and eat without a thought for my financial situation. Mike's already agreed to give me an advance.

I scan over the wine list. The names and years hold no meaning. "Any preference?"

"The Veenwouden Merlot is always good."

Good it may be, but that's not what I asked. "Is it what you like?"

"My favorite."

"May I suggest starting with an aperitif and deciding on the wine after you've made your choice from the dinner menu?" the waiter asks with his nose in the air.

I don't give a fuck about pairing food and wine, but maybe Jane does. I look at her for a clue. She gives a small shake of her head.

"You may not," I say. "The lady will have a bottle of Veenwouden Merlot. Water for me."

"Wait." She halts the waiter with a raised palm. "You're not having wine?"

"I'm driving."

"In that case, a glass will be sufficient," she tells the waiter.

"Certainly, ma'am." With a scowl and a slight bow, he's gone.

I reach for her hand over the table. "You look..." I rack my brain for words, but all I can come up with is a lame, "...amazing."

"Thank you," she says, accepting the compliment gracefully. "I'm glad if you like the dress, because I got it especially for tonight."

For *you*, her words imply.

I can barely hide my satisfaction. I'm the only man for who she's worn it. "I'm flattered."

"Don't."

"Don't what?"

"Don't joke."

It's the furthest statement from a joke. My thumb slide over her knuckles, the silk of her skin soft under my caress. "I never joke where you're concerned."

The waiter returns with food menus and I have to let go of her hand. We both decide on ostrich steak with a wild plum and bitter chocolate sauce. We talk about her work and my studies, our shared interest in advertising the focal point of our conversation. Even though her full, perfectly curved lips mesmerize me, it's not difficult to remain focused on her conversation. She's a skilled talker, but an even better listener. Her interest is genuine, and tonight her interest is in me. She doesn't look at me as the boy from Harryville or the troublemaker who jumped her gate. She looks at the person I am, and most of all the man.

By the time the stuck-up waiter flambés Crêpes Suzette for our dessert, I know the names of her colleagues, as well as the challenges of her job. She knows my objectives for the medium and long term, but not yet for the immediate future. As soon as she's finished her after-dinner coffee, I set that straight.

"I want to come inside your pussy."

Her throat moves with a gentle swallow. She doesn't look around to see if I've been overheard. "Then we better ask for the bill."

"Are you on birth control?"

"Yes."

"What kind?"

"An implant."

Good. There's no chance of forgetting to take a pill. "I'm clean. Do you want to see the blood work results? If you wish, I'll take new tests." I should've offered before I fucked her ass, but she makes me forget crucial things like that.

"I trust you."

Her words spread through me like a fire, lighting my skin with heated satisfaction, but also with guilt. My gaze slips to the bar. I should tell her, but what's growing between us is still too fragile. I'm not risking crushing it, not before it's taken root so deeply she'll never be able to rip me out.

"I'm clean, too," she adds. "I took tests when I found out about my ex-husband's infidelity."

"Did you have other lovers except for Evan and your ex?"

"I didn't cheat on either of them."

"You haven't told me about your ex." Not a subject I should bring up just after I've told her we're going to have sex that will end with my cum in her cunt, but I want nothing between us when I take her to bed.

She avoids my eyes, toying with her napkin. "There's not much to tell."

Her body language says otherwise. "How did you meet?"

"We got together straight after Evan died."

"On the rebound."

She looks up quickly. "You could say that. We were both studying at TUKS at the time."

"If he studied architecture and you communication, you would've been on different campuses."

"I enrolled for BSc Food Science."

This is a surprise. "Food Science?"

"I've always loved cooking."

That part makes sense.

She pulls up her narrow shoulders. "My dream was to own a restaurant."

"Why not attend a chef school instead?"

"My father insisted I get a university degree, something to fall back on if the restaurant flopped. I guess he didn't have much confidence in me." She takes a big gulp of water. "Anyway, it didn't work out. I dropped out before the end of the third year."

"Why?"

Her smile is gentle. "Abby."

"You fell pregnant."

"Yes. Francois had a long and costly degree, so–"

"You worked to pay the bills so that he could study."

"Yes, again."

My anger with the bastard for what he did to Jane escalates to a new level. She only ever had two lovers. The first died, and the second left her after she sacrificed her dream to have his baby. What a piece of shit. He may be better educated and cultivated than my dad, but he's no better than the man who walked out on me, Sam, and my mother. I'm not going to be either of them. I won't let Jane down.

Taking her hand, I pull her to her feet. "Let's go."

There's a sudden urgency in me to be alone with her, to take away the wrongs of her life, and fill her with the pretty words she deserves. And my seed. Coming in her ass was as close to heaven as a devil like me can come, but spilling everything that makes me a man in her pussy is the pinnacle. It deserves to be savored.

The sexual tension is thick in the truck on the way home. It squeezes around my ribcage until I can't breathe or think about anything else. I take the keys from her hand and rush her inside, but that's where the hurrying stops. In the kitchen, I take her bag from her hand and leave it on the counter. Then I kneel to remove her shoes. She offers them freely. I take my time to run my hands up her calves and thighs, worshipping her with my eyes. Straightening slowly, I continue a path over her hips and sides. Her breasts are a beautiful contrast through the silk–soft curves and hard nipples. Her stomach flutters when I place a palm on it. I drag my greedy hands over her arms and push the dress from her shoulders. The silk gathers around her feet, exposing a lace thong and those thigh-high stockings I glimpsed earlier. I run my fingers over every inch of her skin as I remove her stockings and panties, memorizing her curves and learning what makes her gasp. The more I get to know her, the more I feel like I'm getting to know myself, because she's a reflection of what I am. She's an answer to my call. Two damaged souls. The only difference is with her there's beauty in the broken.

Moving behind her, I place a kiss in her neck. Goosebumps break out over her skin. She sucks in a breath as I smooth my palms over her extended nipples, the touch barely there.

"Do you like that?" I whisper in her ear.

It's more of a statement than a question. There's no need to answer. I increase the pressure, massaging her curves. Her back arches, pushing her ass against my erection. On instinct, my hands drop to her hips, pulling her tighter against me as I grind my cock against her. Her skin is supple and warm, flexible under my hands. I knead my fingers deeper, needing to leave bruises, marks, hurt, and possession. I want to stain her and keep her pure. I want the world to know she's mine, yet I can't tell a fucking soul. It drives me nuts. Beyond madness. I want to get rough with her, not like in playing, but the real shit. I don't want to go slow. I want it all. I want it to be so intense she'll scream my name and say it in her sleep. What I want is dirty, depraved, and raw in its honesty, but tonight I don't want to take. I want to give.

Softening my death grip on her hips, I dip one hand between her legs. Her pussy is warm and wet under my fingers. I drape an arm around her breasts and find her lips. Our kiss is gentle and unrushed, an extension of what we've started this afternoon. Holding her to me like this, I walk her to the bedroom. I bring her with me onto the mattress, letting her lie face-down. When I've positioned her in the middle of the bed, I stretch out on top of her, fully clothed. There's not an inch of skin I don't taste, starting at the nape of her neck and working my way down her spine and buttocks to the dips of her knees and the hollows of her feet. I kiss her arms and suck her fingers into my mouth, leaving the best for last. By the time I push her legs apart, she's breathing as hard as I am. It takes every ounce of willpower I possess not to eat her pussy out until she climaxes there and then. Tonight, she's coming while I'm climaxing inside her. I only steal a taste, unable to drag my eyes or tongue away from the sweetness of her pussy.

Before I'm unable to stop myself from going down on her, I push to my knees and start to undress. My instruction is gruff, my voice giving away the thin thread of my control. "Turn around."

She obeys immediately, stretching out on her back with her arms raised above her head. I climb between her legs, stretching them with my hips, and bring our palms together. Our fingers intertwine. Our gazes lock. My cock is painfully hard, pressing on the soft skin of her thigh as I seek the heat of her mouth. The kiss is a gentle exploration, a searing caress that brands my soul. As I take my time with her, foreplay becomes something other than a simple means of getting a woman wet. It's more than a clinical preparation to take my cock painlessly. It adopts a whole different meaning as she lies vulnerable and small under me, not only allowing me to invade her body, but also intangible parts of her past and present.

Her eyes are two huge sapphire gemstones, her gaze clinging to mine as I position my cock. I commit her expression to memory as I slowly, reverently push into her tightness, impaling her inch by inch. Her fingers clench around mine when I hit a barrier. Pulling back an inch, I start to move. Her head falls back, and her hips rock to my rhythm, taking my lead. It's a slow dance of agonizing seduction. Every breath is a battle not to break and fuck her like a madman, but as we move toward our pleasure together, the dance becomes easier. It builds, second by sweet second, until I don't want it to end.

Her fingernails dig into the back of my hands. Her features transform into a mask of pleasure or torment. It's so intense, I can't be sure which. I can't tell the one from the other, because the pleasure is torture. It crescendos. Our release demands a harsher pace, but I fill her with unhurried, deep strokes, giving everything I'm capable of. The effect is earth-shattering. Tremors of a pending explosion wrack my body. The end-result is lethal. The tenderness of the act is more intense than any hard fucking I've done. It binds me to her, my soul intertwining with hers like our fingers. I'm helpless to stop it. I'm helpless to prevent the climax from gathering at the base at my spine. My breaths turn into grunts as I angle my cock so the friction is aimed at her clit.

She lifts her hips and locks her ankles around my ass to assist my efforts. It builds like a tsunami. I can't even speak to warn her. All I can do is grind my teeth and brace myself as the wave hits. It spills through me like a never-ending fountain of brutal ecstasy. I can't move. The release locks me inside her, my cock swelling as I fill her with jets of cum. Shivers run over me. It takes a few seconds before I have the full function of my body back, before I can resume my rhythm to bring her with me to the finish line.

It takes a short while before she's there. Her pussy is slick with my cum. Her muscles clench around my cock as her orgasm hits. It's the sweetest damn sensation. Claiming her lips, I revel in the feeling, keeping our bodies connected. I turn on my side without pulling out, selfishly not wanting to wash my seed from her thighs. Holding her in a steel embrace, I let her fall asleep with sticky semen drying on her legs, until I wake up in the middle of the night harder than ever, still inside her. And then I take her again. And again. My lust for her is an insatiable monster. She won't walk straight tomorrow, and still it's not enough.

Jane

LIKE YESTERDAY, I wake up alone with the hiss of the percolator and the aroma of coffee coming from the kitchen. I'm aching from last night's loving. It hurts when I move. Picking up Brian's shirt from the chair, I pull it on and inhale deeply. The fabric smells like him–pine body wash with a hint of clean sweat. Deliciously male. My skin is sticky and itchy all over. I desperately need a shower, but I need coffee more. Barefoot, I pad to the kitchen.

Brian stands at the island counter, his palms resting on the countertop and a mug standing between them. His jeans ride low on his hips, exposing the deep grooves that cut from his hips to his groin. His naked torso is framed by the first sunlight spilling from the window. With his tousled hair and intense gaze, he drips animal sexuality and dangerous vitality. Arousal flutters in my abused lower region.

He straightens when I enter, his gaze warming with approval as he takes in my attire. "Sleep well?"

"Like a baby."

He prepares a mug of coffee the way I like it and puts it on the counter. "Come here."

His arms fold around me when I stop in front of him.

His gaze turns scrutinizing. "Sore?"

"A little."

He nuzzles my neck. "Sorry."

A gentle bite on the tender skin of my shoulder makes me squeal.

"I couldn't help myself," he says, kissing the spot.

"I'll live."

He pulls away to look into my eyes. "You should rest today."

"I'm not fragile," I chide with a chuckle.

He cups my face, his thumbs brushing over my cheeks. "No, you're not. And yet…"

"Yet what?"

"You're so delicate. So vulnerable." He takes my hand in his and studies the contrast. "So small."

"It only feels like it because you're tall by average standards."

Kissing my knuckles, he lets me go. "Drink your coffee. It's getting cold."

"Did I say thank you for the coffee? You're spoiling me."

"You're welcome."

He picks up his own mug and, turning to the window, takes a sip. A frown plays between his eyebrows as he looks into a distance much farther than my yard.

I place a hand on his shoulder. "I need a shower. Join me?"

He glances down, his eyes slipping to the juncture of my legs hidden under his shirt. "No."

"If you prefer to shower alone—"

"I'll have one at home."

"Oh." I withdraw my touch. "Breakfast, then?"

"No." He walks to the sink and rinses his mug. "Your lawn needs mowing. I'll come one afternoon in the week while Abby's in school to do it."

"You don't have to."

He pins me with a look. "I know."

"I'm moving soon, anyway."

His tone leaves no room for arguing. "In the meantime, you still live here."

He stalks across the floor, takes my face between his hands, and kisses me. It's only the pressure of his lips against mine, nothing more than a couple of seconds. He lets me go as suddenly as he's grabbed me, leaving me cold.

Is this some kind of signal? Is he tired of me? Has he gotten what he's wanted and he's telling me in a non-verbal way not to make a scene? Conditioned by Francois' refusal to fight or enter into any kind of discussion that could stir emotions, I do what I always do. I step aside. I grant him silence.

What is he waiting for? Why isn't he leaving?

His gaze trails over my body, coming to a stop on my thighs again. Oh. I wiggle out of the shirt and hand it to him. He takes it automatically, staring at the shirt dangling from his fingers before blinking at me.

"What are you doing, Jane?"

"Returning your shirt so you can go." Hurt constricts the air in my ribs. I feel exposed, but I straighten my shoulders. I can handle being discarded. "It was fun." I really mean the next words. "Thank you."

His eyes narrow and his nostrils flare. "What are you saying?"

"Isn't it obvious? I'm saying goodbye."

9

Jane

Brian takes a step back as if I'd punched him in the stomach. Emotions pass like shadows over his face. He works his jaw from side to side, scrunching the shirt in his fist. An internal battle rages in his handsome features, and then his expression stills in an obstinate mask.

"No." He closes the distance he's taken, leaving no space between us. "You don't get to say goodbye."

My naked body brushes against a hard wall of muscle. "What?"

"I'm not your toy boy, Jane. You can't sleep with me and kick me out the next morning."

"You're the one who said you wanted to leave."

He scrunches up his face, searching my eyes. "I never said that."

"You implied it."

"How?"

"You don't want to shower or have breakfast with me. You kiss me like we didn't spent the night having incredible sex, and you push me aside as if you can't wait to get out of here."

Gripping his hair, he stares at me open-mouthed for two heartbeats. Then he slams his lips together and grabs my wrist.

"We're going to talk about this," he says, dragging me to a chair.

Before I have time to protest, he falls down in the seat with me in his lap.

"Jane, there's nothing I want more than sharing a shower and breakfast with you, but I haven't seen my family for most of the weekend. If I get into a shower with you, I'm going to fuck you all morning. One, you've had about as much as your pussy can handle for one night. Two, I have responsibilities at home. Three, if I stay a minute longer I might not be able to leave at all. Is that clear enough for you?"

"Oh. I thought..." Embarrassed, I fix my eyes on a spot on the floor.

Gripping my chin, he lifts my face. "You don't need to make assumptions about my behavior. If I have something to say, I'll say it. If my reactions confuse you, you have to tell me. If something– anything at all, no matter how trivial you think it is–bothers you, you owe it to me to talk about it. Are we clear?"

It feels like a dam breaks inside me. The stress of welling years' worth of slush inside rushes away like a flood after the purging rain. I didn't know how much I needed this grant of expression until now. Immense relief stoops my shoulders and leaves me boneless. Right here and now, I fall in love a little. How is it possible that he's so perfect for me?

"Are we clear?" he repeats.

All I manage is a meek, "Okay."

"Okay," he agrees, putting our foreheads together. "Now, where the hell did all that come from?"

"I don't know." Or maybe I do.

"Not good enough. Why did you feel you couldn't talk to me? Are you afraid I won't listen? Do you think I'll judge you?"

"My ex, he didn't–doesn't–like to talk things over."

"I'm not him, Jane. I'm not like anyone you've had." He puts his arms around me, holding me close. "No one can worship you more."

"Who are you, Brian Michaels?"

"I'm everything you'll ever need." He kisses the shell of my ear and buries his nose in my hair. "Come with me."

I turn my face to look at him. "What?"

"Come home with me." Urgency infuses his tone. "I don't want to leave you. Not yet. We can still spend the day together."

My heart leaps with joy. I have no business going to his house or meeting his family. It'll be another unwise decision, because Brian and I can never be more than a secret, but I'm curious about everything concerning him. The hunger to know him is equal to the hunger to be possessed, fucked, and gently loved by him, if not bigger.

"Won't your family mind?" I ask against my better judgment.

"It's just my mother and sister. A friend slept over to keep an eye on them, but he sent a text early this morning to let me know he had to leave."

Questions crowd my mind. Where is his father? Why did a friend have to keep an eye on his mother and sister? How do they spend their Sundays? Most families have big, traditional Sunday lunches. Won't I impose?

Biting my earlobe, he makes all my questions vanish.

His warm breath tickles my ear. "Say yes."

"I'd love to come with you."

He beams. "In that case, we better make the shower quick. I'll do my damnedest not to touch you."

Fifteen minutes later, we're showered and dressed. Brian announces that we'll have breakfast at his place to save time. On the way, I send Abby a text to say good morning. Brian cranks up the music in his truck and places a possessive hand on my knee, which he only removes to change gears. We leave the Sunday quietness of my neighborhood behind and head toward the highway. I wind down my window and let the wind dry my shower-wet hair. The air smells like watermelon. The green perfume of Highveld grass drifts through the open window. It's not too hot, yet. Dressed in a sundress and sandals with no make-up or hairstyle, I'm ridiculously happy. I never want to leave this cocoon of contentedness in the front seat of Brian's truck, except for bringing Abby into my happy place. As with every day she's not with me, I miss her.

Industrial buildings start to fill up the open expanse. Quickly, only concrete and fences remain. Factories billowing long ribbons of smoke into the sky dot the horizon, the biggest of them bearing an ISCOR sign. Iron And Steel Corporation. Half of Harryville and Pretoria West are employed by ISCOR. We cross train tracks black with coal residue and enter Harryville through a narrow tunnel. The deeper we enter into the suburb, the more rapidly the scenery changes. There's Harryville, and then there's *Harryville*.

Brian pulls into a street polluted with noise from the highway. We drive by several houses. The redbrick structures with their peeling tin roofs are sad, but their gardens are pure melancholy. Overgrown grass, weeds, and junk compete for space. The rusted frame of a tricycle stands on what is visible of a garden path. A swing made out of half a tractor tire dangles askew on one rope from the branches of a loquat tree in another garden. The fruit ripened too early. Most of them are peppered with holes where the birds got to them, and the rest is rotting on the ground, the smell of fermentation and decay reaching the interior of the truck fleetingly, but leaving a lingering ambience of dejection.

We stop in front of a house almost at the end of the street. It's the only one with a mowed lawn. There are no flowers or other plants, but the grass edges are neatly trimmed around the fence. Shooting me a bright smile, Brian jumps out to open the gate. He parks under a shade awning at the side of the house. The house is similar to the others in the street, but the red A-line roof is freshly painted. There's a covered porch with steps leading to a back door. The rest of the small building is square.

My nerves get the better of me. What will his family think of him bringing home an older woman? How will he introduce me? How will he explain my presence?

None of these worries seem to bother him as he comes around to open my door and takes my hand to help me out. He doesn't let go as he leads me to the door, and I'm grateful for that point of contact.

"Mom? Sam?" he calls as he pushes open the door.

A young voice sounds from deeper in the house. "Brian!"

Footsteps funnel toward us, and then a girl close to Abby's size flies through the door and throws her arms around his middle. He's obliged to let me go.

He chuckles. "Hey, piglet. You'll knock us both to the ground."

She releases him and plants her hands on her hips. "What took you so long?"

"This is Jane, my lady friend."

Sam turns a frown on me.

"This is Samantha, my sister."

"Hi." I smile, feeling out of place.

"Where's Mom?" Brian asks.

Sam makes a face. "In the lounge."

Either her face or the way in which she said the words alarms him, because Brian utters a curse and hurries from the room, Sam hot on his heels. For a moment, I remain on the spot, indecisive. Something's wrong. What's expected of me? Do I wait here or go see if I can help? He didn't say to stay, so I make a split-second decision and go after them. There's only one door at the right end of the hallway. When I enter the room, the pungent smell of sour and damp hits me before I see the woman lying on her stomach on a sofa bed. Her head is hanging over the edge. Dark hair spills around her face. A puddle of vomit stains the carpet, and next to it stands an almost empty bottle of gin.

"I tried to clean it," Sam says, pointing at a heap of crumbled paper towels.

"You should have called me," Brian says gently, moving to the woman's side.

"Last night, Mom said you were probably with your girlfriend." She glances at me. "I didn't want to bother you."

He wipes the hair from the woman's face, touching her forehead. "You call me anytime, no matter what. That's our rule, okay?"

"Okay," Sam says.

"When did Clive leave?" Brian asks, grunting as he turns the woman onto her back.

"I think it was seven."

"When did she start?"

"She was at it all night," Sam replies. "You know how she gets."

"I'm going to kill Clive. He shouldn't have left."

"I don't think Clive realized," Sam says. "She came out of the bedroom after he'd left, and she passed out not so long ago."

Moving his arms under her knees and armpits, he lifts the woman's limp body. She's dressed in a pink nightdress and fleece robe.

Brian turns to me. "Do me a favor. Can you check if the bed is clean? The first door on the left after the kitchen."

Happy to be of use, I rush ahead of him down the corridor. The room smells of cigarettes, and the sheets are tangled, but they seem clean. I pull them straight as fast as I can and fluff out the pillow so he can lower her onto the mattress. Sam leans in the door, watching us.

"Go dress and brush your teeth," Brian says. "I'll make breakfast."

His sister obeys wordlessly. When she's gone, he sits on the edge of the bed and softly slaps the unconscious woman's cheeks.

"Wake up, Mom. Come on," he coaxes gently. "Open your eyes."

Her long lashes flutter. A few more taps on her cheeks and she lifts her eyelids. Her voice is croaky. "Brian?"

"Do you mind fetching me a glass of water?" he asks me.

I scoot to the kitchen and go through the cabinets until I find a glass, which I fill up under the tap. Brian takes the glass from me with a grateful smile when I return. If she's cognizant of my presence, she doesn't show it.

"Here." He supports her head. "Drink."

It takes a while for her to empty the glass. He leaves it on the nightstand and lowers her head to the pillow.

"Go on. Sleep it off."

He pulls a sheet up to her chin and covers her feet with a comforter. I stand lamely at the side of the bed in the small room while he opens a window and draws the curtains against the bright sun.

A tilt of his head toward the door indicates that we should go. Leaving the door open, he leads me back to the kitchen where he fills a bucket with soapy water, and gathers a sponge and disinfectant.

"Thanks for your help."

"Of course. Will she be all right?"

"Yes." He sighs. "And no."

Without elaborating, he carries his supplies to the lounge and starts cleaning the mess.

I'm standing to the side, feeling both useless and in the way. "Is there anything I can do?"

"If you prefer, you can wait in the kitchen. I'll be done here in no time."

"That's fine." I motion at the soiled sheets. "I can remove those."

"Not a chance, but thanks. I appreciate the offer."

He shoots me a dimpled smile before continuing with his scrubbing. He doesn't apologize or make excuses. He's not ashamed of what's happened or the poverty that screams from the sparse and worn furniture. His self-esteem is too strong to grovel and cower in shame. He's bigger than that. He's bigger than this house and whatever causes his mother to drink, because his reaction tells me this isn't a first. He takes the lack of money and the mishap we walked in on in his stride, dealing with the crisis as the consequences demand, and this makes me fall in love with him a little more.

Done with the carpet, he rolls the sheets into a ball and pops them into the washing machine. I follow him around like a puppy, not sure what else to do. I definitely don't want to wait in the kitchen like someone who's afraid of barfing at the sight and smell of vomit. God knows, I've cleaned up enough of Abby's.

I watch him with no small amount of fascination wash up in the kitchen sink. The house is sorrowful in its lack of decoration and warmth, but it's clean. I don't have to guess thanks to who. That explains my spotless kitchen and neat garden. More questions swarm in my head, but now's not the time to ask them.

"Breakfast," he announces as he dries his hands.

The meal consists of toast and Rooibos tea. We eat at the kitchen table. When the dishes are done–Brian washes and Sam and I dry–he gives Sam permission to watch television. Taking my hand, he pulls me to the porch. He settles on the wall with his back against a pillar and pulls me between his legs with my back resting against his chest.

I drag my hands over the golden hair on his forearms. "For how long has it been like this?"

His chest rises as he inhales deeply. He holds the breath for a few seconds before letting his torso deflate. "If you mean the drinking, since after Sam was born. The real problem started long before that."

If the drinking isn't the real problem, what is? "Have you tried getting help?"

"No."

It's not the answer I expected. "Why not?"

"We all have our coping mechanisms."

He's right. Mine used to be hiding in a flatline relationship with Francois. No highs, no lows. Maybe it's sex, now. I'm not going to argue that one is worse than the other, but alcohol can kill you.

"There are other ways."

"What other ways?"

"Therapy."

"To do what? Replace one addiction with another?"

"You said yourself, we all have our coping mechanisms. Some addictions are healthier than others."

"Her life is tough enough. I'm not going to pile onto it."

I twist in his hold to look at him. "Are you condoning the drinking?"

"Don't judge her, Jane. You don't know what she's been through."

"I'm not judging. I'm concerned. Aren't you?"

Letting go of me, he swings his legs over the wall and dangles them down the side. "More than you can ever know."

"I'm sorry." I place a hand on his arm. "That was an unfair question."

He nods in silent acceptance of the apology.

Dare I ask? "What happened?"

He fixes his gaze on a point in the distance, but I'm guessing he's looking inwardly at a painful memory.

After a long time, he says, "My father walked out on her. Had an affair with one of her friends. He came home one day, packed his bag, and that was that. She just sat there on the couch, smoking a cigarette while he dragged his suitcase to the door. I remember how much her hands were shaking. She couldn't even tip the ash. I clung to his pants, begging him to stay." He swallows loudly. "He told me to grow the fuck up and be a man, so that's what I did."

Oh, Brian. Hugging him from behind, I place my cheek on his back. My heart throbs painfully for the boy he'd been and the hurt he'd suffered. "How old were you?"

"Nine."

Oh, my God. Answers to my questions fall into place. He's been taking care of his mother and sister since his father left when he was supposed to still be a child. No wonder he's so mature for his age. With his mother's drinking, he needs a friend to sleep over when he isn't home. His anxiety this morning to check on his family now makes sense. So does the fact that he never mentions his dad.

"How are things between you and him?" I ask carefully.

His voice is emotionless. "I haven't seen him since that day."

My chest clenches harder.

"My mother was four weeks pregnant with Sam when he left."

If that's the case, Brian could've been nine or ten when Sam was born. That makes Brian nineteen or eighteen, not twenty as he'd said, but this isn't the issue. The issue is something far more shocking.

"Your dad left when your mom was pregnant?"

"I'm not even sure I blame him."

There's so much implied, I'm afraid to ask.

He wipes his palms over his thighs. "One night, my mom came home late from work. She was six months pregnant, two weeks away from maternity leave. Like every other night, she parked in front of the house to open the gate." His voice is factual, as if he's reciting a news article. "As she got out of the car, two armed men jumped from the bushes. They shot her in the stomach and took the car. She survived. My baby brother didn't."

Oh, God. My throat constricts. I can't imagine the trauma of being shot in the most horrific way and surviving only to lose a baby and a husband. I glance in the direction of the bedroom window where the frail woman is passed out on the bed. Brian is right. I have no right to judge her.

"After that," he continues, "she wanted to fall pregnant at all costs to replace the baby they'd lost."

"Sam?"

He nods. "Only, things started getting worse. Mom started having panic attacks, first at work, and then in the shops. She developed a fear of public places. It escalated to a level where she couldn't do her job. Her employer dismissed her for medical reasons. The severance package wasn't even two months' salary, but the company knew she couldn't afford a lawyer to fight them. Her condition got progressively worse until she couldn't leave the house." He points at the top step. "This is as far as she can go."

Agoraphobia. "Did she seek help?"

"A psychologist did a couple of house calls, but stopped when we could no longer afford the fee."

"What about state assistance?"

He scoffs. "When was the last time you read the news? There is no state assistance. The government pension and medical funds have been bankrupt for years. Do you honestly believe there'll be money for psychologists when the masses in our country are dying of hunger and AIDS?"

It's all true, but I can't give up. I can't believe there's nothing to be done.

"Don't you think I would have slaved night and day to pay for a private clinic if I'd thought it would make a difference?"

"You don't think it's worth another shot? There are excellent clinics, places she could–"

"She doesn't want it, and I don't have the heart to have her forcefully removed from the only place she feels safe. She's suffered enough. She deserves to be cut some slack, even if it comes in a bottle."

I don't know what to say. I can't even begin to imagine–

"All she has now is *me*." He straightens, his body lean and imposing as he towers over me. "I'm not going to let anyone hurt her again."

That's why he's working his backside off at the building site. He's not only paying his way through university, but also taking care of his mother and sister. Thanks to Francois' occupation, I know the wages the manual workers and bricklayers are paid. Peanuts. Hardly enough to support a family of three and afford a tertiary tuition, let alone wine and dine a woman–a very lucky woman–at Oscars. However did they survive when his mother's payoff ran out?

"Did your father at least help financially?"

"For a couple of years. When he stopped sending money, I packed groceries at the store after school, but we basically lived off the charity from neighbors. The house belonged to my maternal grandfather. He left it to my mother, so we didn't have to worry about rent. It got easier to find odd jobs when I turned fourteen."

I want to help him, but he's proud. Money isn't something I can throw in his face without offending him. A man like Brian will want to earn his own way.

An idea crosses my mind. Why haven't I thought about it sooner? I'll take it up first thing tomorrow morning, but for now the most pressing issue is still the fact that his mother is an alcoholic with agoraphobia.

"You could stop buying her alcohol," I offer gently.

"I'm not the one buying the alcohol. She orders our groceries online and has it delivered."

"What if you take away the credit so she can't do the online orders?"

"Stop it, Jane. She's my mother, for God's sake." He points at the bedroom window. "Do you know what her life must be like? What the hell else does she have to look forward to but forgetting every once in a while?"

I want to argue, but it's futile. He's doing what he can to make his mother's life the least miserable possible. He's turning a blind eye, hoping it will diminish her suffering. It's wrong, but I understand. I understand the unshakable, deep-rooted sentiment that makes us sacrifice pieces of justice and our very souls for our loved ones. Haven't I done the same for Evan and Dorothy? Am I not trapped within the walls of my past, unable to set a foot over the porch step? I'm no different than Mrs. Michaels. I've only suffered less.

"Brian, I–"

"Brian–"

Sam and I speak simultaneously.

She stands in the door with a hairbrush in her hand. "Can you braid my hair?"

"What's the magic word?"

"Please."

Brian goes to his sister and takes the brush from her. "How about burgers on the barbecue for lunch?"

"Yay." She jumps up and down. "With fries?"

"You're on a diet, remember?"

She makes a face. "You're mean."

"Making you eat the salad you're supposed to would've been mean."

"Are you staying?" Sam asks me.

"Yes." He looks at me over his shoulder. "She's staying."

Despite the way the day started, I enjoy myself with Brian and Sam around the portable barbecue set up in the backyard. While we wait for the coals to be ready, Brian takes my hand and leads me to the far corner of their backyard.

"I want to show you something."

He bends down next to a green hatch hidden in the grass. When he throws it open, a security grid fastened with a chain and lock is revealed. The bars are made of thick iron and the space between them is narrow. It's clearly designed to keep people out. Below is a dark hole.

I peer inside. "What is it?"

Taking his phone from his pocket, he activates the light and points it down. Makeshift stairs lead to a small room with earthen walls strengthened by unevenly spaced planks. The floor is bare soil.

"It's a cellar," he says. "Dug it out myself."

"You dug this?" I'm astonished. "By hand?"

"Took me two years."

"Why do you need a cellar?"

216

"When it's finished, it'll be more of a den than a cellar. I saw this movie when I was a kid about a boy who had a secret den under the ground. Ever since, I dreamt of building a den like that. It started out as a silly project, but as the hole grew bigger and I gained building experience, it turned into a reality. It won't be the cave-room with the treasure chest I imagined, but it can be a place to chill when I need space." The corner of his mouth lifts. "The house sometimes gets crowded."

"I can't believe you're able to build a cellar by yourself."

"Brian," Sam calls, "I think the fire is ready."

"Hungry?" Brian asks.

"Mm." Not so much for food.

As if reading my thoughts, he leans in for a kiss, sucking my bottom lip into his mouth. He lets go slowly, his eyes dark with passion that reflects in my belly.

He lowers his voice, loud enough for only me to hear. "When the cellar is finished, I'm going to fuck you down there. I'm going to fuck you everywhere I can."

Joy infuses with the heat building in my chest and cheeks, because his words imply that he wants to continue seeing me for a considerable time to come.

"Brian," Sam calls again, her tone impatient.

His dimpled smile turns from hot to teasing. "I guess someone is hungrier than us."

Their mother doesn't wake for lunch. He dials someone called Tron to keep an eye on Sam and his mom for the time he'll be absent to drive me home. By the time we go, Mrs. Michaels is still knocked out cold. It leaves an uneasiness in my stomach and worry for Brian, the kind of worry you only feel for people you truly care about.

THE HEATWAVE finally breaks when I pick up Abby at Debbie and Francois' in the late afternoon. The weather is back to a normal spring temperature. Abby meets me at the car before I have my door open. From the look on her face, something momentous happened.

"Hey, honey." I give her a hug and hold her at arm's length. She's wearing eyeshadow and lipstick. She's too young, but I'm not going to make an issue out of Debbie giving her make-up. "You look beautiful."

She bounces on the balls of her feet. "Guess what?"

"What?"

"My period started."

Her first period. My throat clogs up with emotion. She's growing up so fast. She should've been with me. This is something I was supposed to go through with my daughter.

"I haven't told Dad, so I'll appreciate it if you don't mention it."

"Oh, honey. Having your period is nothing to be shy about. It's natural. Your dad's not stuck-up when it comes to women's issues."

"I know, but still. It's kind of embarrassing."

"If you didn't talk to your dad about it–"

"Don't worry, Mom. Debbie got me everything. She took me shopping to celebrate. I got this really cute toilet bag with glitter and a pink flamingo for you-know-what."

"Tampons. They're called tampons and pads." I've always taught Abby to call a spade a spade.

"Whatever. I had a glass of wine–real wine–at lunch with Debbie, because she says I'm a young lady now."

"That you are, although still too young by my standards for wine."

"It was only a quarter of a glass."

How cruel of nature's timing to take this privilege away from me. Debbie shouldn't have been the one. As quickly as the nasty thought rears its head, I push it down. Abby is happy. That's what matters.

"Well," I give her my brightest smile, "shall we get going?"

"I'll get my bag."

Debbie waits alone at the door.

"Hi, Jane. Francois says hello. Sorry he couldn't be here. He had something urgent to take care of at the office."

"Thanks."

I'm about to turn when she stops me with a hand on my arm.

"Can I talk to you for a minute while Abby gathers her things?"

"Sure," I say, reluctantly staying put. "If it's about Abby starting her period, she already told me. Thanks for being there for her." I want to add that she should've called me, but think the better of it.

"Of course. I was going to mention it, but that's not what I wanted to ask."

"Go ahead, then."

"Abby's thirteenth birthday is coming up."

"Yes?"

"Do you mind if I host the party?"

Did the woman who cheated with my husband just propose to organize my daughter's first teenager party?

"Francois and I talked about it," she continues. "I think it'll be a good idea for me to plan it, seeing that we'll be in the house by then. I'm not sure where you're planning on moving, but wouldn't Abby like to have her party in the house she knows?"

The knife twists again. This is not about the house Abby knows. This is about Debbie and I.

"I'm sorry, Debbie, but no."

"Why not?"

"Thirteen is a milestone age in our family."

"I don't see the issue."

"It's her first teenager party. It's my privilege to organize it."

My parties for Abby have always been something special with a theme and a cake I spend days creating. It's our ritual, a rock-solid tradition we've got going. Weeks before, Abby and I already start discussing decorations and party favors. I may not be a perfect mother, but I'm a damn good event organizer, and I'm not giving up on making Abby's birthday special just so that Debbie can integrate into our extended family. Especially not Abby's first teenager birthday.

Tears pool behind her huge, brown eyes. "I'm only trying to do what's best for Abby."

"So do I. Soon, you're going to have your own little girl or boy to organize birthday parties for. You'll understand when you hold that baby in your arms."

She lifts her chin and pulls her lips into a defiant line, but she doesn't reply. Abby saves me from prolonging the painful conversation by coming down the stairs with her overnight bag.

"Bye, Debs."

They hug each other and blow air kisses.

I take Abby's hand, leading her to the garden path. "Goodbye, Debbie. Say hi to Francois for me."

"Oh, Jane," Debbie comes down the steps toward us, "there is one more thing."

"Here." I hand Abby the car keys. "I'll be there in a minute." I don't want my daughter caught in our rope pulling. "What is it?" I ask when Abby is in the car.

"It'll be better if you don't call Abby here."

My ears start ringing. Anger blurs the edges of my vision. "Are you telling me not to call my daughter?"

"Not when she's with us. It makes her feel guilty."

"How do my calls make her feel guilty?"

"She thinks you're calling because you're lonely." Her face is serene, as if she's not twisting that damn knife a little deeper, still. "It makes her feel bad for not being with you."

I'm at a loss for words. Maybe it's true. Yes, I miss Abby. Maybe she feels bad knowing that, but I call for her benefit, not mine.

I don't owe Debbie a thing, but this is my daughter. I'm not going to be unreasonable for the sake of being spiteful. "All right,

I'll talk to Abby about it. If it bothers her, I'll stop calling when she's visiting you."

"There's nothing to talk about, Jane." She places extra emphasis on my name, as if she's scolding a child. "This is our house and our rules. No calls. No text messages. I'm sure you can last for two days. If you insist on disrupting *our* bonding time, you'll leave me no choice but to confiscate Abby's phone for the weekend."

What the–? It takes everything I possess to force calm. "If you care about Abby, as you claim you do, you'll consider what's best for *her*, not you."

Her mouth falls open. She's about to say something else, but I've had as much of this talk as I can handle. I turn on my heel and walk to the car. I don't care that I'm being rude.

"Everything okay, Mom?" Abby asks when I get in beside her and start the engine. She gives Debbie a quizzical glance.

"Perfect." There are still two hours of daylight left. "I want to show you a place I've been looking at for renting," I say on the spur of the moment. I was going to keep the visit a surprise until next weekend when I have Abby, but I'm too excited to share it with her. "If the owners are available, are you up for it?"

She shrugs. "Aren't they all the same?"

I know what she means. We've only been looking at cookie cutter townhouses in copycat complexes.

"This one is different."

"All right. Why not?"

Hilda agrees to leave the cottage open and gives me the code for the electronic lock at the gate so I don't have to disturb them. The farther we drive north, the straighter Abby sits in her seat until we cross Zambezi Avenue, which forms the border of the built-up area the farthest north.

"Where are we going?" she asks, staring with dismay at the gravel road.

"You'll see."

Fifteen minutes later, we pull up at the German doctors' gate.

Abby has gone from dismay to quiet. She doesn't say anything while I take her on a tour of the cottage, showing her the room facing the dam, which will be hers. Mine will be the one at the back, overlooking the hilltops.

"Well?" I ask when we exit onto the deck.

The view of the dam framed by the mountains is spectacular. The smell of a Jasmine creeper infuses the early evening air. A freshness carries on the breeze, cooling down the heat of the day. Frogs and crickets sound around us, reminding me of the Bushveld holidays of my youth.

"You can't be serious," Abby says.

Her words are sticks in the spokes of my excitement. My spirits drop. "Don't you like it?"

She spreads her arms and turns in a circle. "We're in the middle of nowhere."

"Isn't that the point?"

"What about my friends?" She taps a palm on her chest. "How am I ever going to see anyone if we live out in the sticks?"

"The same as how you've seen your friends in Groenkloof. I'll drop you by car or their parents will drop them here. I fail to see how living a short distance outside of town will interfere with your social life."

"What about going to the movies or shopping malls?"

I try to hug her, but she moves out of my reach.

"As I said, I'll take you. It's the same distance to Menlyn Park, whether I drive from here or Groenkloof."

"You don't understand!"

"Explain it, then," I say, perplexed.

"Debbie says I'll soon be old enough to go by myself."

"Go by yourself where?"

"To meet my friends at the mall."

My anger escalates, but it's not directed at my daughter. "How are you supposed to get there on your own?"

"By bus," she says as if it's the most obvious explanation in the world.

"There are no busses, Abby. Not safe ones, anyway. How many times have we talked about kidnappings? Do you know how many girls of your age disappeared this year?"

I'm not saying it to frighten her. It's a reality. When you live in a dangerous and violent country, you need to be streetwise. You need to be prepared. How can Debbie be so irresponsible?

Abby crosses her arms and turns her back on me, staring out over the water.

"Would you rather live in a flat with a brick wall for a view?"

"You don't understand." She sniffs.

"I'm trying really hard."

She flings around. "Have you signed the lease?"

"As a matter of fact, I have."

"So, my opinion doesn't matter anyway." She throws her arms in the air. "Why did you even bother to show me?"

"I hoped you'd be excited. It was supposed to be a surprise."

"Well, I hate it."

My elation at what I'd considered a good find in terms of a home deflates. "All right. You're entitled to your opinion. Give it a couple of months. If you still hate it, I'll find someplace else for us to live."

"Great. That means we'll have to move twice."

"Okay, so we won't unpack except for the most important essentials."

"And live between a mountain of boxes? No thanks."

"You may end up loving it here."

"I doubt that very much."

"Look, this is your home, too. If you feel so strongly about it, I'll pay the penalty for breach of contract, and we can start looking from scratch."

"Forget it." She barges to the door. "Can we go home, now? I'm hungry, and I've got homework."

"Yes, we can go."

I'm beaten to silence. At times like these, I question myself. Am I even a good mother?

Brian

I'M PREPARING Sam's lunch for school on Monday when Tron throws open the back door.

"Monkey sent for you."

My gut turns cold.

I continue spreading peanut butter on the bread as if he's not just told me my life can be extinguished in the next few minutes. Shooting a glance toward the corridor to make sure Sam and my mom aren't within earshot, I say, "I have to drop off Sam, and then I'll be over."

"I'll drop her." He plants his feet wide.

The only way I'm walking past him is if I put a bullet in his heart.

"Sam!" I slap one piece of bread on top of the other and wrap the sandwich in foil. "Time to go."

Schoolbag in hand, she rounds the corner. "Oh, hi, Tron. I didn't know you were here."

"Say bye to Mom," I instruct, taking her schoolbag. I pack the sandwich and an apple before handing her back the bag when she returns. "Tron is dropping you off."

She looks at Tron. "You are?"

Tron gives her his big, harmless, bear smile. "Your bro's got business to take care of."

"Bye, Brian."

She hugs me and bounces through the doorframe ahead of the giant.

He gives me a warning look on his way to the door. "Don't be late. He won't take it kindly."

During the drive to Monkey's dealership, I prepare myself mentally to be beaten, tortured, or killed. Not one is a prospect I look forward to, but I'll sacrifice myself gladly if it'll save Sam and Mom. On a first warning, if I go to him as ordered, he won't touch my family. He'll shunt me around and maybe send me home with a shiner if I'm lucky, or in a body bag if my luck has run out.

The door and windows of the workshop at the back are closed. Not a good sign. Sweat trickles between my shoulder blades and down my spine as I get out of the truck and assess the situation in case I've missed an escape option. Knowing what I know about Monkey, there's none. Lindy must've shot off her mouth about our conversation.

Grabbing the doorknob, I pause to take a deep breath. The metal is cold in my palm from the early morning air. The rest of me is hot, adrenalin coursing through my veins. I close my eyes briefly and push open the door. It takes a few seconds for my eyes to adjust to the somber light. The scene unfolding in front of me isn't what I expected.

A man is kneeling on a plastic sheet spread out on the floor. His hands are tied behind his back and blood is running from his nose and mouth. His head lolls on a shoulder. He doesn't look up or lift his eyes when I enter. He's either close to passing out or dying. My attention moves to the men behind him. Monkey stands at his back, nursing his bloody fists. Two of his goons flank the helpless man, each carrying a gun.

"'Bout time." Monkey spits on the floor and waves me closer.

The sound of my boots echoes off the concrete. Each step I take is the tick of a clock, a time bomb about to explode. I hold my breath in the volatile silence as I stop in front of the beaten man.

"Caught him breaking into Tron's yard," Monkey says. "Not the first time, either."

He kicks the man on a kidney, causing him to grunt and fall face-down.

It takes a dry swallow to find my voice. "Why am I here?"

Monkey grabs the alleged offender's hair and drags him back onto his knees. "To finish him off."

10

Brian

"No." The word is out before I can stop myself.

Monkey scoffs. "It's not as if it'll be the first time you take out a man in cold blood."

"This is different."

He scrunches up his eyes. "How?"

"It's not my fight."

He takes a step closer, scrutinizing me with a tilted head. "Are you saying the neighborhood isn't your concern?"

I'm treading on fragile fucking bird eggs. "I'm saying I wasn't there. I haven't seen shit."

Monkey rounds the man and puts his face in mine. Spit flies from his mouth. "Are you saying I'm a liar?"

"No." I don't back up. Any sign of weakness will cost Monkey's respect, and not even Lindy's pleas will save me. "I'm saying I'm not killing a man who deserves to rot in jail."

The goon on the left smirks. "Tron was right."

"About what?" I spit out.

"You refuse to give your fists' worth to the neighborhood watch."

"The neighborhood watch is trouble. One day, it's going to blow up in your faces."

"The police aren't worth the herpes on a whore's cunt." Monkey snorts from deep in his throat and projects another ball of slime on the floor. "No one is going to watch out for this neighborhood if we don't."

"Save your justifications for someone who cares. Shoot me if you must, but I don't want any part in it."

"Shall I put a bullet in his balls?" the goon on the right asks.

Monkey laughs softly. "Nah. I like his balls. Figuratively speaking, of course. Besides, he needs his testicles if he's to give me grandkids." He looks me straight in the eye. "You've got guts, kid, I'll give you that. Enough to marry my daughter." He grips the back of my neck and squeezes with enough force to crack my bones. "What I don't know, is if you've got enough to take over the business."

Dating Lindy is one thing. Taking over Monkey's business is another. I don't have the right answer, and the wrong one can still get me killed, so I keep my mouth shut.

Monkey lets go with a shove. "Finish him off."

I stumble a step, not sure to who he spoke and to who he referred, but before I can find my bearings, a shot rings out, and the man falls forward for the second time. This time, he won't be getting back up. I stare at the suited guy on the left who shot the poor fucker in the back of the head.

A smile curls his lips. "No one steals from us and gets away with it."

"That'll be a good lesson for his buddies," says the other bodyguard, or whatever Monkey calls them.

Monkey dusts his hands. "Dump the body where the rest of his gang will find it." He gives the corpse another kick for good measure. "Fucking scum."

I've seen enough not to flinch or blink an eye. I've seen all I could the day my mother lay bleeding on the grass with her six-month pregnant belly. I've felt all I could when my father brought her home alive from the hospital only for her to die a little with each passing day. All I feel is pity for the poor dumb dead bastard who was stupid enough to try and rob, and maybe even kill, Tron. Sadly, most robberies also mean killings. The thieves seldom leave the people they rob alive.

Monkey pats my shoulder, his manner almost jovial. "Swing by the office one evening for a brandy and Coke. We'll talk about a job."

"I've got a job."

"Slinging bricks?" He laughs. "No daughter of mine marries a man who can't put a palace roof over her head." He slaps me again, a little too hard, this time. "Stop by sooner than later."

The stench of blood and gunpowder stir memories best forgotten. I turn for the door, pacing my strides. I don't want to make it seem as if I'm running.

"Brian."

I freeze when Monkey says my name.

"You may not have pulled the trigger, but you had your part it in."

The warning is clear. I'm a witness. If I don't go to the police, I'm an accomplice. We all know I'm not going to the police. That makes me as guilty as them.

"I expect you to start courting Lindy soon, and you better do it right."

This is how he's going to blackmail me. My family is only the sword he holds over my head.

If I open my big mouth now, there'll be no one to blackmail and nothing to protect, so I just keep on walking until I hit daylight.

Jane

THE IDEA I had on Brian's back porch has been turning in my head all day, but it's best to approach Toby with matters that require his approval after a drink. I arrange with Loretta to pick Abby up from school and let her stay over at their place for a couple of hours while I corner Toby at our office bar when our working hours come to an end.

I push a Bacardi Breezer into his hands and take one for myself. "I'm drowning. I can't keep up with all the new projects."

"No shit." He takes a long sip, giving me a sidelong look. "You know the solution."

"Delegate." It's Toby's favorite word.

"Exactly."

"Except, I don't have anyone to delegate to."

"You have Candice."

"She's an assistant. She's great with admin, not with creative or strategy."

"No."

"No, what?"

"I'm not employing another advertising officer. We don't have the budget."

Knowing how Toby's head works, I'm ready for this. "I'm not asking for another ad exec. I'm asking for an intern. Call it a trainee."

He turns on his chair to face me. "Elaborate."

"I'm asking for a student, someone who can work part-time with the team. It's a win-win. I get the help I need for a lower budget," which will still be a hell of a lot more than what Brian is currently earning, "and he gets in-house experience as well as a foot in the door for when he graduates."

"*He*, huh?" he says, reminding me he's not a fool. "I gather you already have a candidate in mind."

"I do."

I push the CV I've prepared for Brian over the counter. I hope to God Brian won't mind that I accessed his file via an acquaintance of Francois at the university. I played the card of the agreeable ex-wife. I didn't say it in so many words, but I implied that Francois said I could call him. As it turned out, Brian is an A-grade student. He's top of his class, and his lecturers' notes are glowing with praise for his potential. I didn't want to ask Brian straight out and get his hopes up if Toby was going to refuse the idea. Not just a little guilt eats at my gut as I study Toby's expression while he reads through the document. I'm not even sure how I'll explain it to Brian if Toby agrees.

His eyebrow lifts. "Mm, impressive."

"I know."

"How did you find this guy?"

"One of Francois' connections gave me the information." At least, that's the truth.

"He's looking for an internship?"

I swallow, feeling horrible for speaking on behalf of Brian. "More or less on the longer term, until he finishes his studies."

"He's got…" his eyes scan over the print, "…three years left? So, this is his first year."

"Yes. We should grab him now, before the competition does."

I honestly believe Brian will add value to our team, or I wouldn't have gone to such great, deceiving ends.

"Mm." He drops the paper and adjusts his tie. "I tell you what. Schedule an interview for me to meet your brilliant student. If I like him, I'm prepared to offer him a probation internship with the option to extend on the condition that he passes the year-end exams."

"Thank you, Toby."

I throw my arms around his neck, making him cough.

"Sorry." I pat his back. "I didn't mean to squeeze that hard."

"I'll have an offer drawn up after talking the remuneration over with Bernard. How soon can this, eh…"

"Brian Michaels."

"How soon can Mr. Michaels start?"

"Immediately." I hope.

"Then let's get the ball rolling. While I have your attention, how's Freddy doing?"

"I'm almost done with my new proposal. I'll have something for you soon."

"Good, because Mr. Monroe is getting antsy."

"Don't worry. We've always made them happy. We'll keep on doing it."

"I certainly hope so. Now that you've twisted my rubber arm, I've got a ton of work to get through before I can call it a day." He hops from the barstool. "Are you working late?"

"I'll work at home. I have to pick up Abby from a friend."

"See you tomorrow, sugar." He salutes as he walks through the door.

Before heading over to Loretta's house to fetch Abby, I want to use the time I have alone to talk to Francois. I dial his number from the privacy of the empty office bar.

"Jane, I'm in a meeting."

Francois is always in a meeting. "I won't keep you. We need to talk about Abby."

"Not at the office."

"Can you come by the house on your way home?"

There's a pause. The word *talk* probably made him shut down.

"Can't it wait for two weeks?"

"No. We need to talk alone. Abby is at Loretta's place. I'll have to pick her up soon, so how about in an hour's time?"

"Jane…"

"There will always be times we have to talk about the wellbeing and future of our child."

He sighs. "I'll have to leave the office earlier than planned."

"Just think you're doing it for Abby if it gets too hard."

"There's no need for sarcasm."

"I'll be waiting."

I end the call, feeling like a bitch, but if I don't put pressure on Francois, it'll never happen.

I'm barely home before he arrives. It's the first time since he moved out that he's back at the house, and it's weird to have him ringing the bell. When I let him inside, he stands in the entrance, hands in his pockets, looking out of place. It's the strangest thing to see him there. It's only been two months, but it feels like ten years. He's a stranger to me. He doesn't belong on the Moroccan carpet against the mosaic backdrop of the wall. How does a person you shared twelve years of your life and a child with turn into a stranger overnight? Or maybe he's always been a stranger to me.

"Come through to the kitchen," I say. "I'll pour us a drink."

"All right," he says after a slight hesitation.

This is getting weirder by the minute. It's like we never touched each other or slept together.

"Ice tea?" I ask in the kitchen.

"On second thought, no thanks. Let's just talk about why I'm here, shall we?"

"Debbie asked to organize Abby's birthday party."

His posture turns stiff. "If this is about Debbie, I'm not–"

"It's not about Debbie. Did you know about her idea to throw the party?"

His silence gives me the answer.

"How could you entertain such a notion even for a minute?"

He just looks at me.

"Francois."

"This is why I left the office early? To talk about Abby's birthday party?" he asks in the flat tone that marks his disapproval.

"No. It's to talk about why you don't want me to call Abby when she's at your place. You call her here all the time."

He turns his head a fraction to the side, fixing his gaze on a spot behind me. At least he has the decency to look guilty.

"I told Debbie I'll discuss it with Abby. If my calls upset her, as

Debbie claimed, I won't bother her when she's spending time with you."

His gaze is expressionless when he turns it back on me. "That's a mature approach. Anything else?"

"I know Debbie is part and parcel of your life, but Abby remains our child. If there are decisions to be made, it's between you and me until Abby is of an age to make her own decisions."

His jaw flexes, the standard sign of his irritation. "That goes without saying."

"Then kindly explain to Debbie she can't make promises to Abby that require our approval first."

"Such as?"

"Going to the mall alone, by bus, to meet her friends."

"What?"

"According to Abby, Debbie said she'll soon be old enough."

If there's one thing Francois is careful with, it's Abby's safety. "She shouldn't have said that, if it's indeed what she said. Maybe Abby misunderstood or got carried away."

"Maybe, but I just wanted it to be clear."

"It's clear. I'll have a word with Debs."

"Thank you."

"Is that all?"

Clearly, he's in a hurry. "I'll walk you to the door."

On the step, he pauses. "The lawn is in great shape. For once, the edges are straight. You must've gotten a new garden service."

If only he knew. "Thanks for stopping by."

He stays in place, as if he wants to say something but can't find the words. After an uncomfortable silence, he asks, "Have you found a place, yet?"

"Yes. We're moving at the end of the month, so you can take back the house earlier. Sorry. I've been meaning to tell you sooner, but things have been hectic."

"Oh. Yes. That'll help a lot." Another bothersome silence. "Where is the new place?"

"Leeuwfontein, toward the dam."

"I know where Leeuwfontein is." He frowns. "There aren't any flats out there."

"It's a cottage on a big property."

"I see." He seems to make a calculation in his mind. "I suppose you're not taking all the furniture."

"Only the essentials. Beds, a sofa, the small table, and kitchenware. Nothing else will fit."

"In that case, do you mind leaving the rest?"

I handpicked every piece of furniture to fit with the size and function of each room. A lot of thought and love went into the decoration. Like the house, it's hard to leave the bits and pieces I've collected behind. It's like leaving pieces of myself. It's not leaving behind the walls and carefully selected curtains or custom-built bookshelves, but the *home* I've created. It's what the material items represent that's hard to let go. And I am letting go. A sense of peace dawns on me as I cut the last ties with my old life.

"Sure. The furniture can stay." Although, I can't imagine Debbie being happy with that. I assume she'll want to put her own stamp on the house.

"Great." He offers me a polite smile, the kind reserved for acquaintances. "I'll be off, then."

I'm not aware of the tension in my body until I unlock the tight muscles in my neck and shoulders when my ex-husband is gone. For the hundredth time that day, I check my phone for a message from Brian. Right now, I need a kind word from someone. I need *him*.

Nothing.

After a moment's hesitation, I type, *I've been thinking about you today*, and hit send.

His reply comes a second later. *I've been jacking off thinking about you.*

A grin splits my face. It's vain, but I'm not going to deny being perversely flattered. The butterflies in my stomach agree.

I miss you, princess. When can I see you?

We have to talk about the interview with Toby, but I want to do it in person. *Lunch tomorrow?*

I'll pick you up at 1pm.

No. *Things might get more complicated at the office. Let's meet somewhere.*

Complicated how??

I'll explain tomorrow. Where will you be around lunchtime?

Campus. Hatfield Square?

I'll bring sandwiches.

There's a whole night between now and then. Send me a photo.

Like what?

Anything with your face to see me over.

I hate selfies. *You'll appreciate my face more when you see it tomorrow.* I add a smiley emoticon.

I receive a GIF image of a man banging his head on a desk.

Smiling, I delete our conversation and send a text to Loretta to let her know I'm on my way to fetch Abby, my heart several degrees lighter than a short while earlier.

Brian

THE SQUARE IS PUMPING with shoppers and students, but I spot Jane from a mile away. It's difficult not to, and I'm not the only one. Heads turn as she cuts across the open area past the restaurants with tables outside. It's not just the body-hugging fit of the dress that draws eyes to her perfectly proportioned curves or how her heels emphasize her slender ankles and toned calves. It's more than the sophisticated short cut and striking color of her silver-blonde hair or the way her blue eyes jump at you and arrests every ounce of your attention. It's the way she walks. Her hips don't sway in the pronounced way a woman employs when she's aware of her sexual power, but in a natural, subconscious manner with understated sensuality a thousand times more potent than a catwalk designed to drip with sex.

The fact that she's unaware of how desirable she is makes men want her even more. I see the heat in their gazes as they follow her progress with unshielded admiration. Her gait is sophisticated and poetic, like a ballet dancer's. A Steers bag swings from her hand, the impossibly small diameter of her wrist accentuated by a broad, silver bracelet. Her posture is straight and her gaze direct. She carries herself like a self-assured woman who knows what she wants. It makes a man wonder exactly what she wants, or rather the how, when she's alone in bed. Even with her regal pose, the most noble of men can't help the filthy thoughts that soil their minds as they fantasize about all the dirty ways in which to corrupt her. After all, we're only men. I can't even blame them, but it doesn't stop the possessiveness that rushes through me in a fit of jealous rage.

I could've signaled her from my seat on the fountain wall, but I enjoy stalking her too much, devouring her unsuspecting face as she searches the masses. Then she spots me. Her lips tilt in a reserved smile. A man stops midway in stuffing his face with a shawarma to stare at those full, luscious lips painted with a pale pink lipstick. The only thing stopping me from bashing his head in is that those lips have screamed for me and me alone. It's my name she cries when she comes. I want to rub his chubby, red-cheeked face into *that* and his tzatziki sauce.

"Hey," she says, sitting down next to me with the Steers bag between us. She takes something from the bag and hands it to me. "It's not healthy, I'm afraid. I felt like juicy fat and carbs today."

I'm not paying attention to what's in the wrapper. I'm too focused on her crossing her legs. Her dress rides up an inch, and fuck it, I *know* she's wearing garters under that dress, because that's her style. As she gently swings one leg, her shoe slips, dangling from her toes. It's the most innocent of moves, completely unintentional, but it's more seductive than parading naked. The heat under my skin intensifies, and my cock reacts. My T-shirt and jeans suddenly seem too restrictive. The clothes on my body are like a straightjacket, making it hard to breathe.

I can't resist. I have to touch her. What I want to do to her will make all those other noble men's most perverse dreams look pale in comparison, but out here in the open, I settle for placing a hand on her knee.

"You're perfect. You know that, right?"

She leans back a fraction, blinking at me, but her smile turns broader. "Where does that come from?"

"It came from the minute you set your foot on the square and every man in a radius of visibility started to stare."

She utters a soft laugh. "I love your imagination."

I'm about to argue, but she points at the sauce-soaked wrapper in my hand.

"Eat. It's dripping." She unwraps her burger and takes a big bite.

I steel myself for the familiar aversion to set in, but nothing happens. Is this real? I can eat with Jane without becoming freaked out? Ah, hell. That mouth... The way she chews and swallows before licking a bit of sauce from the corner of her mouth... It makes me think of a time on her sofa and times that haven't even happened yet. And damn it, does she smell sweet. I'm a fuse on a stick of dynamite. I'm a puddle of lust at her feet. I can't look at her walk, sit, or eat and my dick turns hard. I shift, attempting to make my arousal more discreet.

Gently cupping my hand, she moves it away from her knee. "Not in public."

I want to argue. With vehemence. How am I supposed to protect what's mine from the other vultures if I can't stake my claim? Besides, the urge to lay my hands on her skin every second of the time we're together is an overbearing impulse I can't control or deny. It takes all my willpower to abide by her rules and not force my hand. In an attempt to dispel my dark and lustful thoughts, I concentrate on peeling the wrapper from the burger.

"I want to talk to you about something," she says. "Sorry to jump right in, but I don't have much time."

My gut clenches. She can talk about the man on the moon if she wants and have my undivided attention. The only subject I won't entertain is goodbye, but that she already knows from our talk on Sunday.

"How would you feel about applying for an internship at my firm?"

My fist closes around the empty wrapper, scrunching it up into a ball. "What?"

"I need an intern. It'll be part-time, so you can work on a schedule that fits your studies. The pay is good, plus you'll have a foot in the door when you graduate."

"Slow down." My breath comes faster. "Are you asking me to work for you?"

"If you're interested. You'll have to pass the interview, of course. Toby, my boss, is prepared to offer a probationary contract with the option to extend if you perform well at the firm and pass your exams."

In many ways, it'll be the solution to my problems. One, I'll see Jane every day. Two, I'll earn more money.

She dabs a napkin to her lips. "What do you say? The interview is tomorrow. I have to give Toby your answer today. I didn't mean to put you under pressure, but if you accept, you'll get to know Toby. He hates procrastinating."

"How many candidates are interviewing?"

She flexes her foot, fitting her shoe back on, just like a perfect Cinderella with a glass slipper. "Just you."

"Just me, huh? Why?" The dick part of me that's ruled by my cock wants her to tell me it's because she wants to see as much of me as I need to see her, but Jane is too professional for that. Which leaves the one thing I won't accept–pity.

"You're a good candidate. I have no doubt you'll be an investment to the team."

"I don't need charity, Jane. I'll get by fine without it."

She stops eating. "I can't cope with the workload. Whether you decide to give it a shot or not, we're employing an intern. Think about it, Brian. How many opportunities like these happen in a lifetime?"

I chew over the facts in my mind. I don't want a job because of connections. I don't want Jane, or anyone else, to think I'm using her, or worse, that sleeping with her was just a means of getting into her firm.

"How many students enroll for a BA Communication degree each year?" she asks.

"Two, three hundred."

"That's just in Pretoria. Then there's also Johannesburg, Potchefstroom, Bloemfontein, and Cape Town. Make it a thousand five hundred, roughly. How many of those will finish their fourth year?"

"You don't have to validate how big this chance is by numbers. I get it."

"You don't. Statistically, two hundred-and-fifty of those students are going to graduate. The rest will fall out along the way. How many advertising jobs become available each year? Ten. Maybe twenty, if the economy plays along. How many small advertising firms close down every year? Three to four. How many big game players are there? Two, of which my agency is one. If you can land this internship and prove your worth, your career is made. It's not easy with the times we live in. No matter how top your grades are, you're going nowhere unless you know someone, because our world is all about connections. It's sad. It's wrong, but it's reality. Ask me, I know. Winning a job at Orion on your own merit is a noble idea, but it's a fairy tale. We all get in because of who we know. After that, the cards are in your hands. If you fuck up, you're out, no matter who your father or his best friend is.

There's more supply than demand in our industry. Another opportunity like this won't come along."

"You can save your breath. I know all that."

"Then what's the problem?"

"I don't want people to make the wrong assumption."

I don't give a shit, but can Jane handle that kind of scandal? And a scandal it'll be. Most people in Pretoria are a lot less open-minded and tolerant than their liberal cousins in cosmopolitan Johannesburg.

Her face lights up with understanding. "Our sexual relationship will stay our secret. We'll have to be very careful. That's to say if you get the position."

I swallow. That's the problem. Can I be careful? Around Jane, my self-control seems to splinter. More accurately, I don't want to be careful. I want the world to know she's mine.

"Come on, Brian." She shoulders me playfully. "I put my ass on the line for you."

My gaze dips to her backside. I'm going straight to hell for the images I'm conjuring. Yes, I want the job. Yes, I need the money. I crave the time with Jane. Can I juggle my interests so the craving part doesn't drop and bring the whole lot crashing down?

"Say yes," she urges.

I can't say anything different, not when she looks at me like that, except maybe, "Thank you." My hearts expands with more than gratitude. No one has ever cared enough to put his ass on the line for me, except maybe Mike.

She beams at me. "You're welcome."

Just like that, the tension of yesterday's shit with Monkey melts away. My sins dissolve. The darkness of my past lifts. All that's left is a virgin slate. She can write any fucking thing she wants on it. I'll be whoever she needs me to be.

She breaks the uneaten part of her bread into pieces and throws it for the birds. Dusting her dress, she gets to her feet. "Sorry, but I've got to get back to the office before my assistant has a fit. I left her in charge of capturing the print ad schedule into a new software program that'll automate the production line, and it's a mess. We have a few glitches to iron out."

I look at the food in my hand. With my preoccupations concerning Jane, the job, and her body, I've only eaten half of my burger. Stuffing what's left in my mouth, I throw our empty wrappers in the trash and hand Jane one of the two bottles of soda in the bag.

"Where are you parked?" I asked.

"In the covered parking."

"I'll walk you."

I almost take her hand before I think the better of it. Again, stares follow her as we make our way across the square. She's oblivious to the attention, chatting lively about what I should prepare and expect from the interview.

Her car is on the far side of the parking lot against the wall. When she removes her keys from her handbag, I take them to unlock her door, making sure our fingers brush.

She turns in the open door. "I'll see you tomorrow, then."

Taking a step forward, I trap her against the car, the door shielding our bodies from view. The wall forms a barrier on the opposite side.

Alarm flickers in her blue eyes. "What are you doing?"

"I need to taste you."

She glances around frantically. "What? Here?"

One hand goes around her back, pressing her against me so she can't escape. The other slips under her dress.

"Brian, it's not a good idea."

Despite the protest, she gasps as I trail my fingers up the inside of her leg. Fucking hell. Just like I knew. She's wearing a garter. The silk of her stockings changes into soft skin of her thigh as I move my hand higher. Up I go, until the predominant sensation is not the smoothness of her flawless skin any longer, but the heat of her cunt. I slowly trace the line of her slit through her underwear.

She jerks in my hold. When I retrace the line from her clit to her asshole, she inhales and holds the breath, her eyes closing. I move the elastic aside, sweeping the floor for people, but the parking is empty except for us. Holy fuck. She's so wet my finger slips right in, all the way to the knuckle. She arches her back and whimpers, grabbing my shoulders for balance. I wasn't going to finger-fuck her–I swear I only wanted a quick taste–but the lure is too strong. Bracing her back, I bend my knees to find better purchase and fuck her in all earnest.

"Oh, my God." She makes a sound between a moan and a protest. "Oh, my God. Brian, not here."

I drop my head to her shoulder, kissing her neck, and then pull back so I can see her face. "Will that bother you, if someone watches?"

Her eyes fly open, but I'm fucking her too hard to be able to speak. Instead, I draw rhythmic gasps from her as I pound her pussy with the heel of my palm. Voyeurism has always been one of my addictions. The idea of her sucking me off in the middle of a crowded room has me go harder than steel. My balls will be blue until the next time I can sink my dick into her, but it's worth every agonizing moment just to see her face as her climax starts to near and, with the next thrust, spills over. Her pussy is a tight vice around my finger, sucking me deeper and milking what should've been my cock. Her body trembles and her thighs shake as the orgasm takes its toll. She collapses against me, leaning her head on my chest. I keep my finger inside until all the aftershocks are gone, stroking her back while I make her ride my hand for another two beats. Fingers, tongue, or cock, I'll stick whatever the occasion allows inside her. That's how addicted I am. Obsessed.

She straightens with a whimper, pushing on my shoulders. "I–I'll be late."

"In a minute."

Another glance tells me we're still alone, although I'm beyond caring, and anyway, her dress covers everything. I pull out slowly, feeling her inner muscles protest. She holds my gaze as I suck my finger into my mouth, tasting her release, which is a heady mixture of woman, lust, and wicked fantasies. I savor her pleasure with each of my senses–sight, sound, taste, feel, and smell. Only then do I straighten her dress and take her hand to help her into the car. I push on the door button to lower the window.

"Tomorrow at three," she says. "Can you make it?"

I close her door and lean through the open window. "I'll wing it so I can."

"Good." She smiles up at me. "Thanks for meeting me."

"Thanks for lunch." I kiss her lips like I couldn't outside. "Close your window and lock your door."

"Yes, sir."

The comment is said lightly, but it heats my blood. I love her compliance. It does dangerous things to me.

I watch her car until it disappears through the exit. Left standing alone, I almost wonder if it had been a dream. She's so fucking perfect, sometimes it's as if none of this is real. Yet, it's never been more real. The straining hard-on in my jeans is not the only proof of that. So is the hollowness in my chest for the space she left empty.

Jane

It's been a long time since I've felt so relaxed. I'm not sure if it's getting Debbie's meddling off my chest, finally accepting to let go of my home, or the forbidden orgasm in the parking lot, but it feels good to be at some measure of peace. After dinner, I pour a glass of wine and page through my recipe books, hunting for birthday cake ideas.

Abby enters with her school tablet under her arm.

"How's your homework, honey? Need help with anything?"

"No thanks, Mom. It's all done. I'm just revising a lesson for tomorrow's geography class."

Thank goodness Francois is paying her school fees. I'd never be able to afford the private school, even on my salary.

I glance at the kitchen clock. "It's bedtime in an hour. Would you like an infusion?" I keep a variety of caffeine and tannin free herbal teas for Abby. "Here." I hand her the box. "Pick one. I'll switch on the kettle."

When her Rooibos and vanilla blend is ready, she takes a high stool at the counter and peers over my shoulder. "What are you looking for?"

"Ideas for your party. Look at this one." I turn the book so she can see. "It's a sponge cake with peach-flavored icing. The pastel colors are beautiful, aren't they? How about a sleepover with a few of your friends? We can do movies and all the snacks that go with—"

"Mom."

The way she looks at me makes me pause. "What?"

She pulls the mug closer, cupping it between her palms. "I was kind of thinking of letting Debs throw the party, if you don't mind."

My mouth goes dry. I blink a couple of times, trying to process the shock without showing it.

"What about our theme?" I say jokingly, although the last thing I feel like is joking.

"I'm getting a bit old for all that stuff, you know?"

"I do," I say enthusiastically, "which is why I was going to suggest something more grown up like an all-nighter with movies."

"That's...not what I had in mind. The cake and the sleepover, I mean. If it's a problem, I'll tell Debs no. I don't want to hurt your feelings."

I swallow those hurt feelings down. "Of course it's not a problem. I want you to have what you really want."

"You sure?"

"Yes."

"Okay. So, I can tell Debs then?"

"Yes."

She hops off the chair, clapping her hands. "Thanks, Mom."

"Where are you going?"

"To call Debs," she says as if it was obvious.

"What? Now?"

"She'll be awake, don't worry."

"Wait. You haven't told me what you're planning."

"Oh, you'll see. It's a surprise."

She skips out of the room, leaving me with a steaming mug of untouched Rooibos tea and burning rejection. I clamp a hand over my mouth. I'm not even sure what to feel. Like a fool? Like a failure? No, that's my ego rearing its nasty head. This is for Abby. This is what she wants. The least I can do is respect her choice.

11

Jane

As I knew he would, Toby takes an immediate liking to Brian. It's easy to see why. Brian is driven, mature, confident, and energetic. His charm doesn't hurt, either. Judging by Toby's smile, Brian had already won him over with the handshake. Toby has this lopsided kind of smile when he likes someone and a thin-lipped one when he doesn't. Only Erica, the receptionist, and Candice, my assistant, give me uncertain and speculative looks when Brian enters Toby's office and the door closes behind them.

"Isn't that the guy...?" Candice asks.

"That's him. I told you we were discussing advertising."

My explanation shuts her up for now, but I can feel more questions coming.

One hour later, Brian is hired. He's officially my new intern. A thrill comes with the knowledge, and it's not only because I'm happy that he'll be in a better position, but also because I'll be working close to him almost every day.

It's Candice who gets to show him the ropes and introduce him to the other staff in the office.

"Oh, my." Beatrix stares after him, or rather his ass. "Now that's a fine piece of—"

"Please," I say. "What did Alex say about harassment?"

"I'm just saying, not touching." She smirks. "Although, I won't mind feeling my way around *that* body."

Irritation wins over tolerance. "Cut it out. He's not a piece of meat up for auction. Would you appreciate it if the guys discussed your breasts?"

"Honestly? I won't mind."

"You're beyond saving."

"What's eating you?" Mable asks. "It's like you've got the moral police up your ass."

"Just stop, guys. I'm going to work with him, and I don't want you talking about him like this behind his back."

"Ooh," Priscilla teases, "someone's got the hots for her new intern."

"Argh." All I can do is walk away. I'm not jealous. I'm just protecting Brian like I'd protect anyone from being objectified. At least, that's what I tell myself.

Not having a class in the afternoon, Brian starts straight away. Maybe I've been over-optimistic about how easy it would be to work in close proximity. When he strides into my office with a box of promotional items, my heart starts to stutter with a worrying beat. His biceps bulge from the heavy load. The T-shirt does nothing to hide his muscles, and my memory at how those muscles feel under my palms doesn't help my over-heating body.

"Where would you like this?" he asks.

I point at the meeting table. "Over there, please."

As he obliges, I can't help but notice how well his ass fills out his jeans. Urgh. Who am I kidding? I'm no better than Beatrix.

He peers inside the box. "All this is for branding?"

"Yep. We're presenting swag to our Bakers client next week."

More delicious muscles bunch as he crosses his arms. "Swag for what purpose specifically?"

"Christmas gifts for their clients."

He looks into the box again. "Mugs, mouse pads, USB keys, and pens. Not very exciting."

"Do you have a better idea?"

"A factory visit with an all-you-can-eat pass."

I laugh. "Like Charlie and the Chocolate Factory?"

"Why not?"

"I'm not sure their clients want to stuff their faces with cookies, even if they stock them by the pallets."

"Their kids will."

"You mean a family event?"

"What better way to please someone than pleasing their kid, right?"

"Right," I say slowly, leaning back in my chair.

"Instead of spending a fortune on mugs that'll collect dust on a shelf–Because let's face it, who needs another mug?–why not show off the premises and create loyal customers for life? Once you've shown those kids a good time, inconspicuously throwing in some PR with a factory tour, you've got a customer for life. They can have a Bakers cookie party afterward, and why not cross pollinate and invite Freddy? If you want to give swag, give away a starter pack of collectable cards, maybe with a science or cookie related recipe on the back, and include a card in each packet of cookies."

Mm. This could work. "Like football cards?"

"Exactly. Fabricating slime is the fashion, right now. Slime kits are selling like hot cakes for Christmas. Ask me, I'm on a waiting list at five toy stores for Sam. Print a recipe for homemade slime– easy as pie to make–on the first cards. It needs to be something of interest to both boys and girls."

"I like it. I really like it. Can you come up with a few more ideas for the cards?"

"Sure thing."

"I'd like to check what Toby thinks of it, but we need to present a range of cards that'll see them through until Easter, at least."

"No problem."

"Candice has put in an order for a work station for you, but until it's ready, you can use my computer. I want to show you how our print ad schedule works so you can help Candice capture the information in our new program."

Grabbing a visitor's chair, he pulls it up next to me and sits down.

"Shoot," he says. "I'm ready."

He's sitting so close our thighs brush when he leans forward for a better view of my screen. It's a non-intentional touch, hardly worth noting in an innocent situation, but our situation isn't innocent. My heart does a somersault. The distraction makes it hard to concentrate. Discreetly, I move my chair an inch to the side. If I hoped he wouldn't notice, it's futile. He smirks, but says nothing as I run through the print ad schedule and explain the process of booking, confirmation, invoicing, and creation.

When he takes a pen, our fingers brush. His arm presses against mine when he reaches for a notepad. When I'm bent over the light box with a magnifying glass, showing him how to do a print quality check of the brochures, his breath tickles my neck. If I'm lifting a stack of files, his arms come around me from behind to relieve me of the load. No matter where I turn, our bodies are close, too close. I've never been unprofessional, but I can't help my reaction. For the first time, I'm wet at the office, aching for release so fiercely I'm considering tending to the matter in the ladies' room. My only defense is avoiding Brian, which I successfully do for the remainder of the afternoon. I arrange visits to the other departments and make him capture data at Candice's desk.

My plan works well until I slip into the kitchen for a cup of much-needed caffeine. I'm going on tiptoes to reach the cupboard when his body presses up against me. I'm trapped between the counter and his chest with his hard-on growing against my lower back.

"Brian," I cry out softly. "What are you doing?"

The door is open. Anyone can walk in.

"What are *you* doing, Jane?"

"I don't know what you mean." I bump my ass against his thighs. "Get off me. This is not the time or place."

He lowers his lips to the shell of my ear. He doesn't touch them to my skin, but his mouth is so close heat permeates the spot. "You're avoiding me."

I struggle a little harder, but he's trapped me in the cage of his arms, and I'm no match for his strength.

"We're not home," I protest. "I don't mix business and pleasure."

He reaches around me and takes down a mug. "I miss you. I need you."

"Brian, please."

One hand grabs my breast while the other takes the pot of coffee from the percolator.

My breath catches audibly.

"Don't move," he says, kneading my curve. "I don't want to burn you."

I'm paralyzed, helpless, while he hums his approval, plays with my nipple, and pours the coffee.

More heat rushes between my legs. "We can't do this."

"I'll do whatever I want with you, and you'll let me."

His words are filled with self-assurance, which are merited, because he's not wrong. I want him so much I'll let him do anything. God, the sinful things *I* want to do.

Trying to show a measure of self-constraint, I make my voice hard. "You're very sure of yourself."

He adds sugar and milk to the coffee, playing a seductive game of stroking my nipple. "If I'm sure of myself, it's because I know I can please you." He bends his knees and grinds his erection against my ass. "I can make you come right here, on this spot."

My heart is beating erratically, not only from his proximity and dominant touch, but also from fear of being discovered. "You assume too much."

"We both know I'm right." Backing away, he gives me space.

I fling around to face him. "Is that so?" I'm starting to agree, but it doesn't mean I have to admit it and add to his ego. Not just yet.

Slowly, he leans forward. The intent in his eyes makes me stop breathing. Our lips are inches apart. I can't let this happen. Not here. He lowers his head to mine. Instead of kissing me, he reaches for something behind me.

"Avoiding me won't do you any good, princess. It only makes me chase harder." His breath is hot on my ear, his words soft but powerful. "If I catch you, I won't go easy."

"I'm not playing hard to get."

"I didn't say you are. Stop pretending I'm not affecting you and admit the truth. No one can give you what I can."

"That's a rather confident statement."

"Don't forget, I know how you like it."

The air trapped in my lungs rushes out on a gasp. "What?"

"Your coffee." He brings the mug around. "Two sugars and milk."

I take the mug like a robot, stunned to silence as he walks to the door. In the doorway, he turns. "Two weeks are way too long. I need to see you."

"You're seeing me now."

"You want me to be more specific? All right. I need to fuck your tight little cunt. My dick won't last another day."

Blood gushes to my face and then drops to my feet, heating me from my head down. "You know I've got Abby."

"She's got ballet practice tomorrow. That gives us forty-five minutes."

With that promise, he leaves the kitchen.

Brian

NOW THAT I'M earning a better salary, thanks to Jane, I can get a credit card at the bank. Credit allows me a better school for Sam. That's where I start, meeting with the principal of a private school in Hatfield. The fees are steep, but I need to bail my sister out of the dump of a school she's currently in before I strangle a bully or two. The registrations for the coming year have closed, but as my luck would have it, someone cancelled. I fill out the mountain of paperwork and provide the documents required. Then I swing by the building site office to pick up my paycheck. Mike went easy on me, not holding me to the contract period I signed. He's a good friend, but we both know I'll never earn the same money if I continue to work for him. It's when I drive away from the site that I spot the poster on a lamppost near the main entrance of the theater. I slam on the brakes and reverse.

The poster is advertising a symphony concert at the theater, but it's not the information that holds my attention. It's the photo of the star performer, a pianist. I'll be damned. It's the dandy from the bar. My hand automatically moves to my shirt pocket where I used to keep Jane's photo, even if I've been hiding it at home since I started working with her. I cut the engine and get out for a closer look. Sure as hell, it's the same, combed-back, Batman-black hair, fine-set features, and arrogant smile.

Benjamin James.

I've never heard of the dude, not that I'm into arts. Looks like I should've attended the concert Mike wanted to drag me to. I'm so flabbergasted, it takes me a while to register the honking in the street is aimed at me.

"Move your truck or I'll do it for you," the guy hanging out of the window yells.

With a last glance at the face forever committed to my memory, a face that now has a name, I hurry back to my truck. At the first available parking, I pull in and type the name in the search engine on my phone. Various articles come up. The guy is famous internationally. He's done concerts in Venice, Rome, Paris, New York, and God knows where. There's a photo of him with his wife and kid, a stunning, olive-skinned woman and a tall, slender, teenager son, who's said to be following in his father's footsteps. There's another photo of the whole family with a tiny excuse for a dog sitting on a stuffed gold-and-burgundy couch in front of a fireplace in a fancy living room with velvet drapes, a pressed ceiling, and a crystal chandelier. The byline says it's the canal apartment they own in Venice. It's obvious the guy's loaded, enough to have offered me a ridiculously handsome bribe, but that's not what I'm interested in. It's the surname. James. The same as Jane's dead fiancé.

I browse until I find what I'm looking for. Benjamin James' parents. Fuck me. He's Evan James' brother. He said he wanted revenge for the death of his friend. That so-called friend happened to be his brother. Why would he lie about it? To protect his identity? Since he didn't give me his name, it's the only plausible explanation.

I stare at the photo on my screen for a long time. I don't know why Jane cheated on her fiancé, but I'm not going to judge her. I'm the last person to throw stones when I'm living in a glass house. Jane is a good woman, one of the few authentic people I know. Maybe one day she'll tell me her history, or she won't. It doesn't matter. I'm not interested in the past. The only thing I care about is the future.

Starting the truck, I veer back into the traffic, following the road toward Groenkloof. Shall I tell Jane about my encounter with Benjamin? How do I explain not having told her sooner? If I spill the beans, she'll know nothing about how we met was a fluke. She'll know it was a setup from the word go. I know her well enough to know she'll never trust me again. She's had one too many trust issues with the male species as it is. No. I can't risk it. I can't stand to lose her trust or worse, *her*. I'll keep my secrets. So will Benjamin fucking James. He's not going to admit he bribed me to take naked sex photos of his dead brother's fiancée.

As I pass the prison, I confirm my mental vow.

I won't say a damn word.

The only truth Jane needs to know is the truth that matters. That I can't go a day without touching her.

Jane

FORTY-FIVE MINUTES.

It reverberates in my skull until it's all I can think about. It's all I want. Brian's hands on my body. *In* my body.

I need his touch like I've never needed. Every time he fucks me rough, he liberates a chained-up part of me. Every time he loves me tenderly, he repairs a broken piece of my soul.

On pins and needles, I pull into my garage. I'm apprehensive about what awaits and at the same time scared he won't show.

All my worry is for nothing. When the garage door closes behind me, a figure emerges from the dark. Despite recognizing his tall and impossibly strong frame, I jerk in fright. He steps into the headlights of my car, letting me see his face. I drop my bag on the seat and get out.

"Get over here," he says.

His tone tells me the same thing I feel—urgency. I walk over slowly, joining him in the light.

"Tell me," he says.

"Tell you what?"

"Tell me what you want."

At first, the order throws me off balance. I'm used to following, to be commanded in bed, but as I let myself go, feminine power races through my veins. My uncertainty falls away. I know exactly what I want.

Walking around him, I lean against the wall, getting ready for a show. "I want you to take off your clothes."

Holding my gaze with the confidence I've come to associate with Brian, he reaches for the button of his jeans. It's so typical of him to go for his pants first. I smile, but it vanishes quickly when he pushes the jeans slowly over his hips and down his masculine legs. Always commando. Always hard. The Jane from old wouldn't have stared, but this new woman, the woman he awakens in me, looks long and hard, and he doesn't seem to mind. He straightens and pauses, giving me a good view and time to admire his cock. He's got reason to be vain. His body is a sculptured work of art, but his cock is perfect. A perfect fit for me. His balls are heavy. I ache to feel their weight in my palms and taste the heat of his skin, but for now I only watch as he pulls off his T-shirt. His skin tone is equally bronze everywhere, including his groin. I imagine his chest and legs will gain a darker tan with summer on the doorstep. The way he stands there with his cock jutting out and his jeans around his ankles is simultaneously ethereal and dirty. I'd make him use me like this if I wasn't worried he'd trip.

Without breaking our eye contact, he kicks off his trainers and gets rid of the socks and jeans. Fully naked, he faces me again. Waiting.

"Come over here."

He approaches, stopping short of me. Having him at my beck and call is a heady cocktail of desire and power going straight to my lower region. Commanding a dominant male such as the very naked, very compliant one facing me is such a turn-on.

"Closer," I say.

He obeys again, advancing until his cock brushes my hip.

"Good," I praise. "Now go down on me."

With his eyes still locked on mine, he drops to his knees and takes the hem of my dress. Ever so slowly, he lifts the fabric over my hips. I help him out by holding up the dress so he can push my panties over my hips and down my legs. He does so watching me all the while with intense concentration, as if he doesn't want to miss a single nuance of my expression.

When he frees my feet from my underwear, I spread my legs for him. I would never have been this bold before. Somewhere along the line of life, I lost my confidence, but Brian is giving it back to me, little by little, soft kiss by–Oh, my God!–kiss. His tongue strokes over my clit, his lips raining kisses over my swollen folds. With him, I'm rediscovering myself. It's as if every touch is pulling back a layer, unwrapping the masks and pretenses until I'm free to breathe again.

"Oh, God."

Pants. Gasps. Sweet breaths. Freedom. It feels so, so good. My toes curl. I don't care that I'm loud. I let him hear what he does to me as he ravishes me with his tongue, adding his fingers to bring me to ecstasy.

He hooks my leg over his shoulder, stretching me open and touching me deeper. I brace my back against the wall and grab his shoulders for balance.

His dark eyes are scorching me with heat and lust. His voice vibrates against my skin as his lips move over my pussy. "How do I make you come? Fingers or tongue? Pick your choice."

Staring down at him, I take in the sight. He's eating me out with abandon, licking and sinking his teeth into my flesh, moaning as he sucks my clit into his mouth. It's a decadent scene playing out in the car's headlights. We're on our own little stage under the spotlights. It's dirty. It's beautiful. My thighs quiver as pleasure builds in my core.

My tone is hoarse and breathless. "Put your fingers in me."

He sinks two into my pussy and scissors them.

"Ass, too," I command.

His eyes flare. Pupils dilating, he abandons my clit to bring a thumb to his mouth. He sucks until it's wet. I close my eyes, knowing what's coming. Unrivalled pleasure is full inside me as he fills every hole except for my mouth. His tongue goes back to my clit, working in slow circles.

I look back down, searching his gaze. What I find is arousal. Admiration. Approval.

Despite the pleasure rendering me boneless, my voice is assertive. "Now fuck me like you mean it."

He does. His fingers ram into me from two ends while he nips my clit. It's all I need to go over. The force is electrifying. I grit my teeth against the intensity, letting the current snap me in two and sweep me away.

When my orgasm ebbs, he goes softer, allowing me to ride the aftershocks until there's nothing left. He stays down on his knees with my leg over his shoulder and my pussy shoved in his face, waiting for me to tell him what I want him to do next.

"Get up."

Planting a reverent kiss on the inside of my thigh, he unhooks my leg and straightens. He's breathing as hard as I am, his arousal no less than mine.

My gaze drops to his cock. "Stroke it."

Taking his cock in his hand, he pumps twice. His head rolls back. His groan bounces off the walls.

I need him inside me. I turn and bend, hitching my dress up before bracing my palms on the wall. The position puts my ass and pussy on display.

I glance at him from over my shoulder. "You know what I need. Do it."

Fists clenching and nostrils flaring, he stares at me. "Say it."

"Fuck me with your cock."

The verbal command is all he's waiting for. Charging like a beast, he grips my hips and sinks his cock into my pussy. He doesn't wait for me to adjust to the intrusion. Our need is too urgent. He pulls back until only the broad head is lodged in my entrance, and slams back in. The breath leaves his lungs in loud grunts as he thrusts, working a hard but delicious rhythm into my body.

"Yes." I moan. "Now spank me."

He misses a beat, throwing us out of our synchronized grinding and pumping, but he's quick to chase me, pulling my ass back to his groin and impaling me with bruising force. I feel him where it matters, where I don't want it to end.

"You only have to say the word, princess."

A thwack sounds as his palm comes down on my ass cheek. My pussy clenches on his cock, pulling him deeper. The sensations are overwhelming. Heat travels through my skin to my genitals. A succession of beats rain down on my ass. I'm on fire, burning for him. My body contracts, my muscles locking and holding me prisoner, helpless, as my release prepares to explode. Gripping Brian's hand, I move it to the front of my body, between my legs.

"Here," I say. "Spank me here."

Again, he doesn't hesitate. His palm burns on my clit, just where I need it. I come with a scream. His cock twitches and swells inside me. He drives even deeper, and then he roars out his climax. My inner walls grip him hard. He utters a string of expletives as he hammers his release into my body until neither of us has anything left to give.

Falling forward, he catches himself with his arms braced next to mine on the wall, his chest warm on my back. He covers my shoulder with kisses. When we've more or less caught our breaths, he places a palm on my stomach, pressing my ass against his groin even as he pulls out. Warm cum runs down my thighs. We stay like this for a moment, reluctant to move.

It's Brian who steps away first. He kisses the top of my spine through my dress, and then the exposed part at the bottom, just above the crack of my ass. His palm smooths over my ass cheek.

"Fuck, I love my handprint on your skin."

I rest my forehead against the cool wall, not sure my legs will carry me if I stand up straight. Something soft moves between my legs. I glance around. Brian is cleaning me with my underwear. He lowers my dress over my hips and turns me to face him.

"You belong to me." His eyes drill into mine. "My handprint on your skin says so. So does my cum in your cunt."

My eyelids flutter close. I'm lethargic. All I want to do is curl up on his lap.

A soft kiss lands on my lips. "I've got to go if I don't want Abby to catch me red-handed with my fingers under your dress. Naked, no less."

That makes my eyes fly open. He's grinning at me. I check my watch. Shit, we've got ten minutes.

"Don't worry." He picks up his jeans. "I'm out of here."

Guilt suffuses in my throat, making it hard to speak. Anyway, I don't find words. I don't want to treat him like a dirty secret, but I honestly don't know how I'll explain him to my daughter.

He pulls on his jeans, adjusts his semi-hard cock, and zips himself up. I bend to retrieve his T-shirt. When he's fully dressed, he comes to stand in front of me. He's so close I have to strain my neck to look up at him. Rather than kissing me, he caresses me with his gaze, his eyes speaking volumes as they trace the lines of my face.

Our hands touch. He presses something into my palm. My underwear. His smirk is self-assured, but I don't miss the spark of vulnerability in his expression as he says, "Tomorrow."

"Tomorrow," I agree, wanting so much more.

He's already pressing the button to lift the garage door when I remember what I wanted to bring up.

"Brian."

He turns.

"Give me your keys."

He arches an eyebrow.

"The keys to my house," I say. "You can't keep on doing this."

"We'll keep on doing exactly this." His gaze heats on the last word as it finds the sore and satisfied spot between my legs. All the vulnerability disappears from his face. What's left are dark lust and determined intent. "Sorry, princess. Game over. You're no longer in charge."

The garage door has fully opened. The purple light of the evening filters into the garage, carrying with it the scent of Canna lilies. His silent stare dares me to defy him, and maybe I would've if it weren't for Abby coming home at any minute, or that's what I tell myself when he leaves.

Brian

THE MINUTE I GET HOME, I email Benjamin James a message from my phone. I don't even take the time to open the gate and pull into the yard. I do it right there in the street.

Need to talk.

A reply comes almost immediately. *Do you have what I want?*

I slam out the text on my screen. *In person. Now.*

My phone rings a couple of seconds later. I was hoping for a meeting so I could look the fucker in the eye when I told him I knew, but a call is quicker, and where Jane's concerned, I can't wait. I take it.

"It took you longer than I expected," his smooth voice says. "Was I wrong about your charm, or is Ms. Logan a hard cookie to crumble?"

"Tell me again why you want a naked fuck picture of Jane."

"Told you, revenge."

"You didn't say you're her dead fiancé's brother, *Mr. Benjamin James.*"

"Ah. You discovered my name. I suppose it was bound to happen. A famous man can only go nameless for so long."

"Why didn't you tell me you're his brother?"

"Does it make a difference?" His sigh is theatrical. "For reasons that speak for themselves, I was hoping to remain anonymous, *Mr. Brian Michaels.*"

He's checked me out, too. So what? Wouldn't have been hard. My number is listed.

"Take my advice," I say. "Forgive and forget. Move on."

"You don't get to tell me what to do."

"She's suffered enough. Your brother's death was—is—hard on her. Consider your revenge done. Tenfold."

"There are other means than you, Mr. Michaels."

I squeeze the phone so hard the plastic cover snaps with a clack. "If you come near her, you won't have enough fingers left to count to ten. You'll never play the piano again. Do you understand?"

"No need to get dramatic. Just do your job and earn your fifty grand."

"If I catch as much as a whiff of you near her, I'll come for you. Remember that when you close your eyes at night."

There's a smile in his voice. "I'll wait for my goods, but don't make me wait too long. I'm not a patient man, and someone else may be eager for that fifty thousand. Do I need to start looking for someone else?"

"No," I grit out.

"Good. I knew you'd understand. Goodbye, Mr. Michaels."

The line goes dead.

I swear to God, I'll kill him if he sends another prick after Jane. Doesn't matter. No one else is sticking his dick into her. Not for the rest of forever. I'll be there, right beside her, *inside* her, to make sure it never happens.

I'm about to get out of the truck when headlights illuminate our gate. I'm not going for the gun stashed in the house. Not yet. It'll be a damn stupid move to try and break into our house. Everyone on the block and in a hundred-kilometer radius knows it. I've set an example with my mother's hijackers, and I'll do it again.

Shading my eyes with a hand, I squint at the vehicle in my rearview mirror.

Corvette.

Fuck.

This is worse than an attempted burglary. I'd rather deal with ignorant perpetrators.

Monkey and one of his men get out. I have no choice but to meet them.

"Brian," Monkey calls out in greeting, gripping my shoulder.

He's got a pink teddy bear by its ear. The guy with him is carrying a bouquet of flowers, the colorful, cellophane-wrapped kind from the supermarket.

"Since you didn't come to me," he says, "I came to you."

He walks past me toward the garden gate. I want to stop him, to say my mother is sleeping, but it's not even seven, yet. It's the hour most people sit down to dinner.

I rush after them up the path. It's as if I'm looking down on myself from the sky as I unlock the door. I'm watchful. Vigilant. I won't let him or his guy touch my mother or sister. They both carry guns, but armed or not, if I lay my bare hands on them, they'll go home in a hearse.

Monkey steps inside, looking around as if he's inspecting a hotel room for a long stay. His goon stays a pace behind.

"Where's that beautiful mother and charming sister of yours?"

The hair in my nape stands on end. I'm about to say Sam's in the shower and my mom passed out when my mother rounds the corner.

"Monkey." She pulls the ends of her robe close, her mouth slightly agape. Then she starts to ramble. "This is a surprise. Come on in." She moves around the room, pulling books and magazines off the sofa bed and chairs. "Have a seat. How's Ingrid and Lindy?"

Monkey flicks his fingers at the guard who presents the flowers.

"These are for you."

"Oh, thank you." My mother reaches for the bouquet. "That's very thoughtful, but it wasn't necessary."

Monkey wags a finger at her. "Never say you don't deserve to be spoiled. You look good, Jasmine. How's life treating you?"

"Good, thank you for asking." She clutches the flowers to her chest and brushes a strand of hair behind her ear.

He holds up the bear. "I brought something for Sam. Where is that pretty little girl of yours?"

My mother doesn't as much as glance at me. She does nothing to give away her apprehension, and I take my hat off to her for that.

"Sam," she calls down the hall. "We have visitors."

My sister comes down the hallway in no particular rush. Her face, unlike my mother's, is wary. It's not often we have visitors other than Clive, Eugene, or Tron.

Monkey holds out the bear. "This is for you, young lady."

Sam is clever enough to take it and say, "Thank you. She's very pretty."

Monkey looks around again, waiting for something.

"Uh, we were just about to have dinner," my mother says. "You should stay. Sam, set two more places at the table."

"That's generous, thanks," Monkey says, "but Ingrid's waiting for me to have dinner ourselves. I'll just have a quick drink and then we'll be on our way."

"Of course. Gin?"

Monkey pulls a face, which he manages to smooth over with a smile.

My mother hurries to the door. "Come help me, Sam."

When they're gone, Monkey walks to the chair facing the coffee table. He adjusts the sleeves of his jacket and sits down, elbows resting on his knees. The guard remains standing. So do I.

"So." He rubs his hands together. "Are you waiting for me to lick your fucking arse to take a job in my business?"

I cross my arms. "No."

264

"Then where the hell have you been? I thought you were supposed to come see me about that job."

"I was busy getting my life in order."

"Getting your life in order, huh?" He laughs. "Did you hear that?" he asks his guard, pointing a finger at me. "Getting his life in order."

"Yeah. In fact, I already have a job."

Monkey's smile vanishes. "You do, do you?"

"One that'll pay for a palace, as you've put it."

"What's wrong with working for me?"

"I need to prove that I can make it on my own."

"I don't give a horse's arse's damn. You don't need to prove yourself."

"Not to you, to myself. And Lindy," I lie blatantly. "Don't you think Lindy would like to know the guy she marries," fuck, I almost choke, "can make it on his own? No woman wants to think a man is only after her father's money."

He gives me a piercing look. "What kind of job?"

"Advertising."

"You want to be a pansy worker?" he asks incredulously.

"It's where the money is."

"That's what he's studying," the goon adds. "Advertising."

Monkey looks me up and down. "This is for Lindy, eh?"

Fuck. Fuck. I'm going to hell. "Yes."

He sniffs. Silence stretches as he puts his fingertips together and studies his nails. My heart is about to climb out of my throat. If Monkey orders me to start at his business tomorrow, I can't say no. Not if I want my family safe and me not going to jail. The police already have a warrant of arrest with my name on it. The only way out will be to kill Monkey and wipe out his whole gang. It'll be like taking on a war, man alone.

Finally, Monkey looks up. "Fine. Give it a shot. Why my daughter wants a pansy instead of a man I'll never understand."

He gets to his feet just as my mother and Sam reenters, each carrying a drink.

Bowing slightly in my mother's direction, he says, "It was good to see you. Don't be a stranger, now."

"Goodbye, Ms. Michaels," the guard says respectfully, a sliver of pity in his gaze.

My mother's reply comes lamely. "Your drinks."

"Maybe another time."

I move to get the door, but Monkey stops me.

"We'll find our way out. We don't want to keep you from your dinner. Take care."

My mother stares at me when the door closes, her face alight with composed fear and confusion. "What was that, Brian?"

"Nothing," I say. "Go wash your hands, Sam."

"I made bangers and mash," my mother says, but she's looking at me, not at Sam.

I take the glasses on my way to the kitchen. "That sounds great."

It's an even bigger lie than the one I'd spun about Lindy.

Nothing sounds remotely great.

Jane

I FEEL guilty about avoiding Dorothy, and even more so about not thinking about Evan as much as I used to. It's like I'm cheating on his memory, or worse, forgetting all together, which is why I agree when Dorothy invites me for coffee at the Menlyn Park shopping mall on Saturday while Abby is at a tennis tournament.

Dorothy waits in front of Mugg & Bean, wearing a Valentino dress.

"You've been avoiding me," she accuses when I kiss her cheek.

With Benjamin around, of course I have. Well, Brian also took up all my free time.

"Shall we get a table? I'm dying for some caffeine."

I scan the buzzing room for an unoccupied table when my gaze lands on Debbie. She's done away with the dreadlocks. Hair extensions curl over her shoulders. She's looking gorgeous wearing no make-up other than mascara and lip gloss. Clutching a mug between her palms, she's having an animated conversation with her companion. I can't see her friend's face, but the asymmetrical haircut is unmistakably recognizable.

Loretta.

She must've felt my stare, because Debbie's head turns in my direction. Her eyes widen for a split-second before she schools her features. I wish I could pretend I haven't seen them, but it's too late, and ignoring them will be rude.

Dorothy points at a table at the back where a couple is getting ready to leave. "There's a table. Go quickly, before someone else takes it."

We have to pass right by Debbie and Loretta. Taking a deep breath, I stop when we're next to them.

"Oh, hi, Jane," Debbie says, faking surprise as if she hasn't seen me at the door.

Loretta turns her neck so fast she almost spills her drink.

"Janie!" Loretta says. Then in a much colder voice, "Dot."

Dorothy's tone isn't much warmer. "Hello, Loretta."

"This is Debbie," I say to Dorothy, "Francois' girlfriend."

"Fiancée," Debbie says pointedly, holding out her hand.

The light catches a cluster of diamonds on her ring finger. I knew it would eventually happen, but it still comes as a shock. I feel like the world's biggest fool. Couldn't Francois or Abby tell me? Or Loretta?

"Congratulations," I say. "Have you decided on a date?"

She makes a big gesture of laying a hand on her stomach. "We're waiting until after the baby."

"The baby?" Dorothy looks between Debbie and me.

"Debbie is four months pregnant."

I can almost see the calculation taking place in Dorothy's mind.

"Aren't you…?" Dorothy narrows her eyes. "We met at a cocktail party at Jane's house. You're Francois' secretary."

"*Ex*-secretary," Debbie says.

"Did you quit before or after your affair with Francois?" Dorothy asks.

Debbie's dark skin pales a shade. Loretta coughs and hides her face behind her cappuccino.

I grab Dorothy's arm. "Let's get that table before the waitress gives it to someone else. Nice running into you. Enjoy your coffee."

"Wait." Debbie rummages through her bag and produces an envelope. "This is for you, Jane."

I reach for it as if it could be a venomous snake. "What is it?"

"An invitation to Abby's birthday party." She smiles sweetly. "We'd love to have you, of course. If you can make it. I hope you have nothing planned for that Saturday."

Dorothy's mouth drops open.

"Of course I'll be there." No damn question about it.

"Good." She bats her eyelashes. "I'll mark you down on the RSVP list."

"Congratulations again."

I steer Dorothy away before she says more.

"What on earth was that all about?" Dorothy asks when we're seated. "What does she mean by inviting you to your own daughter's birthday party?"

"Debbie's throwing the party, and before you say anything, Abby asked."

"What? That's crazy. Jane, you mustn't stand for it."

"Dorothy, please. This is what Abby wants. Can we just leave it at that?"

She leans over the table. "*That's* the woman Francois left you for? When you told me, I couldn't put a face to the name, but now that I've seen her, I remember her clearly. What a bitch."

"They really seem to love each other."

"First, she steals your husband, then your house, and now your daughter and your friends." She shoots a nasty look in Loretta's direction. "Is she trying to steal your very life?"

"Ralph and Francois are best friends. It's only natural for Loretta and Debbie to socialize."

"May I remind you? Loretta met Ralph because of you. If you hadn't introduced them, they wouldn't be married today."

"That doesn't give me exclusivity on Loretta's friendship."

"I'm sorry, but you're a better person than me. I would've expected more loyalty than that."

"Can we please talk about something else? Tell me how you are."

"Do you really want to know?"

"Of course."

She studies me speculatively, as if she can't make up her mind. Finally, she says, "I'm going to Venice."

"Oh, my God. When? For how long?"

"I'm thinking about Easter. It'll just be for a week. Benjamin and Esperanza are busy, especially now that Benjamin is becoming so famous."

My whole body goes tense. I try to smooth a smile over the rigid muscles in my face, but I guess it turns out more like a grimace, because Dorothy's face falls.

"I miss my grandson, Jane."

"You don't have to justify your actions to me. You're more than entitled to visit your family."

"Benjamin…" She toys with her napkin. "He's been suffering, too."

"I'm sure he has." I mean it. Evan and he were close. "I found a place to rent," I say to change the subject. "You must come and visit." When Benjamin is gone. "You'll like it."

"I'm happy for you."

"I wish Abby was. She's not so fond of the place."

"Give it time. It'll grow on her."

"Oh, and she had her first period."

"There you go. Changing hormones. It's always hard having a budding adolescent in the house. She'll come around."

"The divorce has been hard on her. She adores Francois. It's tough not seeing him every day."

"As much as I disapprove of his actions where relationships are concerned, he's always been a good father."

I look at the friend that could've been my mother-in-law if things had been different. "Am I a good mother?"

She reels. "Where did that come from?"

"Sometimes," I shrug, "I just wonder. Francois seems to be so good at it. No wonder Abby prefers to be with him."

"Francois has always been working. You stayed home and enforced the discipline while he returned from the office to dish out the fun. It's a universal thing with working dads and stay-at-home moms. Believe me, I know. It'll change as she grows older."

"I don't know." I study my hands. "It's just…"

"Just what?"

I dare to meet her eyes. "I wasn't planning on falling pregnant. I didn't want it when it happened."

The unsaid spreads between us. It becomes thicker and heavier until I think she's going to say something to finally acknowledge it, but then the air lifts and the feeling is gone.

"Oh, Jane. It doesn't mean you ever loved her less."

No. From the minute I saw the first sonar, I loved her more than life. I already knew then I couldn't bear it if anything happened to her. Still, there was that moment, that moment when I saw the two lines on the stick, that my heart sank, that I felt–believed–it was a mistake. Could a moment be so tangible as to imprint on an unborn life? Babies sense sentiments, even in the womb of their mothers. What if Abby sensed that for the most fleeting of moments I didn't want her?

"It'll be all right," Dorothy says, reaching for my hand. "You've got to believe that. More importantly, you've got to start living for yourself."

"What do you mean?"

"You've been living for Abby and Francois. Now he's left you, and Abby's growing up. You've got to start thinking about *you* for a change. You can't make your daughter happy if you don't make yourself happy, first."

"I'm not unhappy."

"You haven't been happy, either. Not for a long time."

"That's not true. I've been content."

"Exactly. There's a big difference between happy and content."

What about ecstatic? Is it wrong to be ecstatic at my age? Do I dare behave like a lovesick teenager when there are bigger things to consider, like Abby's future and happiness?

"You know what?" Dorothy says, picking up her bag. "We don't need coffee. We need a bloody stiff drink."

"It's eleven in the morning," I exclaim.

"Who gives a shit?"

She grabs my arm and pulls me to my feet. "Come on. There's a restaurant next door that serves alcohol."

"Now you sound like Loretta."

"Don't you dare compare me to that traitor. She's not worth my old shoes."

"Dorothy! That's nasty."

"Well, sometimes even a lady has to know how to be a bitch."

With that, she pushes me to the door, past my problems and insecurities, if only for a couple of hours.

Brian

I'M HANGING out with Clive and Eugene at Playback while Jane spends the evening with her daughter. These forced separations irk me more than I give on, even to myself. Jane's place is here, with me, or mine there, with her. I don't want to drink and joke with my buddies alone. I want my woman by my side. I want to have fun with her as much as I want to play the serious games of fucking and getting to know her. The real Jane. The one she revealed to me in the bright lights of her car. The one she shows me when I tie her up in bed.

"What's crawled up your ass?" Eugene asks. "You've been brooding and nursing that beer for the last hour."

"Keep the last Saturday of the month free."

"Where are we partying?" Clive asks.

"We're moving."

Clive squints at me. "We?"

"We. Us."

"*We're* moving?" Eugene props his elbow on the counter. "How many *we's* are there in your *us*? Because I see only one, and that's you."

"We're helping someone move."

Clive puts down his beer. "Where the fuck to?"

"Leeuwfontein."

"Ah." Eugene laughs. "It's for your friend, the uptown chic."

"What uptown chic?"

"My dad says he got the place for her like a man does for a mistress."

"Fuck your dad, Eugene. No disrespect intended."

"What uptown chic?" Clive repeats.

"Are you in or not?"

"Yeah, hell." Eugene laughs again. "I want to see this with my own eyes."

"Cut it out or you can mingle with the losers back there in the corner."

"Chill, man." Eugene lifts his palms. "I was just saying."

"No more saying. Are you in, Clive? Yes or no? I need to know if I must ask Mike."

"Yes," he bites out. "I'm in."

I down the last of my beer. "Thank you. That wasn't so hard, was it?"

"Fuck you, Brian. I'm getting tired of you sneaking behind our backs." With that, he sneaks off himself, disappearing into the crowd.

Eugene regards me with guarded eyes. "I don't know what you're brewing, bro, but my dad says you're into this bird."

"What I am is none of your dad's business."

"I'm just saying, because *Lindy*, you know."

"No need to rub it in. I'm already knee-deep, thanks."

He looks over to where Lindy's blonde hair stands out in the crowd. "Monkey is no one to be messed with."

"Tell me something I don't know."

"What are you going to do?"

"Nothing. Lindy will come around when she sees I'm not into her. They always do." She's ignoring me tonight. That's always a good sign.

"If you say so."

Fishing my phone from my pocket, I send Jane a text.

Wish you were here. With me.

She sends back a kiss and a heart with, *I miss you, too.*

I'm done drinking for the night. I'm about to go back to brooding when my phone pings with another message. Expecting it to be Jane, I'm more than a little surprised to see Lindy's face on my screen. She's sent me a pouty-lip selfie. Closing it, I swivel on my barstool, being the bastard who shows her his back I didn't want to be.

It takes all my self-control not to drive to Jane's house and climb through her window while her daughter sleeps in the room next door. I'm suffering from a pussy hangover that's way beyond obsession. There's only one woman for me, and she can't be here.

And the one who is, has the power to destroy the only thing I want more than life.

Jane

THE FUNFAIR COMES to town once a year. We never miss it. This year, I bring Jordan with to keep Abby's mind off the fact that her father isn't with us. Abby misses Francois, and it's making her sad. Jordan is Loretta's daughter and Abby's best friend. Loretta and I gave birth one month apart. The girls grew up together. They've been inseparable since kindergarten.

I watch them scream on all the rides from the rollercoaster to the drop tower. By the time there's nothing they haven't done, we get cotton candy and make our way toward the exit.

Abby stops me with a hand on my arm. "Look!" She points at the fortuneteller's tent. "Can we go?"

"Cool," Jordan says. "I've never been."

My legs are killing me after spending hours in queues, and it's getting dark. I check my watch. I promised Loretta I'd have Jordan back before dinner.

"Please, Mom," Abby insists. "I want to know what's going to happen in my future."

"It's just a show," I say.

Abby is not to be deterred. "It'll be fun."

"All right, but after that we have to go. If we're late, your mom won't let you come with us next time, Jordan."

The girls squeal and jump up and down like toddlers while I go back to the ticket booth to buy another two entries. Unlike with the rides, there is no queue outside the tent. I move the flap aside for the girls to enter and follow. A middle-aged woman sits by a table. The decoration is cliché from the velvet drapes to the crystal ball, and so is the woman's embroidered headband and gypsy-style dress. She looks up from reading something on her smartphone.

"Sit," she tells me.

"It's not for me. It's the girls who'd like a séance."

Her gaze doesn't move from mine. "Eighteen and older."

Abby and Jordan's shoulders slump. She may as well put on a show for them. What difference will it make?

"There's no sign about age," I say.

"It's your fortune or nothing."

I turn to the girls with an apology on my lips, but Abby grabs my hand. "You do it, Mom."

"Why don't we grab a drink before we go instead?"

"You may as well go for it," Abby says. "We're here, anyway, plus you've already paid."

"Sit," the woman says again, already spreading a deck of cards out on the table.

I suppose I could play along for the sake of the girls. I take the chair while Abby and Jordan peer over my shoulders.

The woman spaces the semi-circle of cards. "Pick four."

When I've complied, she turns the cards face-up and places them in a square. I'm expecting some hocus pocus forecasts about my wonderful health and wealth, but not the words she utters.

"Unlucky in love."

I blink at her. "Excuse me?"

She pins me with an unsettling stare. "You're unlucky in love."

The words jar me, because they're not entirely untrue, but she can't know that. Not from four cards. She could've deduced that from my bare fingers. No rings mean no fiancé or husband. I settle back in the chair, a bit more at ease with the knowledge.

"Death," she says melancholically, tracing the design of the first card. "Your great love died."

My heart goes still. My breathing stops. Thank God Abby can't see my face. She doesn't know about that part of my past, and I have no idea how this stranger could've guessed.

"Deceit," the woman continues, pointing at the second card. "The one you replaced him with cheated on you."

Everything inside me goes cold. I want to tell her to stop, but I don't want to make a scene in front of the girls.

The fortuneteller taps the third card. "Soulmates. You met your soulmate."

I stare at the card. It depicts a devil with a spiked fork.

Her brow furrows. "He's a dark one. Powerful where it matters–in spirit. Everything on the outside reflects the inside. He's very tall, yes? Very beautiful. Very young in years, but his soul is old. Very unlucky in love indeed."

My unease grows.

She flicks a nail on the fourth card. "Heartache."

"What?"

"You've suffered death, deceit, and the pinnacle of love. The worst is yet to come. Betrayal." She meets my eyes. "The betrayal of a lover."

The air in the tent is suddenly suffocating. I need to get out. Pushing back the chair, I jump to my feet. "Thank you for the session."

"The devil wears many disguises. His favorite is the one of lover, because it's so effective."

Grabbing Abby and Jordan's hands, I pull them to the exit.

"Be careful who you trust," she calls after me.

I'm not listening any longer. I'm dragging in the dusty night air, moving toward the reassuring reality of fairground music and bright lights.

"Are you okay, Mom?"

I force a smile. "Of course. See? I told you. It's just a show."

The woman spooked me, that's all. I've been stupid. I've been silly to let her get to me. It's a bogus story. She doesn't know a thing about me. Evan may have died, and Francois cheated on me, but there's no way in hell Brian is a devil in a lover's disguise set on betraying me. I almost laugh out loud at that thought. We're set on our path, Brian and I. He's my secret, and I trust him. It's not going to change. Yet, as I make my way to the exit, the woman's warning keeps on turning in my head.

The worst is yet to come.

~ TO BE CONTINUED ~

ALSO BY CHARMAINE PAULS

DIAMOND MAGNATE NOVELS

(Dark Romance)

Standalone Novel

(Dark Forced Marriage Romance)

Beauty in the Broken

Diamonds are Forever Trilogy

(Dark Mafia Romance)

Diamonds in the Dust

Diamonds in the Rough

Diamonds are Forever

Box Set

Beauty in the Stolen Trilogy

(Dark Romance)

Stolen Lust

Stolen Life

Stolen Love

Box Set

The White Nights Duet

(Contemporary Romance)

White Nights

Midnight Days

The Loan Shark Duet

(Dark Mafia Romance)

Dubious

Consent

Box Set

The Age Between Us Duet

(Older Woman Younger Man Romance)

Old Enough

Young Enough

Box Set

Standalone Novels

(Enemies-to-Lovers Dark Romance)

Darker Than Love

(Second Chance Romance)

Catch Me Twice

Krinar World Novels

(Futuristic Romance)

The Krinar Experiment

---

7 Forbidden Arts Series

(Fated Mates Paranormal Romance)

Pyromancist (Fire)

Aeromancist, The Beginning (Prequel)

Aeromancist (Air)

Hydromancist (Water)

Geomancist (Earth)

Necromancist (Spirit)

ABOUT THE AUTHOR

Charmaine Pauls was born in Bloemfontein, South Africa. She obtained a degree in Communication at the University of Potchefstroom and followed a diverse career path in journalism, public relations, advertising, communication, and brand marketing. Her writing has always been an integral part of her professions.

When she moved to Chile with her French husband, she started writing full-time. She has been publishing novels and short stories since 2011. Charmaine currently lives in Montpellier, France with her family. Their household is a lively mix of Afrikaans, English, French, and Spanish.

Join Charmaine's mailing list
https://charmainepauls.com/subscribe/

Join Charmaine's readers' group on Facebook
http://bit.ly/CPaulsFBGroup

Read more about Charmaine's novels and short stories on
https://charmainepauls.com

Connect with Charmaine

Facebook

http://bit.ly/Charmaine-Pauls-Facebook

Amazon
http://bit.ly/Charmaine-Pauls-Amazon

Goodreads
http://bit.ly/Charmaine-Pauls-Goodreads

Twitter
https://twitter.com/CharmainePauls

Instagram
https://instagram.com/charmainepaulsbooks

BookBub
http://bit.ly/CPaulsBB

TikTok
https://www.tiktok.com/@charmainepauls